THE NEW YORK CHARM

UPTOWN LOVE #1

RILEY WINTERS

This one's for anyone chasing their dreams, no matter how big or small. The only opinion that matters is your own.

A NOTE TO THE READER

Dear Reader,

This book explores themes of **alcoholism** and **loss of a parent**, both of which may be emotionally challenging for some readers. The story includes depictions of **alcohol abuse, grief,** and **emotional trauma** (off page), as well as moments of **anxiety and strained family relationships.** Additionally, this novel contains **open-door spice** in chapters 21 and 29.

If you prefer to skip these moments, feel free to navigate the story in a way that feels comfortable for you.

Thank you for being here with me.

1

DYLAN

You would think that I'd be on time for the flight that's about to change my life. Yet here I am, rushing through the airport, nearly knocking over unassuming travelers, making it to my gate in the nick of time. I couldn't sleep last night, my stomach full of butterflies. I've been packed for weeks, and my mom dropped me off at the airport hours early because my anticipation got the best of me.

When it came time to say goodbye to her one last time, I couldn't find the strength to tear myself away. Woodland Heights, Tennessee, was all I had known my entire life, and the two of us had been to hell and back. My mom was my best friend, and the idea that I had to leave her alone made my chest raw with guilt. But I knew I couldn't linger too long because if I did, I'd never leave.

If I thought about her puffy eyes or splotchy skin, I'd break down again, which I can't afford right now. I'm on my way to New York, where I know not a single soul. But that's okay because it's the Big Apple. It's where you go to make dreams come true. At least, that's the American dream that every TV show and movie I've ever watched portrays.

With my headphones in, drowning out the sound of boarding groups being called, I begin daydreaming about my new position as marketing assistant at Thrive Creative Co.

This is what I've been dreaming about ever since I graduated college. It always felt like such a pipe dream, one that I thought would surely never happen. I'm going to have the desk, the cubicle, the view. I'm going to live my very own *Working Girl* life.

Woodland Heights is one of those towns where everyone knows everybody. It's the kind of place where you don't need 'no solicitor' signs on your door because strangers simply don't exist. You're family friends with the mayor, and there's a good chance you'll run into your ex at the market on the corner at least once. Unfortunately, I am speaking from experience. On the upside, I've become a pro at dodging conversation. It's now one of my party tricks.

Before I can fully immerse myself into what my new life is going to look like, I'm snapped back to reality as my group is finally called. I shift the worn-out black duffle bag I've had since I was sixteen further up my shoulder, feeling as if I'm only seconds away from permanently dislocating it. I curse myself for shoving half of my belongings into the bag that I have to carry everywhere I go.

Note to self: buy a suitcase once I get settled.

I nearly drop my phone as they scan my pass to get onto the plane, thanks to my clammy hands, but I catch it with gusto. I'm overrun with giddiness at the thought that as soon as I step onto that plane, my life will never be the same.

After what feels like hours of waiting for the previous passengers to find their seats, I finally make my way down the long aisle of the plane, scanning the seat numbers for 12F. Eight, nine, ten–rows of mostly empty, blue leather seats pass through my vision as I grow closer.

As I approach my seat, I lock eyes with a pair of baby blues that I'd recognize anywhere.

No. It can't be.

My heart immediately drops, and a wave of nausea hits me like a freight train. I look behind me, trying to find an escape route, ignoring that mere seconds ago, all I could think about was being seated. I'm met with a long line of impatient looks, desperately waiting for me to sit so they can do the same. I have no choice but to charge forward.

I turn back around and move toward the seat, my palms dripping with sweat. All I can do is pray that I'm sitting behind him.

As I inch closer, reality hits. Not only is he on my flight, but we're also in the same row. Right next to one another. Our shoulders will inevitably have to touch, and the idea makes my stomach roll.

Why don't planes offer more breathing room instead of packing us in like a can of sardines?

Before I can ask someone to switch with me, I hear his voice, smooth as velvet. It wraps itself around me like an all too familiar blanket on a brisk winter night.

Fucking great.

"Dylan?" he questions, the shock in his voice evident.

Shit, so he did see me. The invisible cloak I imagine covering me apparently doesn't work. I nod, barely muttering out a choked hello. I avoid eye contact, keeping my eyes on the overhead compartment. As I try to swiftly stuff my bag in, it gets caught on the corner, stopping me in my tracks.

"Do you need help?"

Despite averting his gaze, I can see him begin to stand out of the corner of my eye. I know there's a high chance that if I reply, my voice will be that of a prepubescent teenage boy—squeaky and high-pitched, so I opt to keep my mouth shut and give a terse head shake. I shove the bag one last time, fitting it into the small storage bin.

He settles back down into his seat, and I find my seat next to him, my face burning.

The last place I ever expected to see Parker Townsend was on a plane headed across the country. I begin to fidget with the rings on my fingers, nearly sliding one off thanks to the sweat that has accumulated. Even if I wanted to initiate a conversation, the nervous tickle plaguing my throat has my full attention. I do my best to clear it unsuccessfully–the sound that escapes similar to a cat hacking up a hairball. *Perfect.*

What do you say to the man who broke your heart five years ago? The man you haven't seen since the night that he walked out your front door for the last time.

I shuffle in my seat, staring at the small television in front of me, which is currently pitch black and showcasing a very unflattering reflection of my beet-red face. Maybe if I pretend he's not there, he'll get the hint that I prefer silence, and we can enjoy our flight in peace.

"Dylan, you can't ignore me," he tries again, clearly fighting a smile.

Okay, so maybe my plan isn't entirely logical. I didn't account for the fact that he knows me well. One could argue *too* well.

I turn slowly and am once again met with those ocean eyes that make me feel like I'm drowning at sea. He looks different yet so familiar my heart involuntarily clenches.

Parker's once short, dark brunette hair is now grown out, a singular curl falling in front of his face. He has the beginning of a five o'clock shadow that makes him look like a real man—not the boy I once knew better than I knew myself. In spite of the differences, I can spot the dimples on his cheeks that he's had since he was a child. Two little divots that render me powerless any time they make an appearance.

I scan down his body, noticing that he fills out his plain, long-sleeve black shirt, the muscles he's clearly worked hard for, causing the cotton to strain. His left, tanned arm is resting on the armrest, and I catch a quick glimpse of a few small tattoos peeking out from the sleeve he's lazily pushed up.

It suddenly feels like the plane's narrow body is closing in on me as my chest tightens and I fight to catch my breath. When we were younger, he was adamant about never getting a tattoo–he said they were too permanent for him. He must've had the same feeling about us, too. I guess I didn't know him as well as I thought.

Unfortunately, my mind is a traitor, and one glance at his tatted forearm makes me wonder what it would feel like to be curled in his arms again.

No, Dylan. Stop it. You shouldn't be having these thoughts, I scold myself.

I cough a little too loudly, still trying to rid myself of the scratchiness in my throat, and the woman sitting across from us glowers at me. It takes all of my willpower not to roll my eyes at her. How would she react if she were in my position? I'd venture to guess very similarly.

"Hi." It's a pathetic response, but it's all I can muster up.

He breaks out in a grin, which is the epitome of boyish, and my pulse quickens. I mentally reprimand myself once again, reminding myself that I need to play it cool.

"I can't believe it's really you," he says, shaking his head in disbelief.

"I can't either. What are you doing here?" My tone comes out a little too accusatory, like he isn't allowed to be on this flight. I mean, what are the chances, though? It's like fate is playing some sick joke on me. Well, you know what, universe? I'm ready for the game to be over now. I've had enough for the day!

He lightly chuckles as if genuinely amused.

"I'm, uh, actually moving to New York. I was just in town visiting family. I figured I owed them a visit since it's been a while. What about you?"

That's impossible. I rub at my brow, willing my jaw to stay shut. It feels like my brain is short-circuiting, and I have to be very careful with my response because I know I'm seconds away from making an ass out of myself.

"That's nice. I'm moving there, too..." My voice is strained as it comes out, and I drop my hands in my lap.

With that, his eyes widen ever-so-slightly. If I hadn't been staring so hard (cut me some slack), I might have missed the sudden, subtle shift in his facial expression.

"Oh really? So you're finally making your dreams come true, huh?"

The question creates a sense of unease in the pit of my stomach. I didn't want him to know anything about my life. We spent years talking about moving across the country and had countless conversations about what our life together would look like when we made it happen. It was never a matter of *if* that day would come. It was always the *when*. Or so I thought.

Although he was always supportive, he lost the right to know what I'm doing the minute he called it quits.

I nod tightly, trying to avoid having to talk with him any further.

"Good for you, Dyl. I always knew you could do it." He rests his hand on my forearm, a gesture of love that feels like a white-hot brand striking my skin. Thank god I'm sitting down because my legs grow weak at the contact.

Tears fill my eyes, and I quickly turn to face the window to hide the pained look I'm confident I'm wearing.

I know he means well, but it's too painful to hear. I've spent far too many nights with my face buried in a pint of Ben and Jerry's, watching ridiculous rom-coms with a heartache that felt like it was going to kill me. It got to the point where I started going to therapy.

I shudder at the thought of how much money I've spent on my healing, only to have that wound ripped open slowly, stitch by stitch, the minute I see him again. I'm coming unraveled.

I close my eyes, taking deep breaths to soothe the anxiety stirring in my belly. In through the nose, out through the mouth. It takes a few rounds of focused breathing before my heart rate drops and I can open my eyes without a trickle of tears threatening to fall.

"Thank you." I swallow. "I'm starting a new job on Monday."

"Hell yeah. You're making it happen for yourself. There's no one more deserving of it," he responds, that dashing smile reappearing on his face.

I nod, feeling the corner of my lips twitch up as I warm up. We haven't seen each other in years, yet we're already falling back into the ease that was once our everyday lives. No matter how hard I try to fight to keep him at arm's length, slipping back into the uncomplicated conversation that we used to have feels as natural as breathing.

"What about you?" I ask. "What's the reasoning behind your move?"

"I'm starting a new job too, believe it or not. You're looking at one of the newest editors at Blue Bird Publishing." His voice is dripping with pride, and I can feel the skin of my cheeks stretching as my grin grows.

"Wow, you really are becoming a hot shot. Congratulations. I'm sure you're going to kill it." I beam, feeling truly overjoyed that he's also chasing his dreams. A small, whispered voice in the back of my head begins questioning our past. Maybe us going our separate ways was for the best, after all.

He blows out a breath, his eyebrows shooting up anxiously. "I sure hope so. This could be huge for my career."

I nudge his elbow playfully, that jolt of electricity running through my veins again almost instantly. I immediately pull away, hoping he didn't feel it, too.

"You've always been ridiculously talented. I wouldn't be too worried if I were you." The minute the words are out of my mouth, I want to crawl into a hole six feet under the ground. How am I complimenting him already? The *least* I could do is make him work for it.

"Thank you. That means a lot coming from you." He holds eye contact with me for a few seconds too long. I divert my attention away, trying to distract myself from the butterflies running rampant in my stomach again.

Seconds later, the captain comes on the overhead speaker and announces we're ready for departure. Thank god. I don't know how much longer I can make small talk. I already despise it as is, let alone with *him*. What are we supposed to talk about? The weather? The fact that I haven't experienced love in the years we've been separated? I'm sure that won't be awkward at all.

I look out the window and notice we're moving down the jetway. I must've missed the safety briefing while being too engrossed in conversation. Here's hoping we don't crash because I would be utterly useless. Sure, I've flown enough to know the protocol. But knowing that I'm sitting so close to Parker makes me worried that I'd be pushing my way past the panicked passengers, trying to claw my way off the plane so that I don't have to spend my last day on Earth with him.

"If you don't mind, I'm going to listen to some music," I say as I grab my AirPods from my bag and throw them in. Before he can respond, I queue up "Cigarette Daydreams" by Cage The Elephant and turn up the volume all the way. It's the only way I can think of getting out of this conversation.

If he's insulted by my ending the conversation, he doesn't say anything. I see him slide on his own headphones and pull out a paperback book in my peripheral. Why do men have to be so damn attractive when they read?

This is going to be the longest two hours of my life.

❋ ❋ ❋ ❋ ❋

I'M awoken by a flight attendant lightly tapping my shoulder, politely asking me to put my tray table up to prepare for landing. I glance down at my phone and see we're only twenty minutes from our arrival time.

I don't remember falling asleep, but I'm grateful that I did because that very well could have been my own flight from hell if I had been forced to continue talking with Parker.

I sneak a look over at him, and he's still enthralled by the book he brought with him, folded up in the exact position I remember him being in when we took off. As I shift in my seat to put my headphones away, he marks his spot with a bookmark, closes the book, slides his headphones off his head, and places them in the backpack at his feet.

"Have a good nap?" he smugly questions.

A flush creeps up my neck and cheeks. I just had to fall asleep. I can only hope that I didn't drool all over myself or let my head fall onto his shoulder. I discreetly feel around my mouth and chin for any wet spots, but I think the coast is clear.

"I did. I didn't think I was tired, but there's just something about flying that puts me to sleep." I stretch my arms and legs up, trying to get my blood flowing again. My feet have fallen asleep, and it feels like pins and needles are poking my soles.

As I reach my hands toward the top of the plane, I feel his eyes trace my movements, his eyes catching on my shirt, inching up my torso. I simper to myself, regrettably pleased that he can't keep his eyes off.

"I know. If I recall correctly, you slept the entire flight to Arizona. Remember that?"

I let out a small giggle, trying to push away the memories attempting to ambush my thoughts. It was the first vacation we took together, and we spent our days relaxing under the sun. Well, *mostly* relaxing. There may have been some poolside rendezvous, too. I shake my head, clearing away the image. I don't need him catching onto the fact that I'm reliving some of our most sensual moments together–even if they do live rent-free in my head.

"Yeah, I do. What can I say? I feel completely relaxed the minute I step onto a plane."

Except for this one. Although I was calm enough to fall asleep, so clearly, his presence wasn't too upsetting. That or I really need to work on my fight or flight response. Is sleep a third option in times of distress? Because I clearly have that nailed.

I cuss silently to myself for slipping back into the comfort I once was extremely familiar with.

"That a good book?" I question, thirsting to change the subject.

He shrugs. "It's not bad. You'd think I'd spend my time doing anything besides reading since that's all I'm going to be doing day in and day out soon, but I can't stop."

"You've always been a reader. It's one of the things I admired most about you." I bring my top lip between my teeth and bite down.

There I go again. That was the last thing I was supposed to be admitting out loud. These are the kinds of thoughts that you think about internally until you have time to gush in your journal later.

Real slick.

"Thank you, I appreciate that. It's nice to escape reality, even just for a bit." His voice is laced with a tinge of sadness. I'm not sure why, considering it seems like he has everything he's ever wanted.

"I understand that. More than you know." I furrow my brows, deep in thought. I'd love to escape reality. Hell, that's why I'm moving across the country. I need a new beginning—a fresh start.

There's a moment of silence between us, and I feel like I've made things uncomfortable. He doesn't seem to notice because right as I turn to him to fill the unpleasant quietness, he places his backpack back under his seat before turning to me.

I don't get a word in as he asks, "Hey, this may be crossing a line, but since we're both moving to a new city, why don't we grab a coffee sometime? It'd be nice to have a familiar face around every now and then."

No. No, no, no, no, no. That's a bad idea. I've come too far to be pulled back under his spell. I shiver before throwing him a small smile, ready to let him down gently.

"Look, I appreciate the offer, but I think it's probably best to keep our distance. I really do hope that life in the city is everything you hoped for, though. It was nice to catch up, even if only for a couple of minutes."

The grin he's been wearing falters, but before it turns into a full-fledged frown, he catches himself and nods. "I completely understand. If you change your mind, you know where to find me."

The hope in his eyes quickly diminishes, and no matter how hard he tries to pretend, it's clear to see that he's hurt by my rejection. I attempt to take a deep breath and find it hard to fully fill my lungs with air. My knee-jerk reaction is to apologize, but I swallow the urge.

"Thanks."

We spend the next fifteen minutes sitting in silence. As much as I want to spend hours catching up and seeing how life has been (beyond what I've seen during my social media stalking sessions), I need to hold my ground. Falling in love with him was easy the first time. Too easy. And now that he's in the same city, looking as handsome as ever, I know that the likelihood of me falling all over again is extremely high. I'm here to focus on myself for the first time in my life. Not love.

Fortunately, the wait to get off the plane isn't too long when we land. I thank my lucky stars I paid to be in the front of the plane, throw my bag onto my shoulder again, and turn to him one last time.

"Good luck. I hope it goes well for you."

I know it's probably a cold and callous thing to say, but it's all I can think of. I do wish him the best in his endeavors, even if I'm no longer a part of the picture. I always have.

"You too, Dylan."

Before I have time to deal with the swell of emotions I'm feeling, I rush off the plane, ready to put this whole interaction behind me.

The minute I step onto the grounds of JFK, I'm beaming. This is it. Even a run-in with the former love of my life can't take it away from me. I'm ready to start over, and the time is now.

2

DYLAN

By the time I get to my apartment, I'm absolutely exhausted. Despite having napped on the plane, I'm not quite sure if I've ever felt more emotionally drained. An unexpected run-in with your college boyfriend really takes a toll on a person. Who would've thought?

Even though my limbs feel heavy, and I just want to curl up into a ball, my chest lightens as I walk through my front door. This is officially my home.

"Dylan?" I hear a shriek from the bathroom.

"Honey, I'm home!" I call back, bouncing from foot to foot.

Amelia, my new roommate, comes barreling out of her bedroom and tackles me into a tight hug, squeezing so hard I practically suffocate. For such a tiny person, she has an absolute death grip. I give her a quick hug back and gently push her off of me before I run out of oxygen. I gulp down a breath and rub my chest, easing the pain.

"I can't believe you're finally here! How was your flight? Did you have a hard time catching a cab? Tell me Richard, the neighborhood creep, didn't catcall you on the way in. How are you feeling? Do you feel like a local New Yorker yet?" she rambles.

"Whoa, whoa, whoa, slow down." I place my singular piece of luggage down, my shoulder screaming in pain. Most twenty-nine-year-olds have a lot more personal possessions, but I knew the minute I got the job in the city, I was going to treat it like a clean slate. It's not like my thrifted bedding and furniture were worth taking in the first place.

"I can't even begin to explain to you what happened on the way here."

She yanks me further into the apartment and pulls my arm down so I'm sitting on a bar stool near the kitchen.

"Tell me all about it. Did you meet your future husband? Was he the hottest thing in the world?"

If there's one thing that I've come to learn about Amelia, it's that she's long-winded, to put it nicely. I met her on social media a year ago when I began my apartment search, and we instantly clicked. She's quirky, over-enthusiastic, and the life of the party. As someone who's pretty much the exact opposite, it's nice to have someone pull me out of my comfort zone.

Of course, I FaceTimed her as soon as we exchanged numbers. I had to make sure that I wasn't about to get catfished. Or murdered. Or both. The call lasted over an hour. From there, we began talking on the phone every single day. She became my best friend before I even realized it.

She didn't have much competition, though. Most of my friends in Woodland Heights had either moved away or settled down and had kids, making them virtually impossible to reach. I was the last single one out of my friends, and once Parker and I broke up, I became a hermit.

There's something to be said about spending your free time at home rather than out at the bars. As an introvert, staying in proved to me how much I enjoy the peace and quiet of being home.

"That's one way of putting it."

"Ooh, so you did meet someone. Spill." She pulls up the other bar stool next to me and rests her elbows on the kitchen counter, her head resting in her hands as she stares at me with her big doe eyes.

"You'll never guess who I just had to sit next to for the last two hours."

"Ryan Gosling?"

I scoff. "I wish. No. Parker."

Her impossibly large eyes grow bigger, and her jaw falls to the floor. "Like *the* Parker?"

I solemnly nod. "That's the one."

"How is that even possible? I thought he lived in California."

"I thought so, too. Turns out he was visiting family before moving to New York."

"Shut up. That's the most cosmic shit I've ever heard. Do you think that's the universe's way of giving you a sign?" she questions.

I roll my eyes and immediately shut her down with a curt head shake.

"Absolutely not. And you're really not helping right now."

She gets up from her chair and wraps me in a bear hug, again holding me just a little too tightly. We're going to have to work on this whole physical touch thing, but now isn't the right time to bring it up.

"You're right. I'm sorry. How did that go?"

I blow out a sigh. "Alright. We talked for about five minutes before I threw in my headphones to avoid speaking to him for hours. It was the longest five minutes of my life. He looked so damn good, too."

I run a palm down my face, immediately feeling ashamed for admitting it out loud. Thinking it is one thing, but admitting it out loud to my best friend is another.

"They always get hotter after the breakup, don't they? On the plus side, you did, too. How could he not fall in love with you all over again? Just look at yourself."

I give a half-hearted laugh. "Thanks. But I don't know what to do now. I was so excited to get a fresh start and move away from the past. Now, all I'm going to be thinking about is running into him on the subway."

Without batting an eye, she drags me up from my chair and into her small bedroom with her. Soundlessly, she begins rifling through her packed-to-the-brim closet. Aside from being spunky, Amelia is also one of the most fashionable people I've ever met. She could wear a paper bag and make it look couture. I hate and love her for it.

I stand in the middle of her beautifully decorated room gracelessly, unsure of what to do with myself.

My gaze falls back onto the tiny closet. Though the apartment is incredible and offers panoramic views of Brooklyn, it's going to be hard to adjust to the lack of space here, that's for sure.

"There are over a million people in Manhattan alone. That's not going to happen. Now sit," she finally demands, pointing to her bed without looking away from her racks of colorful clothes.

I do as I'm told and sit, legs crossed on her bed draped in the softest sage green comforter I've ever felt. I find myself stroking the fabric mindlessly as I ask, "What are you doing?"

"I'm finding you something to wear."

I glance down at my airport attire. I opted for comfort rather than style with an old pair of black leggings, a grey oversized hoodie, and a beat-up pair of black sneakers. To say that I've looked better is an understatement–and it just gives me another reason to curse at the universe for the bump in on the plane.

"For what? I'm just going to unpack, hop in the shower, and go to bed."

"I love you, but no, you're not. It's only 7 o'clock." She spins around with a very see-through black mesh mini dress with a sewn-in matching black bra and underwear set.

"Um, what is that? There's no way in hell I'm going out. Especially in that."

She shoves the ensemble into my hands and rushes back to the closet to find a pair of shoes to match. Her small stature allows her to buzz around quickly, giving me little time to argue.

"Yes, you are. It's your first night in New York. This is how we do it here. I'm not about to let you sit around and mope about Parker. You know what they say. The best way to get over someone is to get under someone. Now, what size shoe do you wear?"

I throw the dress–if you can even classify the skimpy number an article of clothing–on the bed with a snort.

"I will be getting under absolutely no one. I just want to climb into bed, read my book, and forget the entire thing happened."

It's not that I haven't tried moving on. I dated around a couple of years after we broke up. I had a handful of drunken nights out with the girls that resulted in making out with total strangers. But nothing ever compared to what I had with Parker.

That's why, a year ago, I decided to call it quits and stay single for the rest of my life. It couldn't be that hard, right? Besides, every romantically unattached person I knew only complained about how hard the dating scene was. So, I was really just saving myself the headache.

"Dyl, you're brand new to the city. There are so many hot, eligible bachelors out there. Don't you want to meet them? It will help take your mind off it more than any book could." She places a pair of silver platform heels at the foot of the bed.

I let out a long, low groan. I know she's right, but that doesn't make it any easier. How am I supposed to mingle only hours after my life was completely shaken up?

"Please don't make me. I can go meet guys tomorrow."

"Nope, sorry, babe. I know you're just saying that to get me off your back, and it won't work tonight. We're going out."

She disappears into her bathroom with what looks like a pile of clothes and shoes in her arms. I fall back onto her bed, resting my hands over my face. My invisible trick didn't work earlier, but maybe if I pretend to fall asleep, she'll leave me alone. I can blame it on the jet lag.

I stay as still as humanly possible as I hear her shuffling around.

A couple of minutes later, she emerges in a black lace corset that hugs her curves in all the right places and a pair of tight burgundy leather pants. Her platinum blonde hair is pulled back into a tight, slicked-back bun, and she's donning a smokey eye that makes her blue eyes pop even more than usual.

She looks stunning, which only makes my desire to go out dwindle further. There's no way I should be expected to stand next to her all night. The guys are going to be flocking instantly, and I'm certainly not in the mood to be second best while everyone drools all over her.

I continue to feign sleep, but she's not falling for it.

"I know you're faking it. Get up and get changed. We're grabbing a drink whether you like it or not. On me. Consider it your welcome gift."

I sigh, reluctantly pulling myself up out of bed. I guess one drink wouldn't hurt. But I'm sticking my ground on meeting men. If a man even tries to look in my direction, I'm running the opposite way, whether she likes it or not.

I grab the barely-there outfit Amelia picked out for me and

head to my bedroom to get changed. Not only is her wardrobe incredible, but she's also a damn good interior designer.

My new space is already decked to the nines. The queen-sized mattress rests against an original exposed brick wall, placed on top of a modern, metal bed frame that surely came from West Elm. The cream duvet is minimalistic yet classic, making it the perfect complement for the dusty blue decorative pillows atop it.

Adjacent to the bed is a large window offering views of the Dumbo skyline. I take a second to look out and see the city twinkling beneath the night sky. I sit down on the bed, feeling breathless as I try to wrap my brain around the fact that this is my life now.

If Amelia's dad weren't the rich CEO of a tech company and wasn't trying to pay her off so he wouldn't have to parent her, she wouldn't have been able to afford this apartment. And I *definitely* would not be living somewhere this nice. I'm very fortunate I didn't end up in a windowless cell that many realtors call "apartments" here in the city.

I give myself a quick pinch to bring myself back to reality before undressing and sliding into Amelia's mesh mini-dress. After glancing at myself in the oversize mirror sitting against the bedroom wall, I had to admit that I looked pretty damn good–if you ignore the hair and dark bags around my eyes.

"I'm coming in!" Amelia announces with a quick tap on the door. "Oh my god, that dress is to die for on you. The men are going to lose their minds when they see you. Now go to my bathroom so I can do your makeup."

Before I can debate with her, she gives me a shove. It didn't take long to see that when Amelia wants something, she gets her way, so I don't bother fighting it anymore.

I sit on the closed toilet, and she works her magic with her makeup bag strewn across the bathroom counter. She has every product under the sun, and I'm nervous that I'm going to come out of this looking like a clown. I tend to prefer to keep things very understated. It doesn't help that I've never been great at makeup in the first place.

She rolls her eyes, sensing my hesitancy. "Relax. I know you like the natural look. I won't go too crazy."

What feels like a century later, she pulls back and admires her work.

"God, I'm good," she gloats with a smirk.

I stand up to look at my face in the mirror. My high cheekbones are accentuated with a subtle contour, making me look like I just returned from a tropical vacation. The apples of my cheeks glow with highlighter, and the wing eyeliner she perfected looks like it would have taken me hours. I look less like a zombie and more like a functioning human being.

"You really are. I don't know how you do it. Is there anything you're bad at?"

She purses her lips, squinting her eyes as she contemplates the thought. "I don't think so, come to think of it."

I stifle a laugh and throw my frizzy brunette hair into a loose, low, messy ponytail, letting my curtain bangs fall delicately around my face.

Amelia, chipper as can be, jumps up and down while clapping. "We look so hot! Watch out, boys. It's time to eat your heart out," she calls out to no one in particular. "There's just one more finishing touch we need."

She vanishes back into her bedroom before coming back with a pair of oversized silver hoops. "Here, put these on."

The minute I put them on and take one more look at my reflection in the mirror, I'm bursting with confidence. I haven't felt this hot in years. In fact, I don't know if I've ever felt this hot in my entire life. She's a fucking wizard. It's the only explanation that makes sense.

"Now, into the kitchen to take a tequila shot, and then we're off!"

My stomach churns at the thought, and the confidence I was just basking in disintegrates. I'm *definitely* not ready for this.

✽ ✽ ✽ ✽ ✽

When we walk into Elsewhere, I can barely see. It's dimly lit, with ever-changing colored lights setting the ambiance, and jam-packed. I hold tightly onto Amelia's hand to squeeze past the sea of sweaty bodies.

I know I'm new to the city, but I've researched enough to know that this is arguably one of Brooklyn's hottest nightclubs. And one of the most underground. I shouldn't be surprised that Amelia got us in with no problem, yet I am.

We shove our way to the bar, and within seconds, a hot, tattooed, and bearded bartender comes up to take our order. I can feel countless impatient eyes fall on us. We easily just made the shit list of at least twenty clubbers–there's nothing quite like the restlessness of a drunken crowd trying to order their next round.

"What can I get you ladies?"

Amelia leans against the bar and bats her eyelashes at him. "Two tequila sodas, please."

He flashes us a grin that makes me weak in the knees. "Coming right up." If the men in this city are this hot, then maybe I stand a chance of not dying alone after all.

She turns to me with a smile plastered on her face. "You ready to have some fun?" she yells over the music. Amelia seems completely oblivious to the attractiveness of the bartender, and I'm in awe.

Although I had zero interest in coming tonight, I can't deny that this is amazing. Being surrounded by hundreds of New

Yorkers, everyone dancing and singing along to the music, is electric—so electric that I don't even mind the feeling of sticky bodies rubbing against me.

"Yeah, actually, I am."

She grabs our drinks and hands the bartender her credit card. When he returns to give it back to her, she jots down her phone number on the receipt.

"Call me," she says with a wink.

"I definitely will," he replies, grabbing the tab and tucking it into his shirt pocket for safekeeping.

Looks like I was mistaken. She definitely noticed how beautiful he was, and she definitely just earned herself a date. Or a great night in bed, at the very least. God, she has game. If I ever want to find another boyfriend, she's going to have to teach me a thing or two.

She passes me my drink and pulls me out to the dance floor. Despite there being very little room to breathe, we manage to find a spot in the center. I take a large sip of my drink and instantly hide my pucker. Holy shit, this stuff is strong.

While I do drink occasionally, it's not something I do often. I grew up seeing how much it can destroy families, so I need to be careful tonight. I never built up a tolerance, which means if I'm not cautious, I'm going to find myself on my ass.

I don't mind being a lightweight. It used to bother me when I spent most of my free time at bars with friends, but I've come to realize just how much money it saves me, which I always consider a win.

I begin to sway with Amelia, the music pulsing through my veins. It's euphoric. *This* is what I've been dreaming about ever since I was a little girl. Okay, so technically, I didn't dream of dancing in a club. But being another one of the millions of NYC residents is a high unlike anything I've ever felt before.

As I get lost in the music, I work up a thirst, which I happily quench with my tequila soda. Before I know it, the drink is gone, and I feel my head growing lighter. Fuzzier.

I tried to make it last as long as possible, but it was almost impossible when every song the DJ played was a hit. I could dance all night long, but the last thing I needed to do was blackout and embarrass myself on my first night here. My hangovers also last days now that I'm in my late twenties, and I refuse to spend my first day of work in the bathroom, hurling my guts up.

I open my eyes and see Amelia chatting with yet another good-looking man. This one's got a blonde, surfer look to him. Very different from the brooding brunette who served us our drinks. Amelia's got a little taste for everything, and I can't fault her for it.

I know I got swept up dancing for a second, but it could not have been that long. I can't help but wonder how she finds these men so quickly. Then again, her beauty is so hypnotizing that it draws all walks of life in.

I'm not sure I'll ever get used to being best friends with someone as naturally gorgeous as her. Or the attention that she receives everywhere she goes.

She sees me looking in her direction and shoos the man away. He looks defeated but walks off to find another beautiful woman to flirt with. Typical. She prances up to me and points to my empty cup.

"Time for another?" She lifts her empty cup to show she's finished hers.

I shake my head. "I hate to be a buzzkill, but I'm already feeling this one. I don't know if that's a good idea. Plus, I'm exhausted."

She juts out her bottom lip in a pout but nods. "I understand. We can get going. Thank you for at least humoring me tonight."

She links my arm with hers, and we fight our way to the

exit. As we're approaching the door, I catch a glimpse of a vaguely familiar figure standing to the left of the door. I whip my head around and see a man identical to Parker standing amidst a small group of people. He's even wearing the same black t-shirt that hugs his delicious arms.

Before I can stop to see if it's him, Amelia pulls me out into the dark night.

Not a chance.

What are the odds I see him twice in one day? In a city this big? It couldn't possibly be him.

I debate pulling Amelia back into the club to get one last look, but I know deep down that it's best to leave it alone, even if every part of me says otherwise.

If I'm going to constantly have to be on the lookout for him, my time in New York is going to be a lot less enjoyable than I thought.

3

PARKER

My alarm goes off at 8 a.m. on the dot, causing a shrill beeping to reverberate through my apartment. I quickly shut it off without moving too much. I can't believe it's Monday, and my hangover still has me in a chokehold. One hurried movement and a shooting pain sears through my skull.

I didn't mean to drink that much when I went out, but the minute I saw Dylan out at the club, only hours after sitting through two painstakingly long hours on a plane next to her, my self-control went out the window. I'm not sure what's worse. The urge to vomit that's bubbling in my stomach or seeing the one that got away twice in one day after years of no contact.

I rub the sleep out of my eyes with the palms of my hands and slowly push the comforter down, attempting to climb out of bed. It's the first day of my new job, and while I may feel like shit, I have to go in and make a good impression. I worked my ass off to get where I am today, and I can't ruin that on the first day.

I make my way to a standing position, staying extremely still until I'm confident that I can manage to take the few steps it takes to get to my bathroom without puking all over my new rug. I did pretty well for myself in California, which allowed me to decorate my East Village one-bedroom apartment with fine furnishings. The last thing I need to do is stain it because I'd prefer to drink myself to death rather than sit with my emotions.

I open my medicine cabinet, grab the Tylenol bottle, and pop three pills in my mouth. I need all the help I can get if I'm going to survive the day. I'm the boss now, and I only have one chance to get everyone to take me seriously.

After swallowing the medicine with a large swig of water, I splash freezing cold water on my face. I can physically feel my balls shrivel up into my stomach, but it's worth it when I feel relief from the nausea that's been tormenting me. Within minutes, my teeth are brushed, and the mop of hair I have is now styled.

We're halfway there; I give myself a pep talk.

I saunter shakily over to my walk-in, albeit small, closet and begin to shuffle through the few shirts I managed to hang after landing in the city. I had every intention of unpacking most of my stuff this past weekend, but I quickly derailed those plans.

I'm not one to go out often, but when my best friend Blake texted me inviting me out to meet some friends of his, I figured I should try to be social. He's basically the only person I know in New York, so I might as well try to make new friends. Especially since Dylan immediately shut me down when I suggested staying in touch.

Just the thought of her sends another wave of nausea through me, forcing me to lean against the closet wall to keep me steady. *Shake it off, man.* There's no need to go back to those feelings.

I give my shoulders a little shrug and focus back on the dress shirts sprawled out on the hangers in front of me. I decide on a plain white t-shirt along with a matching light navy blazer and dress pant set. To dress it down, I grab a pair of white sneakers and head back to my bedroom. I swiftly grab my phone off its charger and my work briefcase resting beside my nightstand.

I don't have any food yet, which means I have to grab something on my way into the office. I just hope I can stomach the bagel I've been dreaming about since I landed.

※ ※ ※ ※ ※

As I push through the doors of Blue Bird, I'm met with a smiling face from a timid receptionist.

"You must be Parker. Welcome to the office," she welcomes me warmly.

I respond with the best smile I can muster up and a quick nod, still wary of moving too quickly. Even though I was able to keep my breakfast (which was, in fact, one of the best bagels I've ever had) down, I can't be too sure that the remnants of the hangover are gone yet.

I trudge my way to my office, a small corner space with floor-to-ceiling windows and one hell of a view of Central Park. I don't typically like to gloat, but I know I killed it at my last job. I just didn't think I did *this* well. I have Blake to thank for that, though. We worked together on the West Coast, and after putting in a good word for me, he managed to land me one of the most sought-after positions in New York.

I twist the door handle and swing the door open to find Blake leaning against my empty desk, typing up a storm on his phone. The startle it sends through me causes the room to spin, and I grip the door handle tighter before I lose my balance. When I'm confident I'm not going faceplant, I move my hands to my temples to ease the pressure.

Speaking of the devil.

"Jesus, dude. You can't scare me like that."

He looks up from his phone with a holier-than-thou grin on his face. "Looks like someone really can't handle their alcohol. You okay there?"

I steady myself down in the vacant chair behind the desk. He turns around to look at me, his mouth twisted wryly.

"Maybe if you hadn't insisted on pouring tequila down my throat, I'd be in a much better position than I'm in right now," I snap back.

"You did that to yourself. You looked like you saw a ghost. I was just there to help calm the nerves." He tucks his phone and hands into his pocket and walks to the window, taking in the scenery.

"Well, you certainly did that. I can barely remember anything past the third shot you physically forced me to take."

He sits on the window sill facing me, hands tucked into his armpits. "So you're saying you don't remember getting on the table and dancing to Dancing Queen by ABBA?"

I groan and shut my eyes tightly. That had to be some kind of sick joke. I've been known to do some stupid things under the influence, but I'm not sure I'd ever stoop to that level.

"That didn't happen. You're just fucking with me."

He lets out a deep snicker and grabs his phone back out of his pocket to put it on display. "No, it definitely happened. And I have it all on here. You can guarantee that I will be using it as blackmail when the time comes."

"You're a dick," I retort.

"Is that really how you want to treat the person who got you your dream job?"

"Yeah, yeah. Can't wait to have you hold that over my head for the rest of my life." I murmur.

"That's what best friends are for. Aside from the obvious hangover and the smell of liquor currently seeping from your pores, how are you feeling?" he inquires as he sits on the chair on the other side of my desk, kicking his feet up and resting his loafers on the wood.

I subtly lift my arm, trying to catch a whiff of myself. I thought I drowned myself in enough cologne to mask the scent. I can't smell anything aside from the leathery muskiness of Le Labo's Santal 33, so I ignore him.

"Feeling pretty good. I read all of the manuscripts that you sent over last week. There's a lot of potential there."

He bows his head in agreement. "Good, because word on the street is that there's a new up-and-coming author slated to be a New York Times best seller. I want you to spearhead the project."

There are some benefits to being best friends with your boss, but the last thing I need to do is get work because of nepotism. That's a surefire way to get everyone in the office to hate me right off the bat.

"Why me?"

He lifts a shoulder in a nonchalant shrug. Asshole.

Blake readjusts, resting his elbows on his knees as he leans forward to get closer to me. "I'm kidding. You're great at what you do, and this is the opportunity of a lifetime. I briefly read the manuscript myself last week, and I know it's going to be huge. This could be killer for your career. I already emailed it to you this morning to have you take a look."

Perfect. One day in, I'm already being handed this golden opportunity on a platter. No pressure or anything.

"In that case, I need to get to work. Seems like I've got quite a lot of reading to do."

He stands up, smoothing down his black button-up shirt. "Yes, you do. In the meantime, you should get the ball rolling on marketing. Since you're new here, I already emailed you the name of the agency we've partnered up with in the past."

"Thanks, man. I appreciate it." I grab my laptop from my

briefcase and fire it up, opening my email. Sure enough, at the top of my inbox are multiple emails breaking down everything I need to know about my newest client.

"Good luck today. You've got this." He gives me a little two-finger salute before going back to his own office next door. Once the door is shut and I can finally sit in silence, I click on his first email.

I spend the next three hours in a reading trance. Blake wasn't kidding when he said that this book was incredible. It's unlike anything I have ever read. With some small tweaks, it could be huge.

According to Blake's email, I only have two weeks to get working with a marketing agency to get us ready for the May release date they've projected.

While Blake likes to fuck with me in every way imaginable, I know that he takes his work as seriously as I do, which is why I draft up a new email to Katherine over at Thrive Creative Co.

Being wrapped up in work almost makes me forget about the weekend and hangover from hell. Keyword: almost.

4

DYLAN

My first week at work is pretty uneventful, to say the least. I guess I can't complain. I'd rather blend in the background and coast than deal with constant stress. The one thorn in my side, however, is my boss, Katherine.

I've only been here for five days, but she can't be bothered to remember my name. First, it was Delaney; then, it was Delilah. Yesterday, it was Denise. I guess I should be relieved that I'm flying under the radar enough that she doesn't need to remember who I am. I blow out a sigh, seeing the holes in my own silver lining.

I never expected it to be easy, but I thought it'd at least be a little more glamorous than this. Most of my days are spent taking notes during meetings, grabbing coffees, and planning out social media posts, only to have them constantly edited and rewritten.

As I'm typing away at this week's work, my stomach grumbles, and I glance up at my laptop's clock. 12 o'clock. Lunchtime, thank god. I save my work before shutting my computer and heading down to the office's cafeteria, one floor down.

As I eye today's selection of unappetizing food, I spy Scarlett sitting at a table, enthusiastically waving me over. I grab the most edible-looking sandwich and a bag of chips and join her. She has two iced lattes sitting in front of her, and she pushes one of them in my direction as soon as I'm in my seat.

"Here you go. I figured you could use an afternoon pick-me-up."

I speedily grab it, savoring the first large sip as the caffeine hits my bloodstream. I'm not entirely sure if it's adjusting to the new time zone or the stress of wanting to impress everyone at work, but I've had difficulty sleeping this past week. Of course, the more I can't sleep, the more coffee I drink. The more coffee I drink, the harder it is for me to sleep. It's a vicious carousel ride I can't seem to get off.

"You're an angel," I reply in between gulps.

"I know." She flips her long, loose, jet-black curls over her shoulder.

Scarlett, much like Amelia, is everything that I'm not. She's a perfectionist, a workaholic, wildly ambitious, and Katherine's favorite employee. She's been with the company for three years and has already received three promotions, which is pretty much unheard of at Thrive Creative. Most of us just get ignored.

To be fair, Scarlett's earned it all. She's always trying to be the best she can possibly be at her job, and she's not afraid to do what it takes to get there. That's how she's landed some of our biggest clients. I think she took pity on me when she saw me eating lunch by myself on my first day, so she invited me to join her. Now we meet up at the same table every single day at noon on the dot.

She also happens to be incredibly naturally beautiful. Everything about her screams old money, including the sandy cashmere sweater, matching cream silk midi skirt, and Louboutin pumps she's wearing today. I know that I'll never look like an old Hollywood starlet like her, but being around her gives me a glimmer of hope, as if some of the beauty will rub off on me.

"How are things coming? Has the she-devil backed off at all?" she asks.

I huff out a small laugh under my breath. Scarlett may be the teacher's pet, but she's very aware of the treachery that is Katherine.

"For the time being. But she still hasn't managed to get my name right. As I was leaving yesterday, she called me Denise."

She rolls her eyes and rests a hand lightly on my arm. I feel that same pang of pity that I felt when she first came up to me. The last thing I need is for people to feel bad for me right now. I know how to handle myself. I've had to take care of myself for half of my life, and this is no different. I try to shake it off, reminding myself that Scarlett is one of the only things keeping me sane at the moment.

"I'm sorry. She'll learn eventually. Just give her some time. Soon enough, you'll be on her good side, I promise. It took me at least a year for her just to make eye contact with me," she consoles.

"I appreciate you trying to make me feel better, but you and I both know that's not true whatsoever. You've been her favorite since the minute you got here. I've heard rumblings from everyone else in the office about you, but thank you."

I take a few bites of my sandwich before pushing it away, suddenly aware of my lack of appetite. I hate letting people's perceptions of me affect how I feel, yet I find my mood slowly souring and my control slipping.

"Well, I still think she's the closest thing to Satan that walks on Earth if that makes you feel any better."

With that joke, the heaviness creeping its way into my heart dissolves, and I bring my hand up to cover my giggles. "It does. Thank you."

"Of course. So I was talking to Layla before you got here, and rumor has it that there was a very hot visitor walking into the office earlier. I think Katherine has a meeting planned with him today. You should try to get in on that one," Scarlett says in between bites of her salad.

"The last thing I need to be thinking about is some hot stranger. I'm just here to get good at my job and hope that I don't get my head chewed off on a daily basis. No distractions."

"If anyone is chewing your head off, you better let me know. Because they have to go through me first. Secondly, everyone could use a little eye candy. It doesn't mean you have to act on it. Nothing makes a meeting a little more manageable than something pretty to look at." Her eyes have a devilish glimmer to them.

Although Scarlett and I became close friends quickly, I haven't mentioned anything about Parker. After the plane and club incidents, I thought it best not to discuss it with anyone in hopes that it'd help me forget about it. The only information I've divulged thus far was my relationship status, and I plan on keeping it that way for a while.

"Well, if he's as good-looking as Layla says, I'll be sure to show him a picture of you, which will inevitably lead to him asking me for your phone number."

She takes the last swallow of her latte. "I appreciate it, but I'm on a man sabbatical. It's a scary world out there these days. You can't trust anyone."

I snort. "You're telling me."

AFTER EATING a couple more bites of my sandwich, I toss my trash and head back to my desk. As I turn the corner, I spot Katherine standing next to it, flipping through a file. She must hear me as I approach because, without looking in my direction, she makes her demands.

"Daphne, we have a meeting in the conference room in five. I expect you to be there. Don't be late. This is a big one we can't afford to lose."

I have to physically bite my tongue and dig my nails into my fists to avoid rolling my eyes so far back in my head that they get stuck. The different alias prevails. I'd say, at this point, I should just get my name legally changed, but no matter what I choose, she's never going to remember.

She either knew Scarlett and I were talking about her at lunch because she has superhuman hearing, or she enjoys making my life miserable. I'd bet good money that it's a little bit of both. Something about her seems a little...witchy. She storms off, her sky-high heels clacking against the tile as she walks.

I grab my phone and shoot off a text to Scarlett.

> Me: You can now call me Daphne. Being forced to go into this meeting. Will keep an eye out for this mysterious stranger and report back

As I'm collecting my notebook and pen, my phone vibrates in my hand.

> Scarlett: Good luck in there. I'm sure your notes will be so good that Katherine won't have any choice but to replace me as the favorite. Send a pic of said hottie pls & thx

I grimace at the idea and make my way to the meeting, thinking about the bubble bath I'm going to take as soon as I get home. All I'm focused on is the book I'm in the middle of calling my name until I hit the doorway of the conference room. I come to an abrupt halt as I study the two well-dressed gentlemen sitting alone at the long rectangular conference table, speaking quietly among themselves.

I turn on my heels, ready to flee from the scene and run straight into Katherine's bony chest. I bounce back, doing my best to keep my composure.

"Excuse me? Where do you think you're going?"

Quick, come up with an excuse that'll get me out of this meeting.

"I forgot that I have to send content to a client for approval. It won't take long."

I try to skirt my way around her, but she juts her arm out, blocking me from moving any further.

"You can worry about that later. I need you here now. Unless you don't want to be here, that is. In that case, I can find someone else who can do a much better job."

I back away from her hand, flattening my oversized blazer to hide my shock. Well, shit. That's not the reaction I was expecting. There's really no winning with this one. I'm damned if I do, damned if I don't.

"No, that won't be necessary."

I swallow the knot in my throat and walk back into the conference room, Katherine following close behind. This time, when I walk into the room, I say a silent prayer that Parker won't say anything when he sees me.

He glances in our direction, and we lock eyes, his bulging wide. My throat constricts and I choke on an uncomfortable cough while I take my seat at the other end of the table. I lay my notebook on the table and stare at it so hard I'm convinced I'm going to burn a hole through it.

"Thank you for meeting with us. You must be Mr. Townsend."

Parker recovers from his shock and flashes his million-dollar smile Katherine's way while he shakes her hand.

"And you must be Katherine. It's great to meet you. This is my associate, Blake. I believe you two may have met before."

Katherine returns the affectionate expression, as if being in the vicinity of two attractive gentlemen has transformed her into an actual human being rather than a blood-sucking monster.

"Yes, hello there again, Blake. It's so nice to see you."

Is this some kind of twilight zone? Am I being Punk'd? My eyes rake the room for the hidden cameras that have to be concealed somewhere.

"It's very nice to see you again, Katherine."

Katherine sharply inclines her chin in my direction. "This is Dylan. She's just here to take notes for me, so feel free to pretend she's not even here."

Now I know I'm being pranked. Not only is this the third time I'm running into Parker, but Katherine got my name right for once.

I can feel Blake's eyes physically study me from my waist up, stopping momentarily at my chest before meeting my eyes. He throws a grin my way, and I have to admit, he is attractive. Though, I can't say I'm typically drawn to guys who make it blatantly obvious that they're staring at my boobs before they say hello.

"Thank you for being here, Dylan. It's much appreciated." The sincerity of Blake's greeting surprises me.

I lift my head, give him a weak smile in return, and glance back at Parker. A muscle in his jaw quivers as he grinds his teeth, and he's physically turned away from me, staring deep into Katherine's soul–or lack thereof–to avoid looking at me. I have to admit that this complete one-eighty in his attitude throws me through a loop. Just two days ago, he wanted to meet up for coffee, and now he's doing everything he can to act as if I don't exist.

"Let's get started, shall we? We don't want to take up too much of your time," Parker says as he clasps his hands together and places them on the desk.

Lord, give me the strength to make it out of this meeting alive.

5

PARKER

I stare blankly at my laptop screen, my vision blurring as my eyes dry out thanks to my lack of blinking. I came into this meeting feeling confident that I was going to win Katherine over. Blake warned me about her on the way over, claiming that most meetings he had with her involved a lot of flirting on her end. Of course, I took this with a grain of salt. Blake has a habit of thinking that every woman with a pulse wants to sleep with him.

I stand up, fidgeting with the clicker that I brought as I pull up the first slide of the presentation that I prepared. "As I explained in our emails, we have an up-and-coming author that's said to be the next big thing. We already foresee her on the New York Times Best Sellers list, and it's projected that the book will sell thousands of copies. Of course, this is where Thrive Creative comes in. We need your help with marketing to ensure that her name gets out there properly."

Katherine nods, clicking her pen repeatedly at a frustrating pace. "Of course. Remind me of her name?"

"Evelyn Bennett."

Although I've spent the last five minutes trying to avoid

looking at Dylan, I see her perk up at the mention of the name from my peripheral.

"Evelyn has built quite the social media following for herself. I follow her on pretty much every platform already. She's been hinting at this book for months now. I've been dying to read it," Dylan blurts excitedly.

I chance a full glance in her direction and see a twinkle in her eye. It's the same look that she gets when she's discussing something she's passionate about. She's always been the kind of person who shines brighter than everyone else in the room. My pulse begins to thrum in my throat.

Katherine's head whips in her direction and gives her a threatening look. Dylan sinks back into her chair and puts her head back down to the notebook, jotting notes down quickly. My immediate reaction is to defend Dylan, but I have to remind myself that this is business.

"Sorry about that. Please continue," Katherine mutters.

I bite back the nasty retort that's lodged in my throat.

"Dylan is right. Evelyn has amassed a massive following over the past year. With a combined following of over 150,000 on all platforms, she has the numbers we want to help promote the book. However, she reached out to us because she wants to make sure this is done right. And that's where you guys come in.

"We'd love to collaborate on a social media strategy for the release. We also plan to organize a book tour shortly after the release as long as the numbers look as expected. Her website, although functional, needs an update before we can release any of this information. We're hoping to set up an email drip campaign in a couple of weeks to encourage people to preorder the book, too."

I sneak yet another look at Dylan, whose eyes haven't left her lap since she first mentioned knowing Evelyn's background.

My breath catches as my eyes meet hers again, and I have to look back down at my keyboard.

The pale pink dress peeking out from underneath her blazer makes the green of her hazel eyes pop and her natural rosiness even more prominent. Her silky chestnut hair is styled in relaxed waves, resting behind her shoulders. Every time I see her, it feels like she's somehow become even more beautiful than I remembered.

I toy with the ring on my pointer finger, an anxious cue I've had ever since I was younger, before standing up straight and looking back towards Katherine. This is not the time to get caught up in Dylan's beauty. I can do that in the comfort of my own office. Or when I get home and take a scalding hot shower in search of a release. In more ways than one.

Jesus. Get a grip.

I can't be thinking about stroking my cock while thinking about my ex-girlfriend during a work meeting. What the fuck has gotten into me? I clear my throat, hoping no one can sense where my head has gone.

"Our release date is set for May 31st, which means we only have a couple of months to accomplish all of this. I know it's a tight deadline, but from what Blake has told me, you guys are some of the best in the business, so I know you can handle this. What do you think?"

Katherine puckers her lips, contemplating everything I've offered up thus far before breaking out with a wide grin.

"We can absolutely do that. Thrive Creative cherishes our relationship with Blue Bird and hopes to maintain it. Dylan will start drawing up a strategy as soon as this meeting is over and email it to you by the end of the day tomorrow," Katherine replies.

"We revere our relationship with Thrive as well. We appreciate you guys being on board," Blake counters as he stands up and walks toward Katherine, his palm out and ready for a handshake.

I physically recoil when I see her cheeks transform into a deep shade of red at the typical, professional gesture. I do my best not to judge someone too quickly, but she practically reeks of desperation. Maybe there is some weight to Blake's sentiment about her flirting with anything with a penis.

I throw a quick smile in her direction, stand up, and pack my laptop into my bag. "We look forward to seeing your notes. If you have any questions, I'm just an email away."

Katherine nods and stands to leave the conference room before subtly snapping her fingers in Dylan's direction, calling her as if she's a dog. Though the motion is small, I'm hyper-aware of how Dylan is being mistreated. If this client weren't so important to my career, I would've walked out after the first glimpse of it. She looked uneasy the entire meeting, and I'd bet that it didn't have anything to do with me. For once.

Dylan trails behind her, not bothering to look in my direction again. When Blake is sure the women are out of earshot, he nudges me in the ribs with his elbow.

"Dylan is a smoke show. I'm going to get her number before we head back to the office."

It takes everything in me not to punch him square in the nose as soon as the words are out of his mouth. I love the guy. I do. But I've never been impressed with the way that he views women. As if building up his roster is his biggest goal in life.

"Fuck off," I respond through gritted teeth.

"Whoa, dude, chill out. What's the big deal?"

I throw my laptop bag over my shoulder. "Not every woman wants to sleep with you. What makes you think she'd give you her number in the first place?"

That was a mistake. A troublesome sneer grows on his face as if I'd just challenged him to a game he knows he could win. To his credit, Blake doesn't know that Dylan is my ex. Sure, he'd seen me in rough shape from time to time when we were roommates in California, but I kept my history with her close to my chest. At that point in my life, I could barely hear her name without being on the verge of losing it. So, it was just easier not to say anything at all.

Besides, there were thousands of Dylan's in the world. How would he know this is the one I haven't stopped thinking about for years? That didn't make hearing him say that he wanted to fuck her (in more or less words) any easier to swallow.

"I guarantee I can get her number in less than five minutes. Want to bet on it? The loser has to buy the other a beer after work."

"I'd rather not," I retort as I shove my chair a little too forcibly under the desk and stride out of the conference room. Blake's ego is the least of my concerns right now. I need to find Dylan and make sure she's alright.

I nearly sprint out of the room, scanning the office for Dylan. Because of the layout, I can only see miles of gray, lifeless cubicles. I hold out hope, searching for the top of her hair. That waterfall of chocolate brown hair that's constantly perfect, no matter how little effort she put into it.

I know that she has to be here somewhere. She can't hate me enough to leave for the day. But as I search for her among the scattered workers, she's nowhere to be found.

"Fuck," I whisper to myself.

I clutch my laptop bag closer to my body, tuck my chin, and head toward the front of the office. If I had her number, I'd at least shoot her a quick text and check-in. Maybe I can track her down on Facebook or Instagram. It's not like I haven't been able to before.

As I walk out with my dignity narrowly intact, my mind is fixated on how I'm going to social media stalk Dylan as soon as I get back on the subway. Before I can make it to the large glass front door of Thrive, I accidentally bulldoze my way over a small figure, nearly knocking them over in one fell swoop.

"I'm so sorry. Are you okay?" I ask as I grasp onto their elbow to help them maintain their balance. I let my hand fall the minute I lift my head and see who it is. Dylan.

She hastily takes three steps back, away from me. Though we're no longer near one another, there's a heat radiating off of her, pulling me closer like a magnet. I stifle the feeling, trying to respect the boundaries she's setting for herself.

"We really do need to stop running into each other this way," I quip, a poor attempt at a joke. The corner of her lip twitches, but it's gone as quickly as it came as she pulls her bag back up on her shoulder.

"Are you okay?" I repeat when she remains silent.

"Yeah, I'm fine."

She stands up a little taller, puffing out her chest. I know she's trying to appear more confident, but it's a mediocre job at best. I know because I'm feeling the same way.

She tears her eyes away from mine, focusing on the gray, carpeted floor in between us.

"I was actually just coming to find you. Are you alright? You looked uncomfortable in there."

"It's nothing. Just Katherine being Katherine."

"It's not nothing. She completely steamrolled you. No one deserves to be spoken to the way she spoke to you. You deserve respect."

This catches her attention. She looks up at me, her gaze softening. I fight the urge to take her face in my hand and stroke her cheek the way I once did when she needed comforting.

"Thank you, I appreciate that. It's just part of the territory."

"It shouldn't have to be..." My voice trails off. If there's one thing I know about Dylan, it's that she's stubborn. As much as I want to talk her out of dealing with the demeaning behavior I just witnessed, I know the more that I push, the more her guard will go up. She likes proving to people that she can achieve the impossible, no matter how small the feat. It's always been one of her most admirable yet aggravating traits.

"Looks like we're going to be around each other a lot more than either of us were expecting. Maybe it's a good time to get that coffee?" I try to change the subject.

She lets out a short, jagged breath, and I can see her physically crawl back into herself. She's shutting down on me right before my eyes.

Well, that backfired.

"Thank you for the offer, but I'm not going to work with you. And I still don't want to grab a coffee."

My head rears back, taken aback by her bluntness. My brain has a hard time differentiating between the harsh comment and a physical blow. "Am I missing something? Were you not just in the same meeting as me?"

"I was. But I'm going to tell Katherine that I can't help with the account."

"You think she's just going to let you off the hook because you ask her nicely? I know I just met her, but based on how she treated you in that meeting, I don't foresee that going very well," I argue.

She rolls her eyes at me. I know we haven't spoken in years, but this attitude of hers is new. She's been known to be feisty at times, but more often than not, she was the soft-spoken one that got along with everyone. We rarely fought and never once raised our voices at one another while we were dating. Yet now she's looking at me as if she can't wait to get away from me. And I hate the fact that I'm turned on by it.

"I'll come up with an excuse. Not that it's any of your concern."

I can't help but laugh and throw my hands up in surrender. Yep, I'm definitely hard now.

"Alright there, killer. I figured I'd try one more time. I hope that you can get put on a different account for your sake. But if you can't, I'm sure I'll be seeing you around."

She gives me a small nod with her arms crossed over her chest. "I guess so."

I turn around and push the front door open. But, before I leave, I turn my head around and call after her one more time. She's halfway down the office, and I take my time sweeping my eyes up her figure.

"Hey Dyl!"

She spins around, her fists clenched at her sides. "Yes?"

"You should wear that dress more often. It makes your ass look great."

Before she can respond, I walk out into the frigid February air, a glint of amusement evident in my smirk. If she wants to play that game, so be it. She seems to have forgotten that I love games.

6

DYLAN

I'm still fuming as I make my way back to my desk. I must be a better actress than I thought because Parker seemed to have believed that I was truly upset with him. Speaking to him with such vitriol nearly caused my heart to break into two again, but it's just easier this way. The bigger wall I can build between us, the better I can protect myself.

I truly thought that he was going to lie down and take it until he made that comment about my ass. What was that? And why did I like it so much? God, my heart is such a traitor sometimes. Or should I say my lady bits. It takes everything in me not to picture being underneath him again.

Sex with Parker was always great. More than great, actually. He's one of the few men on this planet that can find the clit. That in itself deserves some kind of trophy–yes, I am aware that the bar is in hell.

I shouldn't have such low standards, but I had my fair share of less-than-stellar experiences during my single days. I've had multiple (yes, regrettably, more than one) men rub my inner thigh and walk away feeling like a champion because I didn't have the heart to tell them they weren't even remotely close. If there were an award for faking orgasms, I'd come in first place every time.

I can't help but wonder if it would be different with Parker now that we've gotten a few more years–and people–under our belt. My mind wanders to what it would be like pressed beneath those muscular, tanned, tattooed arms while he takes his time worshiping my body, licking every square inch of warmed flesh.

Seconds before I run into an open office door, Katherine's shrill voice breaks me from my dirty daydream, dousing me like a bucket of ice water. Why the hell am I picturing a naked tryst with my ex-boyfriend in the middle of the office anyway?

"Diana! My office. Now."

At this rate, I know she's getting my name wrong to get under my skin. There's no other explanation as to why she would have gotten it correct when she's trying to look professional in front of two ridiculously hot men. I roll my shoulders and neck out, resigning to my fate before I march into her office.

I was planning on talking to her about getting out of this project, but I didn't think today would be the day. I figured I'd at least have a day or two to give myself a pep talk. I desperately need a scalding hot shower to help wash away the dread living in my gut from the moment I walked into that meeting.

I lift my chin, feigning confidence as I walk in.

"Yes?"

She's sitting down at her oversized oak desk, which rests against a floor-to-ceiling window overlooking Bryant Park. The sun is beginning to dip below the tall skyscrapers, and if I wasn't terrified to breathe around this woman, I might be able to enjoy the view. The way hues of vibrant pinks and yellows paint the sky and reflect off the glass windows of the towering buildings.

I always thought Woodland Heights had breathtaking

sunsets, but there's something about seeing them in the big city that makes me feel infinitesimal. It acts as a reminder that I'm just a blip on something much greater than my mind can ever comprehend.

"You heard them in there. This is going to be one of our biggest clients to date if everything goes smoothly. I'm going to put Scarlett on this project, but I need you to be there to assist her with anything she needs. I'm putting a lot of faith in you on this one. I don't exactly think it's warranted, but she suggested I choose you to help. Don't make me regret this," she commands, dragging me out of my thoughts.

"About that..." My voice trails off when she lifts her head and shoots daggers at me with one cold look. I'm not typically one to back down so easily when it comes to people like her, but she holds my entire future in the palm of her hand. Between Parker and her, it looks like I'm going to have to find a new therapist earlier than I thought.

"You have something to say?"

"I just don't think I'm the right fit for this project."

"At least you and I see eye to eye there," she scoffs. "But if you refuse to help with this project, I have no choice but to let you go."

"W-what? You can't do that!" I stutter, my voice quivering. I knew Katherine was malicious, but this was a new low, even for her.

"I can and I will. There are hundreds of people out there who are chomping at the bits for your position. It will take me less than a day to find someone more than willing to work on this account. So what's it going to be? Do I need to find your replacement?"

I clench my jaw and count to four, taking steadying breaths. I'm seeing red, and I know if I speak too quickly, I'll jeopardize my job, which is already on the chopping block. This may not be shaping up to be the dream job that I once envisioned, but I still need to make a living. Now's not the time to be rash.

"No. I'll do it. Thank you for giving me a chance."

"That's what I thought." She shoos me away with a quick flick of her wrist.

If I weren't so excited to get home, I'd run to the store to pick up the supplies to make a Katherine voodoo doll. Come to think of it, that could be a fun way to spend the rest of my evening. I bet I could get Amelia in on it, too. All I'd have to do is explain how she spoke to me today, and she'd be stabbing that thing with a vengeance. If Amelia is one thing, it's loyal to a fault.

I find myself laughing under my breath as I go back to grab my purse from my desk, feeling infinitely lighter already. I take one last large inhale, collect my stuff, and leave the office for the day. As I head towards the subway station, all I can think about is how the hell I'm going to explain this to Amelia without having to hear that this is the universe's plan for me.

This should be fun.

✳ ✳ ✳ ✳ ✳

I THROW my keys into the small ceramic bowl on the small entry table and slump against the front door, letting my tote fall off my shoulder and onto the floor. I genuinely thought it couldn't get worse than seeing Parker on my flight, but after seeing him at work and dealing with the devil reincarnated, I'm second-guessing this move.

"Dylan?" Amelia's voice calls out from the kitchen.

"Yeah, it's me." I stride into the kitchen to see her sitting cross-legged at the dining table, chowing down on a bowl of ramen. "Who else would it be?"

"You never know. I've had the locks changed a few times, but I have been known to give the keys to a man after a couple of dates, so you can never be too careful," she replies nonchalantly, mouth full of noodles.

"That's reassuring to hear. Nothing like knowing a random man can pop in at any point in time." A shiver snakes up my spine at the thought. Maybe I should get her self-defense classes for Christmas. I'll look into that tonight.

"It's only happened once. Or twice. Hard to keep up."

"You're not helping." I sigh as I sit across from her at the table. I haven't looked at myself all day, but I know if I caught a glimpse in a mirror, I'd see deep, dark circles under my eyes, pallid skin, and wind-blown hair. I'm still adjusting to the New York weather, and even though the subway station is only a ten-minute walk from the office, the crisp weather really does a number on you.

She looks up at me, dropping her fork immediately when she sees the state I'm in. "What the fuck happened to you?" Lovely.

I groan, cross my arms on the table, and bury my face.

"Hold that thought."

I continue to stare at the ground, making note of the intricate designs of the maple herringbone wood floors. If I wasn't in such a shitty mood, I could appreciate just how beautiful this apartment is. I've lived here for a little over a week, but it still feels like an extended vacation more often than not.

I hear shuffling from across from me, followed by a thud on the table. I glance up to see a bottle of red wine and a wine glass now sitting very close to my face. Before I can move a muscle, Amelia's pouring me a hefty glass. One glass won't hurt–not after the day I've had.

"You look like you could use that."

I don't bother responding. Instead, I collect myself and take a few sips of the Cabernet she poured for me. I cherish how it warms my insides, instantly making the harsh thoughts in my head hazy. I place the glass back down, close my eyes, and bring my fingers to my temples, rubbing out the knots that slowly formed throughout the day.

"Parker showed up at work today. Thrive and Blue Bird are partnering on marketing for a debut author. Katherine wants me to help with the account. She doesn't believe in me, but Scarlett requested me as her right-hand woman, so I don't really have a choice. I tried to get out of it, but Katherine told me I'd be fired if I didn't take the job. So I have to spend the next god knows how long working side by side with Parker while my witch of a boss is breathing down my neck," I prattle.

I gulp for air before taking another large swig of my wine. I already know what Amelia is going to say before the words even leave her lips, and I feel my posture go stiff as I brace myself for the response.

"Okay, Dyl, take a breath. You look like you're quite literally going to explode."

"I feel like I'm going to," I moan as I place my head back into the crevice of my arms.

"I know you probably don't want to hear this, but one of us has to be the voice of reason right now, so I'm taking it upon myself. First the airplane, then the bar, and now this. Do you think this is the universe's way of saying you two belong together? I have a better chance of winning the lottery than all of this. Remind me to go to the store tomorrow to pick up a ticket or two, now that I think about it. Or maybe you can do it for me? If this is the luck you're having, maybe you can rub some off on me."

"Amelia, focus," I chide.

"Sorry. I'm just saying. Chances like these are few and far between. The universe is giving you a message loud and clear. These things don't just happen just for the hell of it."

As much as I love Amelia, this is why I was dreading

coming home. I don't need anyone telling me this is fate. I need someone to tell me that it was, and always will be, Parker's loss. I need the reminder that seeing me is exactly the punishment he deserves after leaving me all those years ago.

"I love you, but that's the last thing I want to hear right now. I need you to tell me how much Parker sucks."

"You know I'm always going to keep it real with you. I pride myself on being honest. As much as I support the "fuck men" train you've been on this past year, I'm having a hard time genuinely understanding why you're struggling with the idea of working with Parker. Just because you two have to work on a project together doesn't mean that you're meant to fall in love again. Of course, I can't think of anything more perfect. But you came to New York to live out your dreams and be the best damn marketing assistant you can be. So why are you letting a man get in the way of that?"

I slam my hand down on the table, causing it to shake on impact.

"Because he's not just some man. He was the love of my life. I already spent months...no, fuck it, years, getting over him. I moved to a new city to start over. The last thing I need is to spend every waking second of my professional career cozying up to him when I'm trying to make the most out of my job!"

She pulls her bowl closer to her to avoid being hit, and the sight makes me flinch. I didn't mean to get this worked up.

With her hands up in surrender, she says, "I get it, Dee. I really do. But just because you two have a history together doesn't mean you can't work together. I know you. You'd never let anything come between you and making your dream come true—even men named Parker. There's no point in letting that get under your skin now."

I let out another discouraged sigh, giving in to her arguments. She has a point, but her judgment is a little clouded. She's the definition of a hopeless romantic (even if she has a funny way of showing it). She also thinks the cosmos are giving her signs every chance they can. Sometimes, I wish I was as delusional as her. It seems like a happier life to live.

Unfortunately, once my dad got sick, I stopped knowing what to believe in. As much as I want to think there's some divine force bringing Parker and me back together, those hopes were dashed the minute he passed away three years ago.

"You're right, Mia. I'm not going to let it ruin the one thing I've worked so hard for. But just because I accept it doesn't mean I have to like it."

"That's what they all say," she sing-songs.

I take one last swallow of my wine, emptying the glass before pushing myself up and off the table. As I move to put the glass in the sink, I find myself swaying on my feet, the wine hitting me harder than I expected. I grip onto the table's edge, steadying myself. The head rush is welcomed after feeling uneasy all day. At least now I can breathe a little easier.

"I mean it."

"I think you're going to change your mind sooner rather than later. Now, if you'll excuse me. I have to get ready for a date."

I glance down at the clock on the oven. How the hell is it only seven p.m.? And how the hell am I tipsy on one glass of wine? My tolerance has *definitely* gone down.

"A date? It's a Tuesday night. Where could you possibly be going?"

Amelia gives an indifferent shrug. "I matched with a guy on Hinge. We're going to grab drinks at Barely Disfigured." She walks over to me and places the bottle of wine next to me before giving me a peck on the cheek.

"Be safe. And for the love of god, whatever you do, please do not give him a key to the apartment. I don't care how great he is," I call out to her as she walks toward her bedroom. I look down at my phone, triple-checking that I still have her location.

She throws her hair over her shoulder. "Don't worry. That won't happen until at least date four. I've learned my lesson."

Amelia gives me no time to lecture her on the dangers of sharing a living space with men she hardly knows before she closes herself in her bedroom, blasting music loud enough that I'm almost positive our neighbors will start pounding on the wall within minutes.

After locking myself into my bedroom, taking a bubble bath until the water grows cold, and changing into my cute pink and white polka-dotted pajama set, I throw myself down on the bed and rub my palms against my eyes, the room still gently rocking as if I'm on a boat in the middle of choppy seas.

I shouldn't let working with Parker get under my skin so much. I'm a grown woman. I can separate work and my personal life…right?

7

PARKER

I spend the following morning, staring at my computer screen, contemplating how to get out of working with Evelyn. If this were any other scenario, I would tell the marketing assistant to stop dicking around and work with me. But this isn't just anyone. It's Dylan. And when I walked out of Blue Bird yesterday, her eyes were full of pure hatred.

Of course, I know her well enough to know it's a front. One she's put up to protect herself. But I'm not willing to make her feel uncomfortable. I don't have much of a choice, though.

I mindlessly tap my pen against the untouched notepad to my right. As much as I care for her, I'm not willing to ruin my career over this. I'd confer with Blake, but I already know how that's going to go. He'd tell me to stop being a pussy, suck it up, work with her, and then try to have sex with her while I'm at it.

I take my laptop out of my briefcase and boot it up. Maybe throwing myself into other work will help take my mind off of it. Ignoring it isn't the best solution, but it's not like I have to make an immediate decision. I've got at least a week before Evelyn sends me the final copy after she makes all the changes I suggested. That buys me just enough time.

My computer immediately pings once it's started, and my inbox is already sitting at fifty emails despite it only being 8:30 in the morning. I take a drink of my coffee, nearly choking when my eyes catch on the name Dylan Jenkins at the top.

I give myself a small pinch on the hand to make sure that I'm awake. I tossed and turned all last night, so I already know that I'm going to be fighting a sleep-deprived haze all day. I do not have enough caffeine in my system yet to deal with this workload. Let alone someone who gets an email from the same girl who swore she refused to work with me with nothing but contempt.

I quickly scan the email. It's short and sweet, leaving no room for interpretation.

Parker,

Yesterday did not go as planned. I think we need to talk. If you're free today, I'd love to meet up for lunch. Text or call me at (931) 529-1740.

Dylan

I sit back in my chair, mindlessly folding my arms over my chest, unable to process what I just read. I know deep down I should turn down the invitation, but I can't help but be intrigued. Less than 24 hours after the meeting, she's already changing her tune. Maybe she realized how overdramatic she was being. Then again, she's always been quick off the mark and hot-headed if pushed too far.

I don't know why I'd expect anything less these days. Perhaps it's because I've changed and want to give her the benefit of the doubt. Regardless, I know what my answer is to this email. I knew what it was before I finished reading it.

I grab my iPhone off my desk and quickly draft up a new text.

> Parker: Hi Dylan. It's Parker. I got your email. I have a free hour at noon if you're available. There's a good sandwich spot near Central Park. Let me know, and I'll keep my calendar open.

Her reply comes back almost immediately as if she was sitting by her phone, antsy for me to respond. It'd appear the game she's playing isn't as foolproof as she thinks.

> Dylan: Noon works great. I'll meet you there.

I shoot her one last text with the name of the deli before placing my phone face down on my desk. This was not how I anticipated to start my morning. Any hope I had of focusing on work has been obliterated, knowing what awaits me in a few short hours.

I stand up, pacing around my office to work off some of the nerves that have found their way to the pit of my stomach. As optimistic as I want to be, there's a very good chance that she won't apologize for our interaction yesterday, which leads me to question whether or not I just agreed to walk into the lion's den.

I hear a soft rapping knock at the door, and before I can acknowledge the sound, Blake is barging his way into my office. I take a deep breath, my chest heaving. Lord knows this is the last thing I need to deal with right now. He may be my best friend, but some things are just better left unsaid, and my lunch with Dylan is at the bottom of my list of current topics of conversation.

"Yes, Blake. Come right in." I grumble sarcastically as I gesture to the seat across from me and sit back down in my chair.

He sits down and kicks his feet up, making himself at home like he always does. "You look stressed, dude. You good?"

I jerk the sleeve of my shirt down in annoyance and run a hand through my unkempt hair. I probably should have spent a little more time getting ready this morning, but I laid in bed, trying to fall back asleep until I needed to leave for the office. I can only hope that I look better than I feel.

"I'm fine," I reply through my clenched jaw. I sit up straighter, wordlessly begging him to leave it alone. I'm in no way, shape, or form in the mood to talk about my feelings.

"Whatever you say. You seem uptight as fuck, but I'm going to let it slide because you clearly don't want to talk about it. Anyways, where did you go yesterday? You stormed out of the office after I mentioned getting that Dylan girl's number and I didn't see you for the rest of the day."

"I worked from home for the rest of the day." I shut down his questioning.

"Why?" he pushes on.

"I wasn't feeling great. What difference does it make?"

He throws his hands up in a defensive position. "Dude, chill. I just wanted to check in and make sure you're alright. You've been acting weird since the minute I picked you up from the airport. I left it alone because I figured you were just worried about work, but you've been wound up so tight all week."

He's right. I have been a dick to him all week because I didn't want to tell him about the predicament I've found myself in. I assumed that after Dylan shut me down on the plane, I'd be able to forget that it ever happened. I knew it would take some time, obviously. I could get over it eventually, though. But after yesterday, it doesn't seem like there's any escaping it, and Blake doesn't deserve to be in the dark after everything he's done for me.

"I know. I'm sorry I've been such an ass. There's been a lot on my mind lately. It's actually about Dylan."

He cocks an eyebrow. "Finally taking my advice and trying to ask her out? If you needed help getting a date with the girl, all you had to do was ask."

"If I needed advice on asking a girl out, you would be the last person I'd turn to, especially when it comes to Dylan." He throws a hand against his chest, acting wounded, but I push forward. "Her and I actually have a history."

He leans forward in his chair, visibly intrigued. "What kind of history? How could you possibly know her if you just moved here?"

I clear my throat, unsure how to break the news to my best friend. I've kept this part of my life secret for so long. I've always been a more private person, but I'm extra protective when it comes to Dylan. It's almost as if not talking about it helped me preserve the memories we shared. I wouldn't have to acknowledge that I fucked up royally if I didn't talk about it.

"She's the ex I've told you about."

He barks out a laugh and shakes his head. "There's no way in hell. She's so out of your league. Besides, you're telling me that you both just happened to move to New York and now have to work together?"

He's not wrong. She is way out of my league. I've known that since the minute I laid eyes on her.

We met at a shitty frat basement party our sophomore year. She was dressed in this slinky little black dress that hugged her in all the right places. While I couldn't tear my eyes away from her curves in that dress, that's not what captured my attention. It was her smile. Even blanketed in the dark, you could spot it from miles away.

Dylan swayed to the music, and I remember thinking how stunning she looked. She seemed so...in her element. Come to find out, she's not a big partier, but she seemed so carefree in that moment. I knew I had to get her phone number by the end of the night.

Spoiler alert: I didn't. When I noticed her slip out to the backyard to get some air, I made some half-assed excuse to do the same. I was a nervous wreck, but I got the balls enough to strike up a conversation. We ended up talking for three hours in the freezing evening air. I gave her my denim jacket, and although I was borderline hypothermic, neither of us bothered to return inside for the rest of the night.

When it came time to say goodbye, I froze. I kissed her cheek and sent her on her merry way. I laid in bed in a beer-induced fog staring at the ceiling until the sun came up, kicking myself for letting this mystery girl walk away. When I fully sobered up, I went on a mission to find out who she was. All I had was a first name and a dream.

Luckily, my persistence paid off, and once I found out her identity, I invited her to another party the following weekend. We sealed the deal with our first kiss on a crowded couch, surrounded by rowdy drunks, and were attached at the hip for years after.

"Yeah, I am."

"How is that even possible? There are millions of people in this city," Blake utters cynically.

"Your guess is as good as mine."

He runs his hand over his stubble. "Something tells me that yesterday at the office wasn't the first time you ran into her."

I shake my head, guilt pooling in my gut. Behind his light-hearted demeanor, I can tell he's hurt. We're brothers. We tell each other everything.

"We were on the same flight over. We sat right next to each other if you can believe that."

His features contort with pain, the muscles in his jaw ticking. "I *don't* believe that. But what I have a harder time believing is the fact that you didn't say anything as soon as you got in the car."

"I also saw her at the bar when we went out that night," I blurt, unable to hold back now that the floodgates have been opened.

"Now you're fucking with me."

"I wish I was."

He blows out a big exhale, placing his hands on the top of his head as he leans back in the chair. His eyes go up to the ceiling, and I see the wheels turning. The way he's processing all of this new information makes the guilt nestle itself deeper into my psyche.

"Well, that explains why you've been so moody lately, and why you were so determined to drink yourself to death when we were at the club. I have to admit, I feel less sorry about that days-long hangover you had to deal with now."

"I'm sorry I didn't tell you. I had no excuse. I've just always kept things about me and Dylan between the two of us. I haven't even told my parents the real reason we ended things. They thought we were going to get married. I think that's one of my biggest disappointments still to this day."

"It's all good, man. Had I known, I wouldn't have pushed so hard about getting her number or trying to sleep with her." I'm relieved he doesn't press about the marriage thing. While I'm finally opening up about it, I'm not exactly in the mood to divulge why things didn't work out between us.

The corners of my lips twitch up, and I narrow my eyes at him. "You and I both know that's not true. If anything, you would've tried harder."

"Yeah, you're probably right." He smirks, and I release a breath of relief. The tension between us immediately thaws at the joke. If there's one thing we've always bonded over, it's his stupidity and inability to stop himself from flirting. He's also great at making light of even the shittiest situations.

"I wish you had told me earlier." His grin fades slowly, and he returns his gaze to me.

"I know. I'm sorry. From here on out, you'll get full transparency on the Dylan front. Speaking of which, I'm meeting with her for lunch in a few hours."

"Is lunch code for meeting up at a seedy hotel to have secret, forbidden sex?" He cocks his head and wiggles his brows.

And there he is, back to his idiotic self.

"No." I fill him in on the events that transpired yesterday before mentioning the email I walked into this morning.

"What do you think it means?" Blake questions.

"I have no clue. I got an email from Katherine late last night that she's putting her best marketing manager, Scarlett, on the project with Dylan. I'm hoping she's coming around to the idea of working together."

"Need me to tag along as a wingman? You know women can never resist my charm. I can talk you up. Make you sound bigger and more important than you are." He flashes me a wink.

"As much as I appreciate the offer, something tells me that's going to backfire. Besides, she already knows how great I am." I return his cocky grin.

"If that's the case, why aren't you two together anymore?" He asks, voice reeking with arrogance.

"That's a story for a different day. The bottom line is I fucked up. And I don't want to make her uncomfortable by forcing her to work with me. Evelyn is the account I need to prove that I'm good at my job. I can't afford to fuck that up too."

"Relax, I'm sure you'll be fine. Just flirt with her a little, show her what she's been missing out these past few years, and you'll be golden." With that, he stands up from his chair, tucking his perfectly styled tie back into his jacket.

"I think I'm going to try a different approach, but thanks for the advice."

He strolls towards the door. "One of these days, you're going to listen to me and realize how wise I am. Until then, I will not be held responsible for your life decisions."

He slides out of the room before I can respond, leaving me chuckling. I glance at my watch. Only three more hours until lunch. I can do this.

✻ ✻ ✻ ✻ ✻

I APPROACH the deli and immediately spot Dylan sitting alone at a booth. I pause to soak in the view of her as much as I can before getting caught. Today, she's wearing beige, twill plaid pants and a black turtleneck sweater. She's got on a pair of thick black square glasses that take up a good portion of her face. I've never seen them before, but I wish she'd wear them more often.

She looks like a true businesswoman, and it's sexy as hell. Between the glasses and the red lip she paired them with, my mind wanders to what she would look like wearing nothing but the glasses and the lipstick.

I discreetly shift the growing bulge in my pants, hopeful that she doesn't notice it as I walk toward her. Her chin is pointed down as she scrolls through her phone, and she's biting her tongue. It's the expression she makes when she's fully focused on a task, and the familiarity of it slows my steps.

She must sense my presence because she lifts her head from her phone and locks eyes with me, making my heart jolt in my chest.

"Hi. Thanks for meeting me," she says as she stands and leans in to give me a hug. I mistake her body language and go for a full frontal, and I'm met with the side of her body, tangling us up in what I can only imagine looks like the most awkward hug known to man. Despite my discomfort, my brain latches onto her scent–rich spices and vanilla. It's hypnotizing.

I clear my throat and take a step back, trying to distance myself from her and the embarrassment of the moment. "Of course. Did you order already?"

"Yeah, I hope that's alright," she replies bashfully, pointing to the sandwich that's blatantly sitting in front of her. I was too distracted by her to notice the food.

We're off to a strong start.

"Of course it is. Let me order, and I'll be right back."

I sprint away, trying to collect myself before she can see the redness creeping up my neck. I'm a thirty-year-old man, and I'm actually fucking blushing over an interaction with a girl. It's humiliating.

I order a classic Italian sub with a soda, and the image of Dylan and I sitting on the beach of our hometown lake plays in my mind like a movie scene. She's laughing, wild hair blowing in the wind, a smudge of Italian dressing coating the corner of her lips.

During the summer, we'd spend most of our weekends on the water, with beers and sandwiches from our favorite local deli. I always ordered the Italian, and she'd get the BLT with turkey, but without fail, she'd eat half of my sandwich. She always claimed it was "just one bite," but I didn't mind. There was something about seeing her so weightless that made me want to give her the world–even if all I had was a couple of dollars and a hoagie to my name.

With stomachs full of food, we'd lay under the sun until we were crisp. We forgot sunscreen on more than one occasion, and we'd do the painful walk of shame back to the car, eager to coat ourselves in aloe to soothe the burn. It's because of memories like these that I look forward to summer every year.

I shake my head, trying to erase the image like an Etch A

Sketch. I snag my food and make my way back to the table, hoping that I don't embarrass myself any more than I already have.

While I open the wrapper of my sandwich, my eyes fall on her food—a BLT. I laugh quietly to myself. Some things never change.

As if she's reading my mind, she says, "Let me guess. An Italian, no onions."

"Am I that predictable?"

She gestures her chin towards her own sandwich and gives a weak shrug. "Some habits are hard to break."

"I guess so." I feel an ache in my chest, the softness of her voice tugging on my heartstrings like a cellist. I can tell by the anguished look on her face that she's reminiscing about those same memories that I just relived.

"So I guess we should talk about why I invited you here in the first place."

I nod, taking the first bite of my sandwich. In the short time I've been in New York, this has become one of my favorite meals for lunch, partially because it's delicious and partially because of the nostalgia. But right now, it tastes spoiled as I chew. There's a gnawing sense of panic that won't go away until I know that she doesn't hate me.

"I talked to Katherine about taking me off the account-"

"That's not necessary," I interrupt. "I don't want to cause any problems for you at work."

She pushes on, fully ignoring me. "It doesn't matter. I have no choice. I either work with you on this, or I'm fired. And as much as I would prefer we didn't work together, I won't jeopardize my career because we have a history."

That shuts me up real quick. Katherine threatened to fire her because she asked not to be on a project? It only took one interaction to tell that the woman was evil. I just didn't expect her to be *this* vicious.

My hands go limp under the table, and I find myself at a loss for words. She went out of her way to avoid working with me, and now she has no choice. How am I supposed to navigate this relationship now? She wants nothing to do with me, and I'm not willing to push her for my own selfish reasons.

"I'm sorry. This is an unfair position for you to be in. I never meant for this to happen."

She hums in agreement quietly. "It's not like you knew that our companies were going to be working together or that my boss is Satan's long-lost daughter. Don't take this personally. Besides, I had some time to think about it. I know how good you are at what you do, and I'd like to think I'm pretty damn good, too. Now's my chance to prove it. What better way to do that than work with someone you're already familiar with?"

I blink a couple of times, trying to keep the shock off my face. She's being so level-headed about this. It's a very different Dylan from the one I met at Thrive.

I school my features back into an even-keeled manner. "So, you think I'm good at what I do, huh?" I challenge. I take another bite of my sandwich now that I'm no longer concerned she wants to strangle me and bask in how the tanginess of the banana peppers complements the assortment of cured meats.

She rolls her eyes. "Don't make me regret this."

I laugh, wiping my mouth free of dressing with a napkin. "I won't. Don't worry. For what it's worth, I think you're great at what you do, too. You've always been talented. Katherine would be an idiot not to see that."

She flashes me a soft smile, and we fall into a comfortable silence. I take another bite of my sandwich, relishing in this moment before her sharp-witted comments resume–they always do. It's one of the many things that made me fall in love with her.

There's something so attractive about a girl that talks back.

If I think about it too much, the erection that made an appearance is going to come back with a vengeance.

As I'm about to ask her how she's settling into her new life, a piercing ring fills the air. My phone vibrates in my pocket, and I raise my eyes to her in a silent question.

"Go ahead."

"Thanks, it will only be a second."

I pull my phone out of my pocket and glance at the caller ID. And just like that, my stomach falls into my ass. *Shit.*

8

DYLAN

I'm not one to typically look at someone's phone while they're texting or getting a phone call. I respect people's privacy. However, when Parker looks down at his phone, his grip on the device tightens, and his coloring goes ashen as if he's seen a ghost. I'd argue that's a dramatic response for a phone call. At least, that's not *my* usual response.

So, naturally, as any other red-blooded human would, I strain my neck forward–a move disguised as a stretch–to see if I can get a glimpse of the name on the other end of that call. Before I can, Parker declines the call and places the phone face down on the table.

"Sorry about that." My eyes catch on his as he fusses with the wrapping of his food. The wrapping of my own sandwich begins rustling as the table shakes ever-so-softly. I chance a glance under it, and sure enough, he's bouncing his leg, causing the entire piece of furniture to move. He's having difficulty sitting still, and it only piques my interest even further.

"You sure you don't want to get that?"

He shoves another bite of sandwich in his mouth. "Positive."

Seconds later, the entire table vibrates again as his phone

rings a second time. Whoever is calling sure as hell is persistent. He immediately declines it, now shifting in his seat. I refuse to break eye contact with him, but he avoids my gaze.

"Everything okay?" I ask, genuinely concerned about what could make a grown man seem this uneasy.

"Yeah, it's fine. Anyways, how are you settling into the city?" He trudges forward, acting as if the phone calls never happened. Of course, it's not that simple because the vibration resumes before I can get a word in.

He lets out a defeated groan, lifts the phone, making a point to keep the screen facing his chest, and points to the door. "Do you mind if I run out and take this really quickly?"

"No, of course not. Do what you need to do."

Parker shoots me an appreciative look and rushes up, answering in hushed tones as he stands. Again, like any other sane person, I slide over to the edge of my seat to eavesdrop. Although I can't hear much of his murmuring, I swear I hear him mutter the name Olivia.

I fall against the back of my chair, the air whooshing out of me. It all makes sense now. The way he went pale the minute he saw the caller ID. The way he turned his phone face down on the table, hiding it from me.

He has a girlfriend.

I don't know why I assumed he was single. He's a good-looking guy. Okay, that's an understatement. He's the kind of attractive you see online that makes you question whether or not people like that exist in real life. Not to mention the fact that he's only grown hotter with age. Between the golden skin from all of the time he spent in the California sun to the stubble that makes him look just the right amount of disheveled, it's sickening how exquisite one man can be. What kind of model-esque man like that wouldn't be in a relationship?

Olivia. It's no surprise that she has a hot name. I bet she's super leggy, looks beautiful without makeup, and doesn't have morning breath when she wakes up. She's probably a model. Or an influencer who only shops at Erewhon and occasionally drinks natural wine because she doesn't want to drink her calories.

Jesus, I'm spiraling. Why do I even care? I take a deep inhale, trying to tame the anxiety that is building. The man is allowed to date. We broke up years ago. It's only natural to move on. I may not have, but I'd like to think that says more about the modern dating scene than it does me as a person. At least that's what I tell myself every night before I fall asleep in my bed–alone.

I peek at the door and see him heading back to the table. I subtly grab my napkin and dab the sweat beading on my forehead.

Act normal. Everything is fine.

"I'm so sorry about that. Ol-" he begins apologizing, but I cut him off, not trusting myself to hear the rest of that sentence. I don't need him to see my jealousy rearing its ugly head only minutes after I agreed to work with him. This lunch is the first time we've spent an agreeable amount of time together, and I'd rather not make it awkward before we dive head-first into working beside one another.

"Don't even worry about it. You don't have to explain anything to me."

"But-"

I interrupt again, "Seriously, it's not a big deal. Anyways, I think you were asking me a question before we got interrupted."

He stares at me for a few seconds too long, eyes narrowed, evidently at a loss of what to say to my gruffness. Good, I'd rather he think I'm rude instead of caught up on the fact that he's with someone.

"Uh, yeah. I was asking how you're settling into life here."

I take a swig of my soda, trying to hydrate my parched throat, but it's useless. I suddenly have no interest in being here. In fact, I'd rather be dealing with Katherine's treachery than be buddy-buddy with Parker.

Time for the classic escape plan. I grab my phone from my purse and look at the screen, which currently displays a whopping zero notifications. He's not the only one who can hide his phone.

"Shit, I have to run. Katherine just texted me saying she needs me in the office right now. It seems urgent." I collect my belongings, wrap the rest of my sandwich up, and stand. I still have half of my food left, but I don't have the heart to take it to eat as leftovers later. My appetite is gone, and I'm not exactly in the mood to eat something with so many memories attached to it. Even if it is one of the best sandwiches I've had in god knows how long.

That's the thing about relationships. Once they end, the little things take on a brand new meaning. That song you used to belt at the top of your lungs in the car together threatens to bring you to tears every time it comes on the radio. You can't put on your favorite sweater without thinking about how he said it brought out the color of your eyes. You catch whiffs of the cologne he always wore, and you're brought right back to the day that you smelt it for the last time while you cried in his arms. Even something as simple as one of your favorite foods becomes tainted.

"You don't want to take that with you to eat later? You barely ate." He eyes the trash in my hand, and my gaze finds his. He's looking at me as if I'm fragile–like one small move will shatter me completely.

My defenses go up, and I'm torn about how to react. On the one hand, I should've known that he'd catch onto my mood shifting. He's always been very attentive. Very caring. On the other, I don't need someone babysitting me. I'm perfectly capable of doing it myself.

I place a light hand on my stomach, feigning an ache. "I'm suddenly not feeling too great. Do you want to take it with you?" I ask as casually as I can manage, but my voice betrays me and wavers.

He can tell I'm lying. I can see it in the way his eyes flicker and in the small step he takes toward me, but he knows better than to argue. "No, that's okay. I hope you feel better. I'll email you after I meet with Evelyn tomorrow, and we can schedule a meeting?"

The corners of my lips twitch up in a pained smile. "Yeah, that sounds great. Thanks for meeting me." I give him a terse nod and just about run out the door, tossing my trash on the way.

As soon as I'm outdoors, I gulp down a breath of frosty air. It burns my lungs, but I'm grateful for how it eases the roaring chatter in my mind. With every exhale, my chest loosens, and the panic slowly subsides. For many, finding out your ex is in a new relationship leads to break-up songs on repeat, tear-filled journal writing sessions, and anger-fueled workouts. Not anxiety attacks. But I've always had a flair for the dramatics–especially concerning matters of the heart.

My anxiety has plagued me for years, and no matter how far I've come to alleviate myself from the overwhelming sense of dread that grips me, there are still moments when the world feels too loud.

I can't help but peek over my shoulder to see if Parker's following me after my sudden goodbye, but he's still sitting at the table, staring blankly at his folded hands resting on the table. Before I can regret my decision, I take out my phone again and text Scarlett.

> Dylan: You mind covering for me if I take the rest of the day from home?
>
> Scarlett: Of course not. Everything good?
>
> Dylan: Long story. I'll tell you tomorrow. Thank you! I owe you!
>
> Scarlett: Just bring me the tea and a latte tomorrow and consider us even.

I tuck my phone back in my pocket and head in the direction of the subway station. Now that I've gotten some fresh air–as fresh as it gets in New York City–I can think more clearly. Parker having a girlfriend doesn't change our dynamic. It's not as if I was running to get back together in the first place.

Although, he was definitely laying it on thick at the office yesterday. Come to think of it, what kind of asshole flirts with someone while they've got a girlfriend? My stomach churns for an entirely different reason now. Parker's always been faithful, and what, that changes suddenly because we have to work together?

I know that we have a past and blah blah blah, but that's no excuse to step out of your relationship. I feel my heart beating in my chest, my frustration rising. My love goggles got the best of me. The sandwich, the compliments—I was blinded.

Now that I've separated myself from the situation, I feel my blood boiling. I'm not going to be the person that comes between a relationship. I whip out of my phone again and draft a text to Parker.

> Dylan: Sorry I had to leave so abruptly. But, I just wanted to let you know that although I've agreed to work together, it doesn't mean that we're suddenly going to become friends again. I spent years without you in my life, and I don't plan on changing that any time soon. I'm happy to be civil, as my job depends on it, but that's where I draw the line. I hope you understand.

Without an ounce of regret, I hit send, turn my phone off, and shove it into my purse, prepared to go off the grid. I know it's brutal, but it needed to be done. I am not going to be a homewrecker, and I'm certainly not going to allow myself to get emotionally invested in someone who has already hurt me.

Once I'm on the subway on the way home, I open my latest read, hoping to replace my current reality with one that's a lot less chaotic. But, as I scan the words, I'm unable to absorb a single thought. Instead, I find myself saying a silent prayer that I didn't just royally fuck everything up.

9

PARKER

What the hell was that? I don't think I've ever seen Dylan try to get away from me that fast. One minute, we were fine, and the next, she couldn't get out of there fast enough. I don't usually take phone calls when I'm in social settings, but the minute I saw Olivia's name light up on my phone, I knew that the only way to get her off my back was to take the call.

Olivia and I dated for about two years, and we broke up three months ago.

She was the first girl I was serious about after Dylan and I ended things. I wanted forever with Dylan, but I burned that bridge and knew I needed to move on. It took time, but eventually, I let my guard down–a decision I unfortunately have to live with for the rest of my life.

When I met Olivia at a bar in Venice, I thought she was cute–in an LA kind of way. Before her, I was drawn to the more down-to-earth girls. The ones who enjoyed spending their weekends hiking and camping rather than going out to the hottest clubs. Olivia was the antonym to that. But my typical type wasn't working, so I figured, why not try something new?

Our first date at Griffith Observatory turned into us spending almost every single day together. I couldn't get enough of her, and one day, without realizing it, all of her stuff ended up moving into my small one-bedroom apartment in Silver Lake. It was perfect. Almost too perfect. I spent every day waiting for the other shoe to drop.

Olivia made me think that maybe my move to California *wasn't* the biggest mistake I had ever made.

I was the one to end things with Dylan, but it had nothing to do with my feelings for her and everything to do with the distance I unintentionally put between us. I think that's the worst kind of break-up. The one where you have nothing but love for the person, but the timing isn't right.

Anyway, it turns out that my gut was right about Olivia because I found out she cheated on me with one of her coworkers—the one she repeatedly told me "not to worry about." Go figure. The worst part is that I caught them together.

I had been working long hours at work and decided to cut out early one afternoon to surprise her with wine and our favorite neighborhood takeout. The last thing I expected to find was her riding him, practically screaming his name for the entire complex to hear. Needless to say, I may or may not have had to clean chow mein off my walls for a week after. The sorry prick is lucky he didn't walk out with a black eye. Or two. Since then, Olivia has been blowing up my phone nonstop, begging for a second chance.

After I found out, I kicked her out, got the job at Blue Bird lined up, and got the fuck out of there. Nothing says running away from your problems like moving across the country. Although distance played a very big role in Dylan and I going our separate ways, I learned to love my life in Los Angeles, so I wasn't thrilled about making the move. But when I saw Dylan on that flight, my entire perspective changed.

My phone vibrates, pulling me out of my daze. I warily pull

it out, almost positive that I'm going to see Olivia's name again. My palms go clammy when I see Dylan's name. I open the text, and my heart stops in my chest.

"*I spent years without you in my life, and I don't plan changing that any time soon. I'm happy to be civil, as my job depends on it, but that's where I draw the line.*"

My breath catches in my lungs, and the blood roars in my ears. I grasp the phone tighter, unable to look away from the screen. If I don't loosen my white-knuckling, it's going to snap in half, yet my mind can't seem to register the intensity of my grip.

What the actual fuck does this mean? For all intents and purposes, I thought we were having an enjoyable lunch. She seemed to hate me a lot less than at the office. I know that's not saying much, but we were at least taking small steps in the right direction. Now, I feel like we're even further behind the starting line. I replay our entire conversation in my head, trying to figure out where things went wrong. Everything seemed fine up until the phone call.

Shit.

I throw my phone down on the table and splay my hands out in a wide stretch before relaxing them, doing my best to swallow the anger rising with every passing second. Fucking Olivia. Still managing to ruin things from 2,500 miles away.

But why would that upset Dylan? She didn't see who I was talking to, and even if she did, it doesn't explain the hostile text. Unless she's jealous, but Dyl's never been the jealous type. She's not one to jump to conclusions, either, especially over something as small as a phone call.

Without giving myself a moment to question my sanity, I shoot Blake a text asking him to meet me at the deli. He responds in seconds, letting me know he'll be here in ten. This could be a misstep, but I don't know what else to do. I have no clue how to fix this, and although Blake may not be the relationship type, he does have a way to get girls to forgive him for even the most despicable mistakes. I've witnessed it firsthand and hate to admit that it is impressive.

As I gape at my hands in shock, I hear the deli door open and my name called. I finally lift my eyes to see Blake striding in my direction.

This is one of the many reasons we're best friends. There are many things we may disagree on, specifically how to treat a woman, but he's always there for me, no questions asked. When Olivia and I broke up, he booked a flight back to California within minutes and numbed the pain with too much whiskey and a Game of Thrones marathon. There's something about watching a grisly battle scene that will make your problems feel exponentially smaller.

He slides into the still-warm seat that Dylan occupied only moments ago.

"What's up? Why the urgent text? Lunch with Dylan go to shit?"

I grimace, though he's not entirely wrong. "You could say that. We were actually having a good time. She agreed to work together in more or less words. I could see her getting more comfortable around me."

He steals my soda from me and takes a swig. "So what's the problem?"

"Olivia called."

"For fuck's sake. What did she want?" His lips press into a thin line.

For someone who has commitment issues himself, Blake has always been very supportive of my hatred for my ex. It may be naive, but it gives me hope that one day he'll settle down himself, though I don't imagine that will happen any time soon. It's not looking promising at this moment, but I consider myself an optimist.

"The usual. Begging for me back, telling me how sorry she was."

He snorts. "She's only sorry she got caught."

I wave my hands in agreement and steal my drink back, draining the last of it. "I know. I shut down the call immediately. Unfortunately, I think Dylan saw who was on the other end of it."

"Why would she care?" Blake asks.

"I wish I knew. That's why I called you. I have no idea what to do now. We were finally making headway, and now we're back to square one. She sent me a pretty nasty text after she left, too."

I pull up our conversation and hand him my phone. He skims it quickly before placing it back down on the table. He leans back and throws one leg over his other, crossing his arms. By the look on his face, it's clear the puzzle pieces are clicking in his mind–and with him, that's never a good sign. I can tell from his body body language alone that he's about to say something stupid. I take a deep breath, mentally preparing myself for it.

"Dude, she's jealous. This is your chance," he says matter-of-factly.

"Did you read the text I just showed you?"

"I did. And it's clear. Now's your window to get her back."

If I had been drinking the last of my soda, I would've spit it out onto the table. Instead, my eyes widen, and I let out a small nervous laugh. This is not the perfect opportunity. And I don't want her back...or do I? That ship sailed a long time ago. I stood on the upper deck of the boat, waving goodbye to a second chance years ago. Based on how she ran away from me, it doesn't appear she's hoping to rekindle things either.

"Absolutely not." I shake my head in dismissal. "Not happening."

"Why not?" Blake leans forward, resting against the table. He grabs the bag of potato chips in front of me and pops one into his mouth. Unbelievable. I shove the bag in his direction in defeat. It's not like I can stomach eating anymore, anyway. "Think about it. The jealousy clearly means there are unresolved feelings there. Now, you can swoop in and show her what she's been missing all these years. You'll be her knight in shining armor."

"Or she wasn't jealous in the first place and realized that working with me is going to be a logistical nightmare."

"As someone who knows women like the back of my hand, I'm telling you, she thinks you have a girlfriend. You should use it to your advantage."

Now I know he's lost his damn mind. "How do I use that to my advantage?"

"You make her fall in love with you again without realizing it. She thinks you have a girlfriend? Act like it. She'll think that you're just being friendly because you're taken when, in reality, you're showing her why she can trust you again. Reminding her of all you have to offer without her thinking you have ulterior motives. It's foolproof."

"That's the dumbest thing I've ever heard."

"Answer me this. Do you still love her?"

"Yes," I blurt out before I can think about my answer, surprising the both of us.

We both freeze, stunned by the admission. After he gets past his momentary speechlessness and shuts his jaw, which had dropped the minute the one-word answer was out of my mouth, he says, "I wasn't expecting that answer right off the bat. I figured you'd at least put up *some* fight. You're making this a lot easier for me."

I sigh, resigning to my answer. There's no point in trying to retract my answer. I've already dug my own grave. Once Blake has his mind set on something, there's no convincing him otherwise.

"I've never stopped loving her. But that doesn't mean we're supposed to end up back together."

"That's exactly what it means. Starting today, Operation Get-Dylan-Back is a go, my friend."

10

DYLAN

It's officially been two weeks since I had lunch with Parker, and I haven't heard a word from him. I know that's something I should be happy about, yet I can't shake the tautness in my chest that's gotten progressively worse with every passing day. This is what I wanted, after all. To keep our relationship strictly professional. I made that very clear. I'm starting to think maybe I made it a little *too* clear.

I've had to lock my phone in my desk multiple times this week to stop myself from texting him. If he wanted to talk to me, he'd reach out first. Although I basically told him never to speak to me again, what sensible person in their right mind would reach out after that?

As I'm going through Evelyn's social media profiles to create a content calendar to prep for this book release, I hear my name called. I turn around to find Scarlett making her way to my desk, latte in hand once again. This woman knows my love language is coffee, and she never fails to bring me my daily caffeine fix. Who needs a man when you have a beautiful woman hand-delivering specialty lattes every day? She even knows just how much milk to add. From my experience, no man is capable of remembering those small details.

While I want to be thrilled that she's bringing me a drink, it's clear to see that she has a hidden agenda. Her lips are pursed, eyebrows raised with concern. No wonder she's bringing me a sweet treat. She's trying to butter me up. She hesitantly hands me the coffee silently with shaky hands.

"Thank you for the coffee. Now, what's wrong? You look like you're about to tell me that you hit my cat with your car."

She scrunches her face up in disgust. "A little morbid first thing in the morning, don't you think?"

I wave nonchalantly. "Maybe. But stop trying to change the subject. Out with it."

"What makes you think something is wrong?" she asks innocently.

"You went out of your way to get me coffee from La Cabra."

"Not just a coffee." She pulls a white paper bag out from behind her back and passes it my way. I peek my head inside to find a perfectly baked, beautifully powdered sugar-coated almond croissant. I have to physically stop myself from salivating at the sight of the delicious pastry. I dream of La Cabra's pastries almost every single night–no, that is not an exaggeration.

I set the bag on my desk with every ounce of self-control in my body, lean back in my chair, and interlock my hands over my lower stomach, unable to be bribed...yet. "Okay, now I know you're really trying to kiss my ass. What's going on?"

She sits down on the edge of my desk across from me and flashes me a strained smile. "Katherine called me into her office last night. She's taking me off the Bennett project."

This jolts me forward out of my seat. "What? Why? You're the only person she can stand. Why on earth would she be taking you off an account? How the hell am I supposed to work with Parker without you as a buffer now?"

Shortly after lunch with Parker, I finally filled Scarlett in on our history. How the not-so-mysterious, hot stranger that walked into our office was actually, at one point, the person I thought I'd spend the rest of my life with. Of course, she swore up and down that she'd be there with me in every meeting, conference call, etc., to help me maintain my sanity (or at least the very little of it that I'm still grasping onto).

I'm sure it didn't help Katherine's image of me as a child who needs hand-holding, but sometimes you do what you have to do to survive. Even if that means your boss thinks you're incompetent. I can't imagine that's far off from her initial opinion of me anyway.

Scarlett presses her tongue to her top lip in contemplation. "That's the thing. She's putting me on a smaller account. She apparently received an email from Blake at Blue Bird, who vocalized his wishes to work with you and you alone. She's strongly against the idea, but she'll do anything she can to impress that man. Not to mention, I may or may not have been in support of letting you take on the account yourself..." Her voice naturally lowers as she prepares for the hell I'm about to unleash on her.

As the words come out of her mouth, The sip of delectable housemade dirty chai latte she brought to buy me off burns my throat, forcing me to wheeze. While I'm gasping for air, she runs over to my side and pats me on the back. I throw my hands up in a gesture to get her to back off, finally gulping down a breath.

"Have you gone mad? You knew I already tried to get taken off the entire thing. What makes you think I want to work on it by myself?" I bite.

She backs up, hands drooping at her side, a remorseful pout on her face. "I know it's not ideal, but Blake asked for it, and as much as I would love to have this one under my belt, this is your chance to shine. Come on, Dyl. Getting opportunities like this so early on in your career is almost impossible, especially with Katherine. I know you're talented enough to knock it out of the park. Now's the time to prove it."

The logical part of me knows deep down that I can't be upset by what she did. It's out of her control, and she wants to see me succeed more than anyone. She's been my cheerleader since the minute I stepped into the office, and as someone who hasn't had many people in her corner over the years, it's been refreshing. Yet I can't help but feel the smallest inkling of betrayal that she didn't put up a bigger fight.

"Why would Blake ask that I'm on the account alone in the first place?" I question in place of vocalizing my hurt.

"I wish I knew." She puts a hand up to her mouth and whispers, "He's either desperate to sleep with you, which I wouldn't fault you for if you did, by the way. The things I would let that man do to me." She blows out a breath as, I can only assume, she visualizes bumping uglies with the man. I roll my eyes as she raises her voice back to her normal volume. "Or, this is some ploy that Parker propositioned to get you two to spend more time together."

My eyes bulge at the thought. There's no way Parker would do that. We haven't spoken in weeks. There's no scenario that I can dream up where he woke up and decided that he suddenly wants to spend every waking second working together.

"That's not possible. He's gone completely M.I.A."

"Well, to be fair, you did tell the man that your life is better without him. That doesn't exactly scream, "I want to talk to you.""

I jut out my bottom lip. "I did not. I simply told him that we're not going to be friends."

"If that's what you want to tell yourself to help you sleep better at night, go for it. But I read that text, and I know that if I ever received that, I would probably crawl up in the fetal position and rot in bed for days."

Scarlett's sitting on my desk five feet away from me, but the blow lands like a slap across the face. I've spent the last fourteen days trying not to think about the text I sent in an envious rage. I *have* been known to be a bit abrasive occasionally, but I thought it was a flaw I was overcoming. Clearly not.

I close my eyes and focus on my breathing, inhaling and exhaling slowly, pleading with my heart to slow its beat against my chest. I'll never fault Scarlett for being brutally honest, even if it's sometimes unbearable to hear.

"Exactly my point. If that text did as much emotional damage as you seem to think it did, I don't see why he'd want to work together one-on-one. If anything, I'd assume he'd be running for the hills. Moving back to LA to get away from me."

"I love you, but stop being dramatic. Besides, I don't bother trying to understand men. It's a waste of my brain power. I think the first step is to reach out to Blake and see if you can set up a meeting. Find out why he requested you and go from there. Either way, I think this is a golden opportunity presented on a platter for you. Who knows how long you'd have to work here before Katherine even considers giving you your own client, let alone someone as big as Evelyn. If you can prove to her that you can do this, maybe she'll give you other accounts. Or at least finally get your name right."

A small giggle floats up from my throat, and I feel some of the unease lift from my shoulders. "It would be nice to be taken seriously for once."

"Exactly. I'm not going to be working closely with you now, but that doesn't mean that I'm going anywhere. You can go to all your meetings with them, and then we can get drinks afterward. Nothing cures emotional pain more than a martini or two. Maybe it won't be as bad as you think."

"I appreciate your optimism," I glower.

"One of us has to be positive in this friendship."

"Hey! I'm positive!" I retort.

"Sure, and I'm the queen of England." She pats me on the head as she makes her way out of my cubicle. "Email Blake. Set up a meeting. If you need anything, you know where to find me."

"Thank you for the coffee and pastry. I love you," I shout after her as she leaves.

"I know!" She yells back.

I take one more long sip of chai. It may not be the liquid courage I need right now, but it's good enough for the time being. I turn back to my email and draft an email to Blake asking to set up a meeting, then go back to prepping the social calendar.

A response lands in my inbox less than an hour after sending it. If there's one thing I've learned over the past few weeks dealing with these men, it's that they're workaholics who will get back to you faster than the speed of light. Despite my dislike for the two, I have to admire their dedication. There are worse people to work with on the biggest account of my life. I'd be caught dead before admitting that to them, though.

Hi Dylan,

Glad the message got relayed! My day is packed with meetings, but I am around for a half an hour or so if you want to swing by the office today around 1. If that doesn't work, let me know and we can get something else on the calendar.

Thanks,
Blake

As much as I don't want to take this meeting, I need to get to the bottom of this. It's also a great excuse to get out of the office. Katherine has me make more coffee runs than I care for, but I savor the moments of peace and quiet while I'm out. Begrudgingly, I can't deny that a meeting at Blue Bird is far better than errands for a boss who views me as a glorified assistant. I might as well be an intern. Let's just hope I can steer clear of Parker.

✳ ✳ ✳ ✳ ✳

BLUE BIRD IS LOCATED in a high rise right on the borders of Central Park—on the 40th floor, to be precise. The elevator ride up couldn't have taken longer than three minutes, yet those three minutes were long enough to send me off the deep end. It's impossible to steady my erratic pulse as I step off to large glass doors.

As I walk in, I see a round front desk with the words "Blue Bird" on the wall behind it. It reminds me of The Devil Wears Prada, and it strikes me that I live in New York again. As someone who had pictures of the Empire State Building on her vision board ever since she was fourteen, I still get moments where I'm reminded how drastically my life has changed. There may have been some hiccups–buff, grossly handsome hiccups–along the way, but it's still a surreal feeling.

The red-headed receptionist seated at the front desk looks like she belongs on the cover of Vogue. She has those sharp, razor-blade cheekbones everyone's paying thousands of dollars to achieve with buccal fat removal. Said cheeks are covered in a smattering of freckles, and to top it all off, her jade green eyes are practically glowing, made even brighter by the deep plum sweater she's wearing.

"Welcome to Blue Bird. How can I help you?" She flashes me a warm smile, and I immediately hate her. Okay, that's not entirely true, but it is truly unfair that there are people walking around this planet as beautiful as her.

I swallow my unwarranted envy. "I'm here for a meeting with Blake Beaumont. My name is Dylan Jenkins."

She looks down at her computer screen, typing away. "Ah, yes. Looks like he's expecting you. Follow me right this way." She pushes her way up from the chair and leads me down the hallway. I do my best to keep my eyes ahead, but I can't help as they fall to her curves. She's wearing a black skirt that many might find far too short to wear to work, but who am I to judge? If I had an ass like hers, I'd probably be showing it off too. The universe really does have its favorites.

We stop at another frosted glass door, and she taps at it softly. I pause, steeling myself to see Parker on the other side. I know my meeting is scheduled with Blake, but you can never be too sure–especially since it's becoming a common occurrence to see him when I least expect it.

"Come in," responds a muffled voice from the other side.

I sag with relief when a voice belonging to a man other than Parker responds. Thank god. The bombshell of a receptionist pushes the door open and throws him her perfectly straight, way-too-white smile.

"I have Dylan Jenkins here to see you."

"Thanks, Blair. Send her in."

Blair. A name fitting for a model. Shocker.

She pushes the door open wider, and I have to clench my jaw to keep myself from gaping at the setup. Sitting behind the desk are nearly floor-to-ceiling windows with half-moon detailing at the top. The adjacent wall is made entirely of exposed brick, covered in colorful prints.

Resting below the art is a sleek black metal bar complete with a crystal decanter full of what I surmise is a whiskey that costs more than I'd ever be willing to spend on a bottle of liquor. I always heard about people stashing a bottle of something or other in their desks, but seeing it in front of me makes the corners of my lips twitch up. How cliche.

There's a long, deep blue velvet couch against the wall, with a glass coffee table in front of it. Surprisingly, there's even a spider plant atop it, and from one quick glance, it appears to be real. Color me impressed.

Situated right in front of the windows sits a long black desk with two mid-century modern chairs on one side and a grinning Blake on the other.

Blair begins to shut the door, but I notice her lingering out of the corner of my eye as if she's waiting for Blake to acknowledge her further. He must notice it, too, because he sends a subtle wink her way. Her cheeks instantly redden, and she closes it the rest of the way. *Gross.*

I was hoping I'd caught him on an off day when his eyes wouldn't leave my chest, but apparently, he openly gawks regularly.

He turns his attention back to me, stands, and gestures to one of the chairs across from him at his desk. "Dylan, thank you so much for coming down. I appreciate the time you're taking to meet with me."

Every fiber of my being wants to roll my eyes at him, but his grin is memorizing. He's attractive in that self-important, womanizing way. Definitely not my type, but I can see why girls would fall under his spell when he turns the charm on.

I take a seat across from him, and he waits for me to be seated before he sits back down. How, unfortunately, chivalrous of him.

"Thanks for finding the time." I clasp my hands together and let them fall in my lap as my eyes wander around the office once again. Blake doesn't miss a beat, refusing to let us fall into an uncomfortable silence.

"You're probably wondering why I asked Katherine to take Miss Kensington off the account."

I let out a shaky laugh. "Yes, I am a bit confused."

He leans forward, resting his forearms on his desk. My eyes

snag on his biceps, straining against the fabric of his midnight blue button-down. It's clear he spends his free time out of the office at the gym, and I hate myself for noticing his physique.

You can find someone attractive and still hate their personality, I remind myself. There's no shame in admiring the view.

"I apologize that you didn't hear it from me first. I was planning on emailing you before my call with Katherine, but this week has been rather busy. It wasn't my intention to make you feel blindsided."

I blink a couple of times, trying to shake away the small butterflies that have begun fluttering low in my belly. It's not my fault that finding a man willing to apologize for even the smallest wrongdoings is nearly impossible in this day and age. I can't be held responsible for my bodily reaction to manners.

"Thank you," I mumble.

"It has come to my attention that you and Mr. Townsend have a history together, correct?"

"I-I guess you could say that," I stutter, unsure how to respond. Is Parker going around and telling everyone in his office that we dated? I'm trying to look professional, and his fat mouth is already jeopardizing it.

"No need to hide it. I think it's going to be extremely beneficial for this account."

"I'm not following." The confusion must be clear on my face because he lets out a low rumble of laughter.

"Parker is new to the team, and Evelyn is a big account to step into immediately. Although I know he can handle this with whomever he's partnered with, I want to ensure things go well. I'd much rather he work closely with someone he's familiar with than a stranger."

"But Scarlett is one of our top marketing coordinators..." My voice fades, and I'm still unsure what direction this is heading. It doesn't fully process that he mentioned the two of us working beside one another.

"Are you saying you're bad at your job?" He lifts a brow, a pompous smile lingering on his face.

I vehemently shake my head. "No, of course not."

"I didn't think so. I had Katherine send me your portfolio before I made the final call. You may not have the experience Miss Kensington has, but you're talented. I'm not concerned."

I sit in silence for a moment while I let it all sink in. This is so well thought out, yet I learned about the decision less than six hours ago. While I am very flattered that he thinks I'm good at what I do, I'm still left with so many questions. Before I can ask a single one, there's a quiet knock at the door. Probably Blair armed with an excuse to see him again.

"Come in." Blake doesn't break eye contact with me but waves his hand, beckoning whoever is on the other side. The door opens, and it's just my luck; it's not Blair. No, it's Parker looking sexy in a tight cream polo and navy chino pants that I just know make his butt look great. I don't know what's in the water over there, but California really made him one hell of a dresser, and I'm not happy about it.

"You wanted to see me?" He asks Blake before his eyes fall to mine.

Great. Here we go again.

11

DYLAN

At the sight of Parker walking into the office, Blake's face breaks out into the largest smile I've seen since coming in myself. The man is practically glowing. It doesn't take much for me to realize that this was his plan all along. He never had any intention of meeting with just me, and all of the compliments were just to soften the blow.

"I did. Please, have a seat." Blake motions to the empty seat next to me.

Parker does as he's told and sits inches away from me, giving me a subtle head nod. From the looks of it, he had no idea that I would be here, either. At least I can't fault him for this.

"I was just telling Dylan that I chose to have Miss Kensington removed from the account because I want you two to work side-by-side on this account."

Surprise flashes in Parker's eyes, but he doesn't let his professional facade crumble. I'm guessing he wasn't in on that decision either. Within seconds, his gaze is stony with anger directed right at Blake. It's not a look I'd want to be on the receiving end of.

"Is that so?" His steady yet hoarse voice sends a thrill through my veins. If I weren't so vexed right now, I'd be able to appreciate just how attractive he sounds.

"Yes. While I think Miss Kensington is extremely talented, you'll benefit from working closely with someone you're familiar with. If all goes well, this account could put your name on the map on this side of the country. Because you represent Blue Bird, I want to do whatever I can to ensure this is successful."

I can feel the heat emanating off of the figure to my right. He's fuming, and I do my best to bottle the sting of the rejection. Yes, I did tell him to back off, but to have such an extreme reaction about working one-on-one together feels a *tad* hurtful.

Blake glances down at his watch and pushes out of his chair, ending the discussion before it can even begin. "While I would love to stay and discuss this further, I have another meeting on the other side of town I need to head to. Dylan, it was lovely seeing you again. I hope you understand where I'm coming from. I want the best for both of our businesses. It's not my intention to make anyone uncomfortable. I know you two will make a great team."

I'm left sitting there dumbstruck. It's not like I can argue with him on this. The decision has already been made, and I want to keep the last shred of my dignity intact. Parker already appears upset enough for the both of us anyway.

"Oh, and last thing." Blake grabs the briefcase he just packed up on the way out. "Dylan, I went ahead and spoke to Katherine earlier. I let her know that you would be coming down here for a meeting with me, and we both decided it would be best to start brainstorming as soon as possible. I blocked out one of our conferences for the rest of the afternoon. You've already been given the green light to stay and work. I look forward to seeing what the two of you come up with!"

And just like that, he's gone.

The room is vibrating with energy, like a thunderstorm ready to break. Parker's head is bowed, and he refuses to meet my eyes. I think it may just be the most unpleasant scenario I've ever been in before–and I've walked in on my parents on multiple occasions. I'm the queen of triple-checking that doors are locked when I have someone over now.

I shift my body to face him, knowing that I'm going to have to be the one to break the unpleasant silence. "I'm guessing you didn't know about this prior to this meeting?"

He lowers his thick, black lashes before swiveling toward me. "I did not. When I came in this morning, I saw that I had a last-minute meeting thrown on my calendar, but I wasn't expecting all of that." He signals to the void that Blake just left. He blows out a large, weary exhale and scrubs a hand down his face. "I'm so sorry, Dylan. Had I known we would get ambushed like this, I would've warned you. Blake has a tendency to do whatever he pleases without thinking about how it affects others."

The corner of my lips quiver in amusement. "That's quite a strong opinion about your new boss."

"He's not my boss. He's my best friend."

"Your best friend?" I ponder.

"We met in California shortly after my move out west. We worked together at our last publishing company and he transferred to Blue Bird about a year ago. He's the one who got me this job."

And just like that, the dots begin to connect in my head.

"This all makes a lot more sense. But wait, why was he ogling me at our initial meeting if you two are so close? Does he not believe in "bro code" or whatever?" I curl my fingers in mock quotations because I'm getting the sense that Blake doesn't abide by these unspoken man rules.

A muscle in Parker's jaw flicks sharply. "He what?"

"I caught him outright staring at my boobs before he even muttered a single hello. Real charmer of a friend you got there."

He sucks in a breath through his front teeth, his brows furrowing. I initially think he's contemplating how to strangle his best friend when he gets the chance until he says, "To be fair, they did look great in that dress."

My jaw falls open in shock, and I slap him gently across the arm. He throws his head back in laughter and places his hand over the spot I just hit, feigning pain.

I feel my cheeks go hot at the sound of his laugh, and a pool of desire begins to grow in my core. The audacity that my body has for enjoying that comment.

I could listen to him laugh for hours. It used to be the soundtrack of my life, the thing that would brighten even my worst days. It's like the sound of birds chirping on a warm spring day when the sun is shining, and there's a slight breeze that kisses your skin. It was the house that I built for myself, the place I felt the safest. Even after all these years, hearing it makes me feel like I'm coming home again.

I clear my throat, hoping to rid myself of the squares of memories that have come together to create a quilt in my mind. Parker notices the shift in my demeanor, and we fall into another torturous momentary silence.

"I'm kidding. Kind of." One look into his devilish eyes tells me he's not joking, and I cross my legs, hoping to keep my libido down to a minimum. Now's not the time or place. "Look, I know Blake rubs people the wrong way, and I will absolutely be talking to him about gawking at you, but he really is a good guy. He's been with me through a lot. And to be fair, he didn't know that you were my ex when he decided to eye fuck you."

"He didn't know about me?" I choke out.

In a flash, the room's warmth is drained and replaced with a bone-chilling iciness. I wrap my arms around myself protectively. He's kept me, us, and our history a secret all these years, as if I was just another girl he dated. Not the one he went ring shopping with.

"He knew how messed up I was over a breakup. I just never told him the details. I never thought I was going to see you again. It just felt easier to keep some things to myself…" His voice tapers off as he loses confidence.

For the first time since we ended things, I can see a glimmer of pain in his eyes. I can hear it in the way his voice breaks as he speaks about it. The only other time I've seen him show an inkling of emotion was the day we went our separate ways. Unfortunately, I remember it like it was yesterday.

I've tried to scrub it from my memory for years, but there's something about that kind of heartbreak that lingers with you for the rest of your life. No matter how many people you meet, sleep with, or try to forget with, it sits buried deep in your soul.

When he came over that October afternoon, I immediately knew something was wrong. He was aloof and wouldn't look me in the eye. We were supposed to go apple picking that day. I dressed up in a new sweater I had just bought, in a shade of teal that he had once said was his favorite color on me. I had picked it out just for him.

We made plans to move in together earlier that year, but Dad passing away from lung cancer the previous year put all of my plans on pause.

Mom didn't take it well and began using alcohol to cope with her grief. She went from one of the happiest, most vivacious people I've ever met to escaping reality at the bottom of a bottle. So I stayed home to take care of her. While she eventually did make a full recovery after some time in rehab, the journey to get there was a long one. I felt like I was drowning, and there was no life preserver in sight.

To make matters worse, Parker got a job in California. He applied on a whim, said he had no chance of getting it. We had both wanted to get out of town, so I couldn't fault him for trying. I think we both knew deep down that getting the job was a very real possibility. He was smart, driven, and had an impressive resume with internships and a nearly perfect grade-point average. They would've been foolish to turn him away–which is why it was no surprise to me when he broke the news that they had extended him an offer.

He had every intention of turning it down to stay with me, but I knew I couldn't ask him to sacrifice his dreams. Despite living across the country from one another, we made it our goal to see each other as much as possible. In the beginning, we saw each other once a month. As time progressed, our visits became few and far between.

I knew the distance was making things tense for us. Stolen kisses turned into clipped conversations over the phone. Laughing until our stomachs hurt, up until 3 a.m., turned into unanswered texts. We were always quick to apologize and work through our fights, but it tested our relationship unlike anything we had gone through together up until that point. I thought it was just a hurdle, one that we were strong enough to get through if we just practiced a little patience.

That is until we stood on my front porch, and he told me he couldn't do it anymore. That moment has echoed through my thoughts like a horror movie countless times throughout the years—the way he avoided my gaze the entire time he spoke, how stoic he was as he broke the news that his schedule was only getting busier and that it wasn't fair to me to keep things going . It was cowardly. But more importantly, it was one of the worst days of my life.

I cast the unhappy thoughts aside, trying to focus on the man sitting in front of me with puppy-dog eyes. I nod my head in understanding.

Sometimes, it's easier just to tuck away your innermost hurt and hide it from the world–even those who know you best. After his rented Toyota Corolla pulled away from my house that day, I didn't leave my bedroom for weeks. I couldn't bring myself to say the words out loud. We weren't strong enough to make it.

I divert the conversation. "Well, it looks like we're going to be around one another a lot, so we might as well get started."

He coughs quietly, visibly upset that I'm not pushing the topic further, but decides against saying anything. "Definitely. Hey, instead of using that conference room, why don't we take a walk?"

"Really? Don't you think we should get started on this? We've got a presentation with Evelyn in a couple of weeks."

He loosely shrugs his shoulders. "Being outside always helps me get the creative juices flowing. Besides, if I had to guess, you've already gotten a head start on this presentation. Am I right?"

My cheeks heat, and I bring a hand to my face to cool myself down before he can notice. While I don't want to give Blake any credit for forcing us together, there is something to be said about working with someone who knows you better than you know yourself.

I've always been an overachiever. It was one of the things Parker always said he admired most about me. I blame being a double Virgo. I was destined to be a kiss-ass since the minute I was brought into this world.

"I may or may not have already brainstormed a few social media ideas to help us promote the book..."

"A few?" He lifts a brow in question.

"Okay, I've got a content calendar planned for the next six months. So what?"

He beams up at me, his smile as bright and warm as the sun. "That's the Dylan I know and love. Looks like we've got plenty of time to get some fresh air."

My heart lurches in my chest at the words. He pushes out of

his chair, leaving me no time to think about what that "love" comment means before he's out the door.

※ ※ ※ ※ ※

It's an unusually warm March afternoon. The city is thawing under the bright light of the sun, but the trees that line the sidewalks of Central Park are still bare. I can't wait for the warmer days when the trees are in full bloom, but there's something magical about the way you can see the city skyline behind the naked branches. Traces of greenery have begun to sprout, and the idea of the leaves making their appearance for the first time this year is oddly comforting. No matter how harsh the conditions get in the winter, there's always spring—the chance to start over.

That's what this move has been—my chance to bloom.

"So, tell me what you have in mind for marketing so far." Parker's gruff voice pulls me out of my musings. I glance over at him, strolling beside me. His hands are tucked in the pockets of his pants as he walks slowly to match my pace. My eyes trail up to his dark, loose curls, blown by a light gust of wind. He looks so effortless, as if he's lived in New York his entire life.

It's never something I've admitted to him, but I've always been jealous of how he can chameleon his way into any setting or scenario. That never came naturally to me, and I've always struggled to fit in.

"Well, we already know that she has the following needed to promote this book. But those numbers don't necessarily correlate to buyers. I've already shared the calendar that I've put together with Scarlett, and she thinks it's a great start. I'll share that with Evelyn so she can get a head start sharing blurbs of the book, behind-the-scenes moments, hints about writing book two, that kind of thing." I twirl a strand of hair around my finger, suddenly shy, discussing my work.

"While we're getting all those posts scheduled, I'm going to be working with the web designer Scarlett put me in contact with. It's no secret that her site needs a facelift. Once we get that fleshed out, I'm going to create an email marketing campaign to get the ball rolling on preorders. I've already begun putting together a list of influencers to send early copies to, so once those physical copies are ready, I'll send that list over to you. Oh, and I'm also in the process of organizing a release party here in the city with the help of our PR team."

I look down at my feet when I realize I'm rambling. I'm met with utter silence. Perfect. I've bored him to death. Without looking up, I can feel his eyes on me. I flick my eyes up and meet his stare. It's not a look of judgment that I'm met with. No, it's one of admiration.

"Sounds like you've got this in the bag." He nudges me with his shoulder. "I wish you could see yourself from my eyes sometimes. You'd stop being so hard on yourself. You're talented as hell, Dylan. It's time you start believing in yourself."

It's moments like these where my heart is tugged right back in his direction. He always knew exactly what to say when I was feeling down. If we hadn't been dating in college, I'm not sure I would have graduated. There were countless long days following all-nighters spent studying where I didn't feel good enough. All I wanted to do was finish with honors to make my dad proud, but imposter syndrome got the best of me more often than not.

As my mind wanders, I can't help but wonder who else he's given these same pep talks to. *Olivia.*

That reality brings the runaway train of my thoughts to a screeching halt. He has a girlfriend. There's a reason I was trying to distance myself from him in the first place.

"Look, I appreciate that. I really do. But you have a girlfriend, and I don't think it's fair to her for you to speak to me that way. I'm okay with working together, but that's all it is. Work. No compliments. No walks down memory lane. Strictly professional."

"Dylan, we need to talk about-"

I cut him off him, feeling a wave of panic start to wash over me with every powerful beat of my heart. I refuse to have another anxiety attack in front of him. It's been years since he's last seen me in that state, and I don't want him to know I have yet to overcome it. "No, it's okay. I shouldn't have eavesdropped on your phone call, and for that, I'm sorry. But I heard you talking to her the other day at lunch. I'm happy for you, I am. I hope it works out for you two, but let's focus on this project, and then we can go our separate ways for good, alright?"

As I speed up to get ahead of him, I feel his fingers curl around my bicep. I'm lightly jerked backward, and I meet his eyes, a grave expression on his face.

"I wish you would let me explain myself." He frowns.

I glance down at my watch. "I'm sorry, I really should get back to the office. I don't need Katherine chewing my head off for a third day in a row."

With a wince, he lets go of my arm. "Okay, I understand. Can we at least set up a meeting later this week? I'd love to go over what you've got. In a more formal setting."

"Sure, just send me a calendar invite. I'll make time."

"Alright, sounds great. Thanks for humoring me with this walk."

With that, I turn around and walk in the direction of my office, leaving Parker behind.

12

PARKER

Blake received an ear full as soon as I got back to the office. I knew that no matter how hard I protested against "Operation Get-Dylan-Back," he would do something stupid, and he did not disappoint.

I really did try to tell Dylan the truth about Olivia, but she left little room to get a word in. I don't know what's worse. The fact that she won't let me tell her the truth or the fact that she thinks I've turned into the guy who willingly skirts on the line of flirtation with other girls who are *not* my girlfriend. I am, and always have been, a one-woman kind of man, and thanks to Olivia, it's proven to have bitten me in the ass.

Ever since our stroll through Central Park, Dylan and I have exchanged a series of passive-aggressive emails. I'm doing my best to play nice, but her responses are always short and to the point. As of yesterday, we finalized the last of the edits for Evelyn's book, which means it's ready to go to print, and it's time to ramp up marketing. We've got a meeting this afternoon, and I've felt a sense of dread from the minute I woke up.

It's not that I don't want to see her. Hell, there's nothing I'm looking forward to more than meeting with Dylan. However, I am fully prepared for it to be like pulling teeth. Thank god Evelyn, Katherine, and Blake will be there as buffers to save me from the pain of sitting in suffocating silence while she does her best to ignore me. Although, I don't trust Blake not to do something wildly stupid to help get us together. I can only hope he's professional enough to know that he shouldn't meddle when we're around a client.

As I make my way into the all-too-familiar Thrive office, I'm met with a frightening smile from Katherine, standing at the front desk, hands on her hips, as if she's been waiting for me to show up.

"Ten minutes early? I've always loved a man who takes showing up on time seriously." She bats her eyelashes at me, and I refrain from shuttering at the motion. She's laying it on thick, and the meeting hasn't even begun. What are the chances I can get through this without a call to HR to report harassment? Slim to none, but I try to remain wishful anyway.

I throw a timid grin her way, hoping to tame the beast. "I know how important this meeting is. I'm very much looking forward to seeing what Dylan has to present and how Evelyn feels about it all."

"I had Dylan share her work with me this morning. It's all very impressive, really. We're so lucky to have her."

She's lying straight through her teeth, but I don't call her out for it.

I'm not privy to much of Dylan's life lately, but we have spoken about work, which includes her relationship with Katherine. Or, as she sometimes refers to her, the Wicked Witch of the East. It doesn't sound like the relationship has improved since our last meeting here a few weeks ago, which frustrates the hell out of me.

Not only can I not say a word because I could lose my job, but I also know that Dylan doesn't want me fighting her battles. I lost that right, and I don't foresee getting it back.

I do my best to mirror her smile, willing it to look natural despite the fact that I want to be as far away from this office and Katherine as possible. "Dylan is quite good at her job. I don't doubt that she'll blow us away."

Her face twists into a sneer of what I can only assume is jealousy. But as quickly as it appears, it's gone. So the ice queen doesn't like it when I compliment Dylan. Interesting. Maybe I will have a little fun with this meeting after all.

"Why don't you follow me into the conference room? Once everyone arrives, we can go ahead and get started."

"Of course, lead the way."

I follow her into the conference room, where Blake is already sitting, scrolling through his phone. He hears us enter and lifts his head to cast us a shit-eating grin. I try to look good by getting here early, and this asshat still has me beat.

I sit down next to him with an icy glare. At least I don't have to endure more of Katherine's flirting while I wait for the others to show up. I would rather sit through hours of Dylan's terrible reality TV shows that she stays up late binging than sit through that torment. I don't know if that's saying much, though, because there's something weirdly addicting to Love Island... but I digress.

Katherine leaves the office without another word.

"You would get here earlier than me. Kiss ass," I murmur under my breath.

"Just remember that the next time you wonder why I'm your boss."

"Whatever. I'm just glad you're here. I'm not sure I could stomach sitting here in silence while she makes eyes at me and shows me pictures of her three cats. She hit on you, too?" I tilt my chin up in question.

"Of course. But are we surprised? Look at me." He sweeps a hand up his body. "Who wouldn't want to hit on me? After all of this is said and done, I may have to take her up on her offer to grab drinks."

"Are you out of your fucking mind? She's as evil as they get."

"That remains to be seen. Besides, she's hot."

"You've officially lost it."

"What can I say? I like a challenge, and I like older women even more."

"This is why you're going to be alone forever." I shake my head in disbelief.

"As long as my bed stays warm, I have no problem with that." The smile on his face turns into a self-righteous smirk that makes me want to deck him.

If he hadn't proved to me that he does have a heart–albeit very deep down–there's no chance we would've stayed friends this long. My relationship with my mom has always been rocky, but she instilled values in me from a young age. She went out of her way to raise a gentleman, and if she saw how Blake talks, she'd have a heart attack. While I'll never deny that I would love to be as detached as Blake sometimes, it's not in my genetic makeup.

The door to the conference room opens back up, and Evelyn walks in, followed by Katherine and Dylan. Evelyn is beautiful, don't get me wrong. Her snow-white, freckled skin is contrasted by her auburn hair, and her large dark brown eyes resemble those of a deer. But it's not her that takes my breath away.

Dylan is wearing a red cardigan paired with a black skirt, and she looks angelic. The sweater's scarlet hue brings out the rogue coloring of her cheeks, and her lips look extra sultry, thanks to whatever kind of gloss she's wearing.

I can't tear my eyes off her as she sits beside Evelyn. When she finally returns my stare, I see the corner of her lips lift before she looks back at Katherine. Out of my peripheral, I see

Blake staring me down. My phone, which is sitting facing up on the table, lights up with a new text.

> Blake: Dude, stop staring. You're making it way too obvious

I swiftly shove it in my pocket, thankful that Dylan is sitting too far to read it. *Real subtle,* I chastise myself. Fortunately, I don't have time to think about how overt I'm being because Katherine begins the meeting.

"Evelyn, thank you so much for meeting with us. We're very excited to share everything we've been working on these past few weeks. Dylan, why don't you fill her in on the marketing strategy you've put together?"

"Of course, thank you, Katherine." She stands up and begins AirPlaying her screen onto the projector at the end of the room. "As you know, Evelyn, I've put together your content calendar for the next few months. We've also gotten approval for your site redesign. But we've also been working on a lot of other things that we think are going to help make publishing day as successful as possible." She clicks through the slides.

"The new site will be unveiled at the end of the week. I've already set up a drip campaign along with a newsletter sign-up pop-up ready to gather as many emails as possible. Once the site is live, we will post a giveaway of sorts on your social media platforms to help gain interest from the get-go. The first 100 people to preorder the book through your site are guaranteed a signed copy. The following 500 people to preorder are entered to win a signed copy. We want this to feel exclusive–help your audience feel a little competition. When they preorder the book, we'll also ask them if they want to join the newsletter where you'll share behind-the-scenes snippets, quotes, sneak peeks of the next book, and more."

As Dylan is speaking, a rush of pride swells in my chest. She's come a long way since she was that girl in college in our small town. We spent countless late nights talking about our goals and what we wanted in life, and here she is, making them a reality. She's kicking ass at it too. I gaze over at Evelyn, who is enthusiastically nodding, noticeably impressed.

"I've been emailing with Parker for the past week, and we'll be sending physical copies out to select influencers. We also opened advanced reader copy sign-ups on Monday, and the requests have already started flooding in. Your videos help with the marketing, but theirs will, too. Lastly, we're putting the final touches on a party to celebrate the publication. I included all of the details in the email I last sent you, but as of right now, it's looking like it will be two weeks from now at Somewhere Nowhere. Do you have any questions on anything so far?"

"No, this is great. The social calendar you've put together is already getting so much attention. I've gained another 5,000 followers in just the past week. I can only imagine what everything will look like on release day. Everyone seems super excited. Myself included. Thank you so much for your help, Dylan. I wouldn't have been able to do even half of this on my own." Evelyn offers a genuine smile.

I peer over at Katherine and see her fake grin plastered on her face as she does a mediocre impression of a boss who's pleased with their employee. This only fuels my pride even further. Dylan's not only made our client incredibly happy, but she's also sticking it to Katherine, which is just the cherry on top of the sundae.

Dylan returns Evelyn's friendly expression. "Of course. We still have a lot to do, but I think all of these efforts, combined with your existing social media following, will make this a huge hit. I've already got a copy downloaded and plan on spending the rest of the evening curled up with a glass of wine reading it."

"I like you already. I have a good feeling we're going to be great friends." It's not hard to see the gleam in Evelyn's eye.

"Thank you for that, Dylan. Excellent job." Katherine responds snappishly as she stands up, cutting Dylan's chance to respond in the bud. Dylan sheepishly tucks her chin before sitting down and folding her hands into her lap, morphing into the timid girl I see her transform into every time Katherine is around.

I know that we're not friends, but after this meeting, we need to have a discussion about this. She's better than cowering from a soon-to-be has-been. If this keeps up, she'll be taking over for Katherine in no time. I just hope I'm around to see it.

"Does anyone else have anything to add?" Katherine looks around the room in question.

"I would just like to say a quick thank you to Dylan as well. That was an extremely well-thought-out presentation. You've made Blue Bird proud to be partnering with Thrive." I give Dylan a sincere smile of my own, and I'm rewarded with the same. Meanwhile, I can feel the venomous daggers Katherine's throwing my way. Poking the bear may not be the smartest, but I couldn't help myself. What's the worst she's going to do? Fire us? We're the ones who hired her agency.

"Yes, we're very lucky to have her. Anyways, thank you so much, everyone, for coming by. We will all be in touch soon," Katherine signals, officially ending the meeting.

As everyone begins shuffling out of the conference room, I lightly grab Dylan's arm, preventing her from leaving. She immediately looks up at me, and I can see her eyes soften as they register who's touching her. My heart jerks at the touch, and the idea of pushing her up against the wall and finally kissing her runs through my head like a semi-truck. I remove my hand before I can do anything I'll regret.

"I just wanted to pull you aside and tell you how proud of you I am. I know I said it in the meeting, but that was primarily to kiss Evelyn's ass and piss Katherine off." She lets out a low huff of a laugh. "I meant it, though. That was perfect. Evelyn seems thrilled."

"Thank you, that means a lot. I thought I was going to throw up the entire time."

"Well, I couldn't tell. You looked like you've been doing that your entire life. Regardless of how the release goes, I think you just solidified your place with Thrive. Katherine is going to have no choice but to promote you when this is all over."

"One can only hope."

Her eyes dart back to the door as if she can't wait to get as far away from me as possible. The gesture, though miniscule, cuts through me like a knife. I just wish we could end this hot and cold routine once and for all. It's giving me whiplash. However, I'm not one to accept defeat that easily. All I can do moving forward is prove to her that I'd never hurt her again.

"Hey, before you go, I just want to say that you shouldn't let Katherine treat you that way. You deserve better. I saw you crawl back into your shell in that meeting when she dismissed you. I'm sorry that she made you feel that way. You proved that you're good at what you do. You should own it."

"Yeah, well, that's easier said than done. She is my boss. I say one wrong thing, and she can fire me. I need this job, at least for a little bit. I don't plan on staying here forever, but if I can blend into the background long enough to get some experience, my life will be much easier. Then I can move on."

I brush my hand against hers as we slowly head toward the door, a small motion of support. "I know. You've always been the one to keep the peace. It's admirable. Just don't let her walk all over you, alright? You're better than that."

"I'll try not to. Thank you. It was good to see you, but I've got to get going. Publication party planning calls."

I give her a nod and a small smile as she walks toward her desk. It may be in my head, but I swear, as she's walking away, she's standing a little taller. And that's all I can hope for.

13

DYLAN

"So?! How did it go?" I walk up to Scarlett, perched on the end of my desk, waiting for me to return from the meeting.

I dramatically fling myself into my chair and throw my arms over my face. "Really well, actually."

"Oh, thank god. Then we won't be needing this." She pulls out a small flask of some unknown liquor from behind her back. "Although, you seem like you may need it anyway. Are you alright?"

I look from the small bottle to her face. "Do you just carry that with you everywhere you go?"

She lackadaisically shrugs. "Of course. It's mandatory if you work here. Dealing with Katherine calls for tequila pretty much 24/7. Just be thankful she doesn't blow up your phone on the weekends. My liver is going to hate me if I'm not careful. Now tell me, everything good?"

I stifle a laugh and ignore the flask she's holding out to me. As much as I would love a drink right now, I know that using alcohol as a crutch isn't going to make me feel any better. I wave her off delicately, and she pulls it back to her chest. "It was great. Evelyn seemed thrilled with the ideas I came up with."

"Then what's the issue?"

"Parker."

"Ahh, do tell." She jumps up onto my desk, folding her feet underneath her crossed legs. Her stiletto heels have been abandoned by my feet.

"He's being so... nice. I don't get it. I mean, I do. He's always been a nice guy. But I've been so mean to him to guard myself from getting hurt again. Yet he seems completely unfazed. It's maddening."

"I'm not seeing the problem. Look, I may be on the hating men train and won't be getting off any time soon, but it kind of sounds like he's a good guy who just wants the best for you. Don't you think you've been a little rough on him?"

I stare at her, slack-jawed. I haven't known Scarlett for that long, but I do know that she's always the first to vocalize her distaste for anyone of the opposite gender. She briefly mentioned that she was previously married a few years back, which ended poorly, but it must've really done a number on her because she's about as pessimistic as it gets when it comes to love.

"I'm just trying to protect myself..." My voice cracks, and I instinctively bring a hand to my throat to bring myself some illusion of solace.

"Aw, Dyl, I know." She hops off the desk and drapes her arms around my shoulders. "You're doing what's best for you. Anyone would if they were in your shoes. Maybe just lighten up a little. There's nothing wrong with being friends with the guy if he really does seem to have good intentions. Besides, you said he has a girlfriend. That's enough to help you keep yourself an arm's length away from him. It seems like no matter how hard you try to keep him out of your life, he's here to stay in some capacity."

As she speaks, I feel her phone vibrate in her pocket against my ribs. She stops mid-thought and begins drafting a text.

We sit in silence as she continues without looking up from her phone. Her fingers are flying, typing god knows what to god knows who. Whatever it is, she seems to be enthralled. The giddy grin on her face would be infectious if I weren't so suspicious.

I let out a pointed cough, trying to recapture her attention. She pops her head back up to look at me.

"Sorry about that." She smiles and tucks her phone back into her back pocket. I don't miss that she's put a small distance between us, so I can no longer feel her phone when it goes off.

"Texting someone important?" I pry with a skeptical gaze.

"No. Of course not. Just my mom."

"Mhmm, sure. Is there a new man in your life? Is that why you're getting so soft on me all of a sudden?"

She scrunches her nose and sticks out her tongue in disgust. "Absolutely not. That ship has sailed. I'm just saying that if you and Parker are going to be working together, and he's proven to you that he's going to continue to be nice to you no matter what you throw at him, you might as well not let it get under your skin." She redirects the attention off of her.

"You're probably right, and I hate you for it."

"No, you don't. Look, your first love is always going to be complicated. His showing up in the same new city as you is something straight out of a rom-com. That's automatically going to make you question whether or not the universe is playing tricks on you, and hell, maybe it is. But you're both different people than you once were and now is your chance to have him in your life on a friendship level. I understand his having a girlfriend complicates things even further, but that doesn't mean it's worth hating the guy. You're wasting your own energy."

My eyes narrow into slits. "God dammit, I hate when you get all wise on me."

"I'm sorry. It's part of my DNA. My grandma always told me I had a knack for it. She also said that in my past life, I was some kind of stoic philosopher...so maybe her words don't mean much. Anyways, do you want to cut out of here an hour early and head to hot yoga and then maybe grab a juice? I need to detox myself of my poor decisions last weekend."

"Scar, it's Wednesday. I think it may be a little late for that." I begin packing up my laptop and all of my other belongings into my work bag. I'm more than happy to get out of here as soon as possible, even if it means exercising and drinking some colorful liquid that probably tastes like dirt.

"With that attitude, it is. I rarely go out and still feel like I'm suffering the consequences. God forbid I let loose every once in a while."

"Once in a while? You broke out a flask of tequila in the middle of the office." I pucker my lips, immediately regretting the condemnatory tone in my voice. Fortunately, she doesn't seem to take offense to the abrasive comment.

"It's for emergencies only. I don't need your judgment." She twists the lid off and throws it back, taking a shot. When she's finished, her body shudders, and she smacks her lips in revulsion. "Fuck, I wish I had a lime."

With a laugh, I put one hand up in the air and the other on my heart. "I would never judge you. Scout's honor."

"So? What do you say? A little sweat sesh may clear your head of this Parker stuff."

"I could use a break now that the presentation is over."

"Hell yeah, you could. Let's go. I'll let Katherine know. Save ourselves the headache of her finding out and giving us an earful."

"Have I ever told you I want to be you when I grow up? Maybe then she won't hate my guts."

"She doesn't hate you. It's more of a strong dislike."

"Oh, thanks," I mutter under my breath. As she strides towards Katherine's office, her giggle is carried away with her.

✻ ✻ ✻ ✻ ✻

AFTER RUNNING by Scarlett's apartment and borrowing a workout set from her because my place was too far away, I got my ass handed to me in hot yoga. I was never the athletic type. I dabbled in different sports throughout high school, but nothing ever stuck.

By the time I was in college, I had basically given up. Of course, when you're in college and you have the metabolism of a child, you don't have to worry about working out or eating healthy. No matter how much you stuff your face or drink yourself to death, you never gain a pound. I took those days for granted. Now, it's all about watching what I eat and trying to have some semblance of a workout routine (news flash: it's non-existent).

Luckily, ever since moving to the city, I've been walking more than ever. Unluckily, that doesn't correlate to being naturally great at hot yoga. By the time class is over, I'm dripping with sweat and wheezing at a mortifying volume. Meanwhile, Scarlett seems almost unbothered as we walk out into the cool air, trekking for a green juice.

"How are you not dying? Please don't tell me you're one of those people who's just naturally good at every workout you try," I whine.

"Absolutely not. I've been doing yoga for years now. When I first started, I nearly passed out on multiple occasions. It took me a couple of months to build up my stamina. But I like the way it helps me clear my head. It's become my safe space."

As I glance over at her, her cheeks the softest shade of pink from exertion, I notice a sense of serenity I've never seen before. In the moments we've spent together at lunch and coffee, she's always seemed so tense. I knew she put everything into her work, but I assumed it came easily. At least, that's how it appeared as an outsider looking in. She always has her shit together–not one hair out of place.

Now, I'm seeing her in a new light. Her shoulders sit further down from her ears as if a weight has been physically lifted off of them. Her eyes are glowing brighter. She's gliding down the sidewalk, her steps lighter.

When I take the time to think about it, I understand that feeling. Being in that room, contorting my body into positions that I didn't believe were physically possible for me, helped take my mind off of everything that I've been dealt lately—being unhappy at work, knowing deep down that my feelings for Parker are still there, stifling said feelings because I can't afford to have my heart broken again. I feel lighter than I have in weeks.

"I know what you mean," I reply.

She looks over at me and offers me an unadulterated, joyful smile. It's different from any other smiles I've seen from her in the past, and my chest grows heavy at the idea that I've never noticed the front she puts on for everyone. "I know that I'm good at my job. I've worked hard to get to this point. But sometimes it feels like I'm suffocating."

"Really? You've made it look easy from the moment I met you."

She playfully rams her shoulder into mine as we walk in step with one another. "Well, maybe I should change career paths then. Because I spend more time at work than I do with friends, I haven't gone on a date in over eight months, and I couldn't tell you the last time I took a vacation."

"For what it's worth, I wasn't kidding when I said I want to be you when I grow up. You're a badass, and I aspire to be that dedicated. Just don't forget to take care of yourself, though."

"Don't worry about me. I'll be okay. That's why I work out five days a week. I may be working around the clock, but that isn't going to stop me from getting a banging body. The feeling less insane thing is an added bonus, too." Her tone is casual, but I can tell deep down that she's being serious. I make a mental note to spend more time together outside of work, even if I have to force her.

"Trust me when I say you've succeeded there, too."

She peeks down at her figure, and her mouth crooks up with a sense of achievement. "Thank you for listening to my sob story. I didn't mean to bring the mood down. I'm sorry. I promise I won't do that again."

I step in front of her, grabbing hold of her shoulders to stop us in front of the juice shop. "Don't ever apologize for that. I appreciate you telling me. If you ever need someone to talk to, you know I'm here for you."

She leans in to hug me but stops herself right before she makes contact. Her nose wrinkles, visibly repulsed by the noticeable sweat marks on her clothes. "I know you are. Thank you. I'd hug you, but I am soaked in sweat and probably smell terrible."

I grab her anyway and pull her into a tight embrace. "Don't worry, me too. We can reek together."

She's barely able to keep the laughter out of her voice as she squeezes me back and says, "Let's just hope we don't run into any deliciously hot single men while we're here. We stand no chance."

I open the door of Joe & the Juice and let her in before me. I amble over to the fridge full of vibrant juices and study each and every single one individually. As much as I need to eat more fruits and vegetables, there's something about drinking a juice made of cucumber, celery, kale, and olive oil that sounds less than appealing.

"You know, for someone on a strike against men, you sure talk about dating and finding a hot guy a lot," I jest.

"Am I not at least allowed to look?"

I giggle, grab an appetizing-looking juice that I'm ninety percent sure at least has strawberries in it, take Scarlett's juice out of her hands, and head up to the register to pay. After handing the cashier my card, I give Scarlett her juice back and grab a seat by the large window facing the bustling city.

"Of course, you can look all you want. But I think deep down there's a part of you that wants to do more than just that."

"Like sleep with them, no strings attached? That's a given. I'm a woman with needs. I'd be doing myself a disservice if I didn't try to find a man to keep me occupied every now and then," she agrees.

Scarlett pulls out her phone again, stopping my chance for a response dead in its tracks. This is the second time today. It's as if whoever is on the other side of these texts has her in a trance. Either she's already hooking up with someone or hiding something much bigger from me. Unease coils in my belly as the last sip of juice I took grows tart in my mouth.

"You tried to play it off earlier, but I'd argue that you've already found someone to fulfill those needs of yours." I motion my head towards her phone, and her eyes lift to meet mine.

If I didn't know any better, I'd say there's a flash of shame in her expression, but I don't want to press the issue. If she is interested in someone, she'll tell me when the time is right. That doesn't explain the complaining about the lack of dates, though. I screw the lid on my juice and push it away from me, no longer interested in it.

She slides her phone back into her crossbody bag and adamantly shakes her head, grabbing my hands. "If I were seeing someone, I would tell you. I promise. I'm like the Sahara down there, and I don't anticipate that changing in the near future."

"If you say so. But if you do catch feelings for someone, just know I'm here to talk about it. I want to see you happy."

"I know you do. And I appreciate it. You're the first person that's come into my life in years that I know I can trust. If I finally break my dry spell, you'll be the first to know."

While the smile that has grown on my face is authentic, I can't help the sinking feeling that there's something she's not telling me.

14

DYLAN

I peer down at my watch, which reads eleven forty-five. I have fifteen minutes to make it across the city for Evelyn's photoshoot. Although this isn't typically expected from someone in my position, Evelyn specifically requested that I come to help her pick out outfits. She emailed me her phone number, and we've been texting ever since.

I know she's *technically* a client, but it feels like there's a fast friendship forming. How's a girl supposed to say no when someone compliments your outfit and asks you to be there to help them with photos that are going to be used all over her social media accounts? Could this be considered a conflict of interest? Maybe. But becoming Evelyn's friend has felt natural.

No matter how close we get, I still want to impress her. It's my name that's going to be the talk of the town when everyone sees all of my hard work pay off, and this release becomes one of the biggest debut releases anyone has ever seen–which it will be because I'm manifesting it. Okay, so obviously, I didn't write the book. But, with the social media strategy that I put together, Evelyn has gained another 10,000 followers in the past week, and that number is only going up. That has to count for something.

I fling myself into the subway before the doors shut and nearly crush me. I'm already running so behind; the last thing I need to do is get severely injured on my way to the shoot. I snort as I sit, thinking about what Katherine would do if I ended up in the hospital–probably tell me to rub some dirt in it and come to the office. The laugh I chuckle to myself turns into a small shudder.

She's lightened up a little since the presentation, but I've let myself become the office punching bag, and any reminder of it strikes a nerve. I've always prided myself on being ambitious.

Out of my high school graduating class of a little over one hundred, only a handful have left Woodland Heights. Most stayed home, got married, and had babies. I never envisioned that for myself. The fact that I left town is a miracle in itself. There was a point in time when I wasn't sure if it was possible. Mom spent all her days buried in bed, a bottle of whatever she could get her hands on placed on the nightstand next to her.

The day she agreed to go to rehab, the pressure on my chest eased immensely, and I no longer felt like the room was closing in on me. There were no guarantees that it was going to stick–that she was going to stay sober–but it was a step in the right direction after a year of constant panic, unsure of whether or not she was going to live to see another day.

With each passing day, the idea of leaving town felt more like a possibility. She kept getting stronger, relying less on outside substances to find joy. Eventually, she was approved to move back home. While she still attends AA meetings at least once a week, she refused to let me stay home to take care of her. She told me that she wanted me to be selfish for once and chase my dreams. So, I applied to some jobs here in New York, never expecting to hear back.

Now, it's been a couple of months, and I can't see myself living anywhere else. Something inside of me clicked the minute I stepped off that plane. I feel more at home with millions of strangers than I did in the small town I grew up in.

A pang of guilt runs through me at the thought of my mom at home by herself. She's since gotten into Pilates, joined a local book club, and started casually dating (which I haven't entirely accepted yet), but I can't help but envision her sitting alone day in and day out. I pull out my phone and shoot her a quick text, letting her know I love her and will be calling her after the photo shoot right as the overheard speaker calls out my stop.

12:02.

I push my tote bag higher onto my shoulder and break out into a full sprint towards the photoshoot. By the time I arrive, my lungs are on fire, and I'm choking down as much air as possible, but it's only 12:10, which means I'm only ten minutes late. It's far better than the twenty minutes I was expecting. Despite despising being late (yes, I am the stereotypical Virgo in many ways–that being one of them), I give myself a small pat on the back. Sometimes, you have to celebrate all the small wins you can get.

I rush over to the water station and pour myself a cup, chugging it to help ease the burn. After two refills and a quick fan with a flier I find lying around, I feel more level-headed and ready to support Evelyn. It doesn't take long to find her near a rack of clothes, throwing pieces onto the ground in a frenzied tornado as she paces.

"Everything okay over here?" I ask tenderly, trying not to set her off the deep end even further. She spins on her heel to face me, placing a hand on her chest.

"Oh, thank god, you're here. I'm on the verge of losing it."

"I can see that. Take a breath."

Evelyn sits on a nearby flimsy cardboard box, which slowly

crumbles under her weight until she's resting on the floor. She lets out a sigh and runs a hand down her face. I place a hand on her shoulder, getting down to her level. It's bizarre seeing someone who's usually so put together look like they're moments away from an absolute meltdown, especially over something so trivial.

I think back to my hot yoga date with Scarlett, where I had the same realization about her. Knowing that everyone in my life is putting on a polished facade soothes a restlessness I didn't realize was weighing on me up until this moment.

"Hey, what's going on? It's just a photoshoot. You've already written the book. That's the hardest part. Now's the fun stuff."

She puffs out a breath and looks up at me, tears welling up in her eyes. "I know, I know. I think it's all just hitting me now. Everything I've worked so hard for these past couple of years is about to be in front of everyone. What if they hate it? What if I fail?"

I slide closer to her and grab her hand, giving it a light squeeze of encouragement. One singular tear falls, and she lifts her shoulder to wipe it off her cheek before any more can spill.

"Hey, don't cry. Your makeup looks too good to cry. Look, I've read the book. It's one of the most magical stories I've read in a long time. And that's saying something because I've built quite an extensive library, " I joke. "I laughed, I cried. It had everything I could ask for in a book. And if someone can't see that, they aren't worth your time anyway. You can't please everyone. There are going to be some people who probably don't like it. But I promise you won't fail. Besides, who did you write this story for? Them or yourself?"

She swallows the lump in her throat and wipes one last stray tear. "I've wanted to be a writer since I was a little girl. I've dreamed of being someone's favorite author for as long as I can remember. When I was younger, I would spend hours daydreaming, writing short stories about everything I could think of. My poor parents. I made them read everything I wrote, but they would tell me how talented I was every single time, without fail. They acted as if everything I wrote was the best thing they'd ever read in their entire lives.

"But even with parents who supported every one of my dreams, I never thought the time would come to publish my life's work. To put my heart and soul out there for the world to read it. I just wanted to prove to myself that I could do it. That my dreams weren't silly," she sniffs.

"Your dreams are never silly. I think what you're doing is incredibly brave. Putting yourself out there is extremely vulnerable. I see your passion and how much you love the story you've crafted. It was clear from the moment I picked it up. Because *you* love it so much, others will love it, too. There's no doubt in my mind," I console.

She pulls me into a tight hug, making my wobbly on my feet. I rest my hand on the ground, trying to stay upright as I return her embrace.

"Thank you, Dylan. You're right. I can do this. No matter how scary it is."

"You absolutely can. Now, let's get you an outfit picked out and photo-ready."

I look down at my watch again– we're now almost thirty minutes behind schedule. My eyes travel over to the photographer, who's doing his best to look busy, not wanting to interrupt us during this emotional moment. Standing up, I brush off my pants and lend Evelyn a hand to stand.

"Here, try this out." I grab a simple yet sophisticated high-collared black dress that beautifully contrasts with her marble skin and russet waves. She's naturally beautiful, and I don't want to take away from that for even a second. Without a word, I usher her into the nearby bathroom and lean against the wall, waiting for her to finish up.

"Looks like your ability to give one of your world-famous

pep talks hasn't gone anywhere." A booming voice calls from behind me, sending all my thoughts scattering like leaves in the wind.

What's he doing here?

15

PARKER

Dylan pushes herself off the wall, forgetting about Evelyn in the bathroom entirely. It wasn't my intention to eavesdrop on their conversation. I figured the photoshoot would be fully underway when I got there, seeing as I was almost twenty minutes late. When I arrived, I noticed Evelyn and Dylan on the ground, and it didn't feel right to interrupt.

When I was going through college, Dylan always went out of her way to make me feel better, even when she was going through some of the lowest moments of her life with her parents. I can still remember the feeling of laying in bed together, my head on her stomach, the light rise and fall of her chest, as she talked me off of a ledge.

Growing up, I never had anyone to turn to. My parents were constantly at each other's throats, the sounds of yells filling our halls more often than laughter. Their arguments occupied most of their time, and it never felt like they had enough for me. By the time they got a divorce when I was fourteen, I had all but emotionally shut down. I rarely let anyone in, and I never wanted anyone in my life to see me struggling. It was easier to internalize all of my emotions than to let anyone see that I was anything but happy.

Dylan changed that, though. After months of patience, I finally felt safe enough to open up. In the blink of an eye, she was home personified. Even when the world felt like it was crumbling all around me, she stood there steadfast, the foundation stronger than the storm.

Whether I was overwhelmed, sad, or frustrated, she was my anchor when I felt myself drifting into the darkness. I know I never made it easy on her, but she never failed to make me feel invincible.

I never thought that I would experience that kind of love in my life. The kind that I had only seen in the movies my mom would force me to watch when I was a kid. Though it didn't take much–I cherished any time I got with her when she was in the mood to be a parent.

With Dylan around, I felt like I could do anything. Five years later, she's still making others feel the same way.

"What are you doing here? Stalking me now?" she asks, her eyes narrowed. I didn't want to surprise her, but emailing her to let her know that Blake requested I be here didn't feel like the smartest idea either. I know there's no reason for me to oversee this shoot, but Blake is still technically my boss, and with his head still very much on the Operation Get-Dylan-Back mission, I don't have much of a choice.

I fold my arms and ankles, leaning against the wall inches away from her, my lips twitching up at the corners. "If I were, you'd never know. I'm stealthier than that." I pause for dramatic effect, and this gets a smile from her. "Blake suggested I come by to see how everything is going." I glance around the room at the lack of work being done. "Seems like that was the right call, seeing as I'm running late, and the photoshoot hasn't even begun."

She casts an exasperated look up at the ceiling and grips my wrist, yanking me away from the bathroom door where Evelyn is still getting changed. "Don't let her hear you. We got off to a rough start, but we're making progress."

"I know. I saw what you did out there. Thank god you were here. I'm not sure I would have made it through college if I didn't have those motivational speeches of yours." I lift my chin towards the direction they were sitting in.

I catch the small grin that she's trying her hardest to hide from me. "Hard to believe coming from someone who graduated summa cum laude." My eyes trace the outline of her plump lips as she says, "cum." The meaning behind it is entirely innocent, but my mind and cock, which twitches beneath my zipper, betray me at the double entendre.

"Ah, yes, but if it weren't for all of those all-nighters with you, who knows where I might've ended up."

"Right. Now you're just a hot shot with what I'm guessing is a strong caffeine addiction, the typical Manhattan bachelor pad that most people only dream of affording, and the inability to take a day off. I really should give myself a pat on the back," she counters.

I try my hardest to keep my features neutral. I don't need her to know that she has me read like a book–and that when she puts it that way, my life sounds, well, kind of miserable. "I think you'd be surprised by my so-called bachelor pad. I have a couple of plants, you know," I say defensively.

"Fake, plastic ones don't count."

"If you don't believe me, then why don't you come over and see for yourself?" My voice is full of challenge, and the fire in her eyes tells me she's not opposed to the idea.

Before she can respond, Evelyn comes barging out of the bathroom, dressed to the nines, beaming. If I hadn't gotten here in the midst of her breakdown, I'd have no idea that it ever happened in the first place. I wasn't lying when I said Dylan was a pro at soothing you when you need it most.

Dylan rushes over to her, clapping her hands together. "You look incredible! You ready?"

"Very," she replies.

Evelyn follows Dylan out onto set, where Dylan gives her hair one last fix before coming back to stand next to me. Despite not having a choice about working with Dylan on this project, there's no one else I'd rather partner up with. I know that this will be successful because of her and her alone. Between Evelyn's talent and Dylan's hard work and dedication, the two don't need me. I'm just here to get the book into the world's hands.

I slide my hands into my pockets to prevent myself from getting closer to her. My skin itches with the innate desire to close the distance between us.

"I know I've said it before, but thank you for your help on this. Evelyn is lucky to have you. Thrive is, too. We all are."

"You have to say that. Your team is the one that hired me," she mumbles.

"I don't. Technically, we hired Thrive. Before that first meeting, I had no idea that you would be a part of that decision. That just happened to be a very fortunate added bonus." I shift to face her, blatantly ignoring the photos being taken in front of me. I twiddle the ring on my thumb that's currently shoved deep into my pants to help subdue some of the nerves suddenly overtaking me.

"You have a way with people that I'm not sure you'll ever understand unless you see it from my point of view. If it were anyone else, I'm not sure Evelyn would've ever come out of that bathroom. Just trust me on this for once, alright? I know that I hurt you, which is something that I will forever regret. But I would never lie to you. Especially about your talent."

"Well, thank you. I really appreciate that." Her voice trembles. Her cheeks are now flushed a deep shade of pink, yet when I try to look into her eyes to gauge how she's feeling, I notice her eyes are misty with tears threatening to pour over.

"Dyl, I didn't mean to upset you." I reach out for her wrist, bracing for the moment she shakes me off. But it never comes. She lets me lightly hold onto her arm, and I take advantage of the moment, bringing her closer so we're only inches away from one another.

My fingertips tingle as I envision holding her in my arms in a way that was once so familiar. I know that if I try, it will scare her off, and I'm trying to take things slow, no matter how hard I try. She still hasn't even given me the opportunity to tell her about Olivia. I'd never want to make her uneasy because she thinks I'm crossing a line that only I know doesn't exist.

She takes a deep inhale through her nose and lets it out through pursed lips. "I'm alright."

"Are you sure?" I ask.

She nods, and I test the boundaries further by pulling her closer so our bodies are pressed against one another. Her hands loosely snake around my waist, and my breathing hitches. My heart is racing a mile a minute, and I know if she gets too close, she will hear it pounding. I never thought I'd be the kind of guy who gets worked up over a hug, yet now that I'm here, I never want to let go.

I run a hand down her hair, smoothing it down, and I feel her grip tighten around me. A feeling of déjà vu sweeps through me like a hurricane. The last time I held her like this was one of the worst moments of my life. She was gripping my shirt, knuckles white as she refused to let go, cheeks stained with a combination of mascara and tears. I've never felt pain like that before, and it's a feeling I've relived many times on sleepless nights. You hear of people dying from broken hearts, but I always believed that to be a myth. It wasn't until that day that I understood just how possible it is.

She lets out a low hum and pulls away from me, jerking me out of my melancholic stupor. My hands fall to my side, and I curl my fingers into a tight ball. I push down the urge to word vomit just how much I need her back in my life–how much I've fucked up.

I know deep down that it's not the right time. I've seen enough rom-coms to know that the grand gesture has to be timed perfectly. Until she trusts me again, I need to pace myself. That doesn't stop me from feeling a seed of gratitude for getting one step closer to that moment.

"I'm sorry. Got a little carried away there." I chuckle softly, trying to make light of the situation.

She lets out a little sniffle and flashes a smile in my direction. It feels like a knife to the heart. The things I would do to see that smile every day for the rest of my life.

"It's okay. I needed that. I feel like I've been running a mile a minute lately."

She turns back to look at Evelyn, who's now staring at us with a knowing smirk on her face. The photographer is snapping away, oblivious to the fact that Evelyn caught that entirely too personal interaction.

Dylan must also be unaware that we were caught because she strides over to the computer to look at the photos taken while we were in our bubble. I curse under my breath.

So much for keeping it professional.

16

DYLAN

"Dylan, can you come into my office?" I hear Katherine's voice call from her office, which is tragically closer to my desk than I'd prefer. Ever since the presentation, she's been surprisingly...nice. Okay, that might be the wrong word for it. But at least she hasn't been down my throat. It's almost like she's starting to realize that I am a perfectly capable human being who isn't half bad at her job. *Almost.*

I close my laptop and rise from my desk, throwing Scarlett a pleading look to save me before entering her office.

"Please, take a seat." She signals to the seat sitting in front of her desk. As much as I hate her, there's no denying that her office is beautiful.

It's the definition of feminine. There's a modern white desk fitted in the center of the room, with two baby pink velvet chairs sitting across from it, finished with white feathered pillows. Instead of floor-to-ceiling windows, there's a built-in bookshelf behind the desk filled to the brim with brightly colored books, plants, and knick-knacks. It's far superior to the lackluster cubicles that fill the rest of the office.

Of course, Katherine spent most of the decorating budget on her office. While she works on her throne, the rest of us peasants are typing away in small boxes that, at moments, can feel unfathomably claustrophobic.

I sit down in one of the velvet chairs, the fuzzy pillow tickling me through my black silk blouse. Now that spring has fully arrived, I'm no longer bogged down by layers. I've been counting down the days until the beginning of summer when I can freely wear cooler clothes without freezing my butt off.

As much as I love the winter, growing up on the lake in the summer made me a lover of the sunshine. I dream of the days on the boat, catching fireflies in the backyard, and stargazing under the summer stars.

I know that New York is different than Woodland Heights in almost every sense of the word, but I still find myself wishing for the warmer months.

"Yes?" I anxiously smooth down my wide-length trousers, knowing damn well that they're completely wrinkle-free. I spent twenty minutes ironing them this morning to be sure of it, but there's something about Katherine's presence that makes me jittery.

"I got a call from Evelyn this morning," she starts, and my throat constricts. If she has any issues with me, it could be the end of my career as I know it. "She spoke very highly of you and how you helped manage the photoshoot."

I gingerly rub the knot in my chest and relax in my seat, my posture becoming lax as I sink into the relief. That is good news, but something tells me there's more to it.

"I should congratulate you, I suppose. It appears that Ms. Bennett is quite appreciative of the work that you've done for her so far."

I sit in silence, waiting for the moment when Katherine finally praises me for my hard work, but it doesn't come.

"Because of this, I talked to the PR team who's been

working hard on putting together a short, two-week book tour for Evelyn. I'd like you to join her. It's primarily the East Coast."

"Um, thank you," I reply, unsure how to feel about the opportunity. On one hand, I should feel thankful that she's giving me yet another chance to prove that I know what I'm doing. On the other hand, she's sending me away from other clients I could take on if I were still in the city. This feels like a trap.

"Parker will also be joining you to ensure it all goes off without a hitch."

"Excuse me?" I leap forward to the edge of my seat, positive that I misheard her.

"You'll be leaving in exactly," she looks at her computer and then back up to me, "one month to assist Evelyn on her book tour. It's clear she trusts the two of you, and I'm putting a lot of faith in you. A lot is riding on this release, and if it's not a bestseller, then we're all fucked. So, I need you to do everything in your power to make sure this goes well. Blue Bird has invested a lot of money into this tour, and if it's unsuccessful, it reflects poorly on us."

"Then why are you asking me to go and not someone like Scarlett?"

"If it were up to me, I would be asking Scarlett. Unfortunately, Evelyn sees this as the best option, and I'm not going to argue with her when she's one of our biggest clients right now."

I dig my nails into my palms, trying to bite back the feeling of hurt. I knew that Katherine didn't think highly of me, but to outright tell me that this isn't her choice brings a swell of pain that I wasn't expecting to feel.

"That's all. You can go now." Katherine ushers me out with a flick of her hand, closing the window for a retort.

I stand up and rush out of the office, fighting the prickle behind my eyes. My vision blurs, making the short journey back to my desk difficult.

Don't cry. It's not worth it, I lecture myself. I tumble into my chair, hands covering my face.

"Hey, hey, what's wrong?" Scarlett's voice, although soft, startles me.

I bite the inside of my cheek, willing the tears threatening to overflow to stay put, and pull my hands away from my face to look up at her. She bends down closer to my level once she notices my mental state.

"After working my ass off, Katherine still doesn't think I'm good enough for this job."

"I'm sure that's not true." She tries to comfort me by placing her hands on my shoulders, but I'm numb to the consolation.

"She actually just told me. Straight to my face." I throw my hands toward Katherine's door, unwilling to look in that direction, knowing that if I do, the tears will finally fall. Until I moved to New York, it took a lot to ruffle my feathers. These days it feels like I spend more time crying than I do enjoying myself.

I refuse to run away from the city just because I loathe my boss and I'm forced to see Parker 24/7, but I've never been more excited for a project to end. Maintaining a low profile has proven to be impossible.

Scarlett's eyes blaze with anger as her soothing hold becomes a tight grip on my shoulder. "Do you need me to go in there and kick her ass?"

I let out a halfhearted, watery laugh. "No. Just because she hates me doesn't mean you need to lose your job."

"I've been going to Jiu-Jitsu classes on the weekends. It'd be nice to have some real-life experience," she responds nonchalantly.

"I know you're just saying that to make me feel better."

"No, I'm not. It's been a great stress reliever." She shrugs, and my eyes widen. Scarlett is one of the most unpredictable people I've ever met, and the idea of her taking down Katherine–although I'd never condone violence–sends me into a fit of giggles. I don't stop until there's a stitch in my side, and I'm gasping for air. As I wipe away tears of laughter, I look up at her to see a giant grin on her face.

"Feel better?" She reaches down and squeezes my hand.

"Yes, thank you. But please, don't beat anyone up. The last thing we need in the mix of this shit show is a lawsuit."

She throws her hands up. "You just say the word, and I'll be there. I think I speak for the entirety of the office when I say that Katherine needs to be put in her place."

"I love you."

"I know," Scarlett sneers.

I lean back in my chair and take a sip of the watered-down latte I got first thing this morning, wrinkling my nose at the bland flavor. The clock on my desk reads 4:50 p.m.–thank god the day is almost over. I grab my closed laptop and put it into my bag, gearing up to leave for the night.

"I have to go on the book tour with Parker," I confess.

"Excuse me? Why didn't you lead with that?" Her head whips back with surprise, and she plants herself on the floor of my cubicle. It looks like, despite the workday being done in ten minutes, she's making herself comfortable. I sigh and plop my bag back on my desk.

"Oh, I don't know. I thought Katherine telling me I suck at my job was a little more important at the moment," I huff.

Scarlett shakes her head disapprovingly and tucks a loose strand of hair behind her ears, scooting closer to me in the process. "Well, you and I both know that's just not true. She sees your potential and isn't willing to admit that because she has an ego the size of Texas and a heavy dose of control problems. But I am sorry that she made you feel that way. You don't deserve that."

"Deep down, I know you're right. It's just hard not to take it personally sometimes."

"Trust me, I understand. That's why I'll be here every step of the way to tell you to ignore it. If you keep up the work you've been doing, you'll be coming for my job sooner rather than later."

"I love you, but I think I need to hold your hand when I tell you that you're delusional."

"Not delusional. Just someone who sees that you're great at your job. You being one of my best friends is just an added benefit for me." She winks. Hearing Scarlett unexpectedly refer to me as one of her best friends brings a bubble of joy to my heart. "Now, why don't you tell me about this book tour over a martini? There's a new spot right around the corner with a killer happy hour that I've been dying to try."

I leap out of my chair at the mention of leaving and grabbing a drink. If I'm going to survive this next month, I'm going to need a hell of a lot of girl time and a martini or two.

"You're speaking my language." I grab my oversized bag that, quite frankly, weighs too much for everyday use, extend a hand to Scarlett, pull her off the ground, and link arms with her as we head out of the office.

17

DYLAN

When we walk into the swanky bar, I'm immediately drawn to the sexiness that it exudes. The dimly lit room is decorated with black and white marble-like tiled floors, inviting rust orange velvet chairs and half moon couches, and low gold tables, each topped with a tealight candle. The arched walls are lined with tall palms and birds of paradise, giving the ambiance a tropical feel. The bar, situated on the right-hand side of the room, has countless bottles of liquor displayed, with even more plants draped across the top.

As we're led to our booth, I feel like I've been transported halfway across the world. I can't keep my eyes from wandering as we take a seat.

"Why didn't you tell me it would be this gorgeous?"

"It's beautiful, right? I learned about it a couple of weeks ago, but my schedule has been too crazy to stop by."

Being friends with Scarlett has its many perks. Aside from her being the ultimate ride-or-die friend, she's also the queen of finding the hottest restaurants and bars in the city, so it comes as no surprise that this is another one of her recommendations.

I grab the menu and begin scanning my eyes down, immediately stopping when I spot the martini made with olive oil-infused vodka. That's all I need to see to know that this is going to become a new after-work staple.

I hand the menu to Scarlett, who only takes seconds to look before closing it, having settled on the same cocktail. Shortly after the waiter comes by, and we order our drinks, she leans forward, resting her entire upper torso on the table.

"Okay, tell me more about this tour. Why is she having you go on the tour when Evelyn is perfectly capable of handling it herself? Especially if Parker is already going to be there?" she wonders.

"Your guess is as good as mine. She said that she spoke with Evelyn, and she seems to think it's best that I be there to oversee. If it were up to Katherine, you'd be on the job."

"I doubt that."

"Oh no, those were her words exactly."

At that moment, the waiter drops off our drinks and I swiftly pick it up, careful not to spill a drop, as I take a big gulp. The vodka warms my throat, immediately making me feel airy–like I'm floating on a cloud. Fuck, that's delicious.

"God, that's good," Scarlett vocalizes my same thoughts as she places her drink back down on the table and picks up her phone, tapping around on the screen before setting it back down face down. "Is this the worst thing that can happen? It seems like you guys have been getting along pretty well lately. One could argue you two might have even started a new friendship?"

At that, I take another large swing of my martini, letting the burn settle my mind. And my tongue. "Ahh yes, more Team Parker talk."

"Babe, I love you. You know that I've got your back one

hundred percent, no questions asked. But I feel like you're letting him dictate your life. I understand it was shocking initially to learn that you two had to work together, but it's been over a month now. I feel like your life would be so much easier if you'd stop being so stubborn about working together." She raises her pointer finger to hold that thought while she swallows another sip of her drink.

"From what I've seen, you've both been on your best behavior, and I know that your job is important to you. You wouldn't do anything to jeopardize it. So why not just lighten up a little? Sure, you'll be on tour, but it's not like you guys have to share a hotel room or anything. This isn't some romance novel of yours. You two can work together in a very professional manner and make Katherine eat her words."

As her words settle in, I find myself chewing loose skin on the side of my nail. A habit that I've had since I was a little girl. When I take a step back and think objectively, Parker and I have formed somewhat of a friendship–even if it is somewhat surface-level. We know we work well together, and ever since I put my foot down after lunch, he has been very well-mannered.

The real question is whether or not I can stomach being friends. We're already halfway there without realizing it, so there's no reason not to. He's in a relationship and seems to be doing well in life, and I'm working on getting to that same point in my own.

Work gives me the migraine of a lifetime, but I have loved every second of the city so far, and I'm willing to make those sacrifices, knowing that one day, I'll no longer have to deal with Katherine and will meet the love of my life.

I huff out a breath and take the last dreg of my martini, feeling infinitely lighter than I did when I sat down. As I'm about to ask Scarlett, who has also just finished her drink, if it's a more-than-one-drink kind of night, I hear a familiar voice from behind me. Before I glance over my shoulder to see the owner, I catch the look on Scarlett's face. She's absolutely incandescent, hearts in her eyes.

I twist my body, gripping the back of my seat to see Blake strolling in, looking as good as always. His white cable knit polo is tucked into a pair of navy chinos. The ensemble is finished off with a pair of chocolate brown oxfords. If I didn't know any better, I'd think he was a model that just got done with a shoot for J. Crew.

Where Parker is a little rough around the edges, Blake is a pretty boy. It makes me question–in what world are two best friends *that* good-looking? I don't know what the world had planned when it brought them together, but it gave them far too much power. If Parker were single, I'd be half tempted to buy a billboard in Times Square warning the women of Manhattan about the two of them, especially when they're in the same room.

I turn back to Scarlett, who's discreetly touching up her lipstick in a small compact that she carries with her everywhere she goes. I clear my throat quietly to catch her attention, and she immediately puts the mirror back in her purse and tries to look uninterested in Blake, who's now walking over to our table. I give her a gentle kick under the table, lips pursed.

"Did you know that he was going to be here?" I hiss.

"Of course not. Now, be nice." She fluffs her hair and throws a dazzling smile in Blake's direction.

"Well, look at what the cat dragged in." Scarlett leans forward, making a point to push her cleavage together in her low-cut, vintage designer dress.

"The cat has great taste. Can't blame it for trying to show off." He slides into the booth beside Scarlett, forcing her closer to the table next to us. She lets out a giggle you'd expect to hear from a schoolgirl, and I can't help but stare, stupefied, as heat rises to the apples of her cheeks. It's official. I'm in the twilight zone. Scarlett and Blake are visibly flirting in front of me as if I don't exist.

"What are you doing here?" I ask, striving to keep my voice as calm and collected as possible but failing miserably. I've kept it together around him in every other setting, so I excuse this one slip-up.

"I was told they have great martinis. I had to check it out myself." He offers me a genuine grin before throwing an arm on the back of the booth behind Scarlett. My eyes flash to his hand, which has begun rubbing small circles on her bare shoulder.

Our waiter returns to the table, and I immediately order another drink. If I have to sit here and witness Scarlett and Blake eye-fucking one another, I need a little more in my system. When it's Scarlett's turn, she orders herself a second.

"I'll have two of whatever they're drinking," Blake courteously says to the server as he points toward our empty glasses.

My blood runs cold, but I try not to panic. Why would he be ordering two when Scarlett clearly just ordered a second right in front of him? I bounce my leg, hopeful that the movement will help ease some of my anxiety (it doesn't). It wouldn't be the end of the world if Parker showed up–especially now that I've decided to give us a true shot at friendship. Though, I say that in the *loosest* way possible.

"Do I have to spend the evening watching you two eye fuck one another the entire time? That's not what I agreed to when I said I'd go out for a drink after work," Parker's voice calls from behind me.

Well, I guess that answers my question. I let out a titter under my breath despite myself, happy to know that someone else feels the same way I do about how this happy hour is shaping up.

"Guilty as charged. I was just admiring the view. Can you blame me?" Blake croons, his eyes not leaving Scarlett's once.

She turns to me, eyes wide, face flushed, lips pressed together tightly to hold back a smile I know she's dying to show. I've never seen someone this anti-men completely fold under the attention of one of the most promiscuous men to walk this planet.

Parker rolls his eyes and grabs a chair from the empty table next to us. Before bringing it over to our table, he bends closer to me and nods to the vacant space beside me. "Hi. Is it alright if I sit next to you?"

Curse him for being polite. I'd expect nothing less.

When we were together, he was always the one opening my doors, paying for dinner, and surprising me with flowers when I least expected it. Growing up in a small town, you quickly learn that men are raised to treat women with respect. I've been avoiding the dating scene like a plague, but I can confidently say that the men here in New York do not share that same sentiment.

"Of course." I shift my chair to the left, making room for him. He pulls up next to me and sits down before glancing back in my direction, holding eye contact with me for a second too long, yet I can't look away.

"Hi," he whispers again. The intensity of his gaze has me in a chokehold that leaves me tongue-tied. His eyes fall down to my lips, and I slowly lick my lips under the pressure of his unwavering stare. The movement is small, but I notice how his chest expands with an inaudible gasp.

"Hi," I whisper back. Any logical person would say something else–keep the conversation going. But it feels like my brain has turned into mush, and any thought I've ever had has been erased from my mind.

"You're going to give us shit when you two won't stop drooling over one another? Should I ask them if they have bibs?" Blake's voice snaps me out of my trance. He's wearing a sneer, and I suppress the urge to roll my eyes. The worst part is that he's not wrong, and I hate him for that. I sneak a look at Scarlett, and she's wearing the same look on her face.

"Shut up, man." Parker laughs, shaking his head. Our waiter returns and drops off our four martinis, and I quickly but carefully reach for another sip. Now that Parker's here, I have to walk a very fine line between easing my apprehension and getting too tipsy and making a fool of myself.

"Did you hear the news?" I spin back to Parker, who's now leaning back in his chair, one leg crossed over the other. He looks completely at ease with how close we are to one another. Meanwhile, I'm trying to get my resting heart rate back to normal, or else I'm going to end up in the hospital.

"What news?"

"I'm going on the book tour with you," I blurt out. There's no use in sugar-coating it. Besides, there's a good chance he already knows about it.

Unfortunately, I chose an extremely inopportune time to tell him this, and judging by his reaction, he had no clue. As soon as the words are out of my mouth, he's choking on the martini he just took his first sip of. I pat him on the back, doing little to ease his sputtering coughs.

I know I didn't take the news well either, but I at least didn't have a visceral reaction in front of the other person involved.

He hits his chest and sets down his drink as his breathing slowly steadies. I shift to the side of my chair, trying to put as much space between us as possible. His eyes flicker with regret as they meet mine, and I internalize my own.

"I'm sorry. That was an overreaction. I just wasn't expecting that."

Scarlett chortles. "You could say that again."

I glower, but she doesn't look in my direction to catch the venom I'm directing at her. I need a breather.

"If you'll excuse me. I need to use the restroom." I push out of my chair and beeline it to the bathroom.

That went very differently in my head.

18

PARKER

"I don't think that could've gone any worse, dude." Blake is shaking his head, laughing loudly at my misfortune. Scarlett covers her mouth, trying to stifle her own laughter. I groan and flip him off.

"Yeah, no shit. Thanks for stating the obvious." I squeeze the bridge of my nose, trying hard to keep my annoyance at bay–annoyance with Blake and annoyance with myself for freezing up. "It's not like I planned on choking. I just had no idea that she was going to drop that bomb on me."

"If it makes you feel any better, she didn't either. Katherine pulled her into the office today and broke the news. She had a similar reaction." Scarlett says soothingly, placing a delicate hand on my arm.

"Oh yeah, that feels great to hear," I deadpan. "Wait a second. Is that why you said we were meeting them here for drinks?"

I scowl at Blake, who's back to wearing his boastful grin. One look at him, and I know this was a setup. I don't give him time to respond as I say, "You know what? Don't answer that.

How did you know? And more importantly, why didn't you tell me earlier? It would've been nice to get a heads-up."

"I may have told him." Scarlett raises her hand bashfully. My anger with Blake immediately disintegrates. "I texted him as soon Dylan told me."

I squint at them, shaking an accusatory pointer finger in between them. "How long has this texting been going on?"

Blake throws back the last of his martini. "That's none of your concern. Now, how are you actually feeling about Dylan joining the tour?" I spot it instantly, the way he brushes me off all too easily.

"Well, of course, I don't mind. I love any excuse to get closer to her, but I'm not sure she feels the same way. Especially after learning that she had a similar reaction."

"I think you just need to give her time. It's clear there's still something between you two. Blake told me all about Operation Get Dylan Back. This could be the perfect opportunity to get closer," Scarlett replies.

Great, now Scarlett is in on it.

"Did either of you have anything to do with this?" I inquire.

Scarlett's intentions are probably pure, but I have less faith in my best friend. He's not afraid to pull some strings to get what he wants.

Blake crosses his arms on the table, his pinky slowly stroking Scarlett's hand. The gesture is subtle and so unlike him that it catches me off guard. But I don't have time to address it as he says, "I swear, scout's honor, that I did not meddle for once. We both know that I asked you to go to make sure everything was running smoothly, but I had no idea that she was going to ask Dylan to join. This is all Katherine. I could kiss the woman for it." I catch the frown on Scarlett's face at this, and she pulls her hand away from his touch. I need to ask Blake what's going on between the two later.

"Katherine may love me, but I don't have that much pull. If I had to guess, Evelyn said something to her," Scarlett replies, not an ounce of defensiveness in her voice.

I can't help but feel a prick of sadness for the girl when I think about her with Blake. Despite not knowing the full extent of their relationship yet, I know that Blake chews and spits girls out as soon as he gets bored with them–which is typically after sleeping with them for the first time. Scarlett seems too genuine to be getting wrapped up in his shit.

Without turning around, I feel a pair of eyes bearing into my back. I can feel Dylan hesitating to return, but I don't move, waiting for her to come over to me in her own time.

It's a wild thing. To have been separated from someone for years, only to be aware of their presence whenever they're near. It's as if my body hasn't forgotten what it's like to be that physically close to someone I love, and it wants to remind me of all of the mistakes that I've made.

Without looking at me, she sits back down next to me, remaining on the edge of her seat so as not to sit too close to me. I wish I had a time machine to go back and redo that whole interaction. Within seconds, I watched her walls build right back up, but I'm intent on bringing them down and keeping them down once and for all.

"I'm sorry. I know I was a total dick back there. It wasn't my intention to make you feel like I didn't want you on the tour with me. I was just caught off guard," I murmur.

"I'd say. I thought I was going to have to give you the Heimlich there for a second." There's a trace of humor in her voice, and I feel my tense muscles loosen up.

Thank god.

"Are you CPR certified? I can force more martini down his throat if it means giving him some mouth-to-mouth action." Blake nods at me, flashing me a quick wink before Dylan can see. What a fucking idiot.

"Have I ever told you that you're a moron?" I quip back.

To my relief –and disbelief–Dylan breaks out into a large grin directed at Blake. I don't want to give the man credit, but he has a knack for making women feel better instantly. It's a secret talent that he uses to his advantage far more often than I care for. Unfortunately, I'm thrilled it worked this time around.

"Want to test it out yourself? See if I'm any good at saving lives?" There's a twinkle of mischief in her eyes, and I know where this is headed. Most men would take this as flirty banter, but I know Dylan is gearing up to hit him where it hurts.

"Is that your way of saying you'd rather kiss me? Because if so, at least wait until Parker's not around. The poor man is sensitive." His arrogant grin is almost enough to get me to break, but I know I have to keep my facade up if I want to watch her tear him down.

She leans closer to Blake from across the table, folding her arms in front of her. Blake's eyes fall to her chest for the second time, and I bite the inside of my cheek until it bleeds to keep myself from ruining the build-up. Dylan can handle this herself.

I still hate seeing him ogle her, though.

"You'd like that, wouldn't you?" She curls her finger in a "come hither" motion, and Blake does as he's told, just like a dog. How predictable. "I am CPR certified." She pauses a moment before the punchline. "Sadly, your case is beyond medical help."

There she is. My Dylan.

Blake lets out a raucous laugh and matches her posture, pointing a finger at her while looking at me. "Feisty. I like this one." A warm surge of pride fills my chest, and without thinking, I mutter under my breath, "I do too."

I must be louder than I thought because Dylan's eyes find mine, and I prep myself for an earful. Instead, her cheeks are dimpled, and her mouth is tilted up in a quiet smile so beautiful it deserves a spot in a museum. If it were ever on display at

The Met, I'd spend thousands to sit and stare at this piece of art.

"How about no one pours anything down anyone's throat, and we make it out of this bar alive?" I reply.

"Ugh, you're no fun. I'd kill to have my tongue down someone's throat right about now," Blake wails. Scarlett physically blanches beside him as she moves an inch away from him yet again. It's as if whatever spell he had her under has finally been broken, and she remembers exactly what kind of guy he is.

"That's disgusting," she vocalizes her distaste.

Blake has been known to turn these types of comments into an opportunity. Why go for a girl who's clearly expressing interest when you can focus all your attention on changing the minds of the ones who hate you?

"So you're saying you're not volunteering?"

"Absolutely not."

As the two of them go back and forth, I use the opportunity to lean toward Dylan and whisper in her ear, "I really am sorry, you know. There's no one else I'd rather be stuck with for two weeks than you." My eyes flicker down to her arms, now covered in goosebumps. I'm hit with a burst of satisfaction, knowing I still have this effect on her.

"There's no need to apologize. I'm sorry for my abrupt bathroom visit. I just needed to catch my breath for a second. It's been a whirlwind of a day."

"You don't need to be saying you're sorry. I'd imagine learning that would be quite a shock."

"It was. But from the looks of it, I'm not the only one who was just learning of it, too. I should've been more understanding of your reaction."

I pull away and stare at her, awestruck. Only this girl would hear that she has to go on tour with her ex and apologize to *me* for being the one to break the news. She feels the weight of my gaze and lifts her napkin over her face, hiding her nose and lips.

"What?" she whispers.

I may not be able to see her perfect mouth or her button nose, but the limited view makes her hazel eyes pop. At first glance, they look green, but this close, I'm mesmerized by the flecks of gold. They remind me of the sun setting over an open field in the spring—the time of day when the sun brushes its lips against your skin, and the butterflies flutter freely.

"You're beautif-" The words are out of my mouth before I can think about their weight, but I catch myself before finishing.

Surprisingly, she doesn't shy away from my bluntness. She lets out a nervous titter and brings the napkin back down to her lap. The apples of her round cheeks are painted pink, and I'm run over with the need to make her feel like this for the rest of my life.

"I can't seem to get it right around you today, can I?" I grasp the back of my neck, suddenly needing something to do with my hands.

"Don't worry about it." She leans her shoulder into mine, closing the gap between us. "And thank you."

The table has gone completely silent, and I tear my eyes away from Dylan's to see Scarlett and Blake staring at us, eyebrows raised in amusement. I feel a blow to my shin underneath the table, and I mask the groan of pain with a cough.

Blake begins miming a heavy make-out session with an invisible woman sitting in front of him, and I return the favor with a swift kick to the leg before Dylan can catch wind of his actions. Unsurprisingly, it just makes the asshole laugh.

I look back to Dylan and realize how close we've gravitated towards one another. Our chairs are touching, and she's got her elbows resting on the arm, centimeters away from my own. The sound of Blake's chuckle must startle her because she lurches her chair away from mine and looks over at him, dazed and confused.

"Sorry. Scarlett told me a funny joke. Didn't mean to scare you."

"I did no–" Scarlett tries to defend herself, but Blake hurriedly covers her mouth with his hand. "Why don't we track down the waiter and get this bill taken care of?"

She nods silently, and Blake pulls her to her feet and out of the booth.

"Oh, here. Take my card!" Dylan fumbles through her bag and pulls out her wallet to hand to the two. Blake waves her off without muttering a word and walks away.

"Just let him go. He's got a thing about always paying for a woman's meal or drinks. He won't let you, no matter how hard you try to argue."

"That's oddly... nice of him?" she puzzles.

"Shocking, I know. He's not as bad as he seems. You just have to get past the whole sleeping with anything with legs thing."

She leans back into the chair, placing her hands on her lap, and it feels like all of the air has been siphoned out of the room now that she's no longer close. "If I'm not the one sleeping with him, I don't care what he does in his free time. I think he could learn a thing or two from you, though."

"I'm working on it, trust me. Let's just say this: if you had met him in California, there's no way he would've walked out of here without a knee to the balls." I curl my lip up with distaste.

"And you call him your best friend because?" she taunts.

"The guy's been there with me through hell and back. He may rub a lot of people the wrong way, but he's also the kind of guy that'll be there the minute he gets that SOS text."

"Well, for what it's worth, if you're willing to call him your best friend, then he's got to be a half-decent guy. You've always been a good judge of character. Just don't expect me to spend my free time with him." Her eyes are wrinkled with a genuine smile, and with it, I feel us crossing a threshold. Not only can we coexist, but this feels like the start of a genuine friendship.

I'm not dumb enough to think that this means we'll fall in love again tomorrow, but it feels like it did all those years ago. It's something I wasn't aware that I was painfully searching for until I had it again.

"Don't worry. I won't subject you to that kind of misery." I joke.

And just like that, the musical tune of her laugh has me fighting off the urge to kiss her.

One step closer.

19

DYLAN

"Mia, help!" I rush into Amelia's room, doing my best not to have a complete meltdown about the lack of clothes in my closet. Growing up in a small town, you didn't have to worry about wearing the hottest designers or staying on top of the latest trends. I lived in jeans and a t-shirt or the occasional sundress. New York is a whole new ballgame, and I am grossly unprepared.

"Oh my god. What is it?" She jolts, looking up from her vanity, mascara now smeared across her eyelid.

"Shit, sorry. I didn't realize you were in the middle of doing your makeup."

She grabs a Q-tip, licks it, and begins scrubbing at the black smudge. "It's fine. But this better be worth it. I'm supposed to meet up with West soon, and I have to take the subway." Her face contorts in disgust.

For someone who loves the city, you would think that taking the subway would be a common occurrence, but Amelia despises it. She says it's "too dirty" and there are "too many people." Ironic, considering we're on a floating island with over one million other humans. This is just one of the many things she chooses to do that I've learned not to question.

Apparently, Amelia likes this West guy enough to take the subway. If only he knew how big of a sacrifice that was for her.

The girl walks more than anyone I know. There have been multiple instances where I've seen her tackle over twenty blocks for the sake of avoiding public transportation.

As much as I'd love to be like her, there's something about the subway that I find oddly comforting. I've seen some of the craziest stuff–like someone eating a full-blown seafood boil and far more feces than I care to admit–and yet I wouldn't change a thing. It makes me feel less alone. That's how I feel about the city altogether.

Even when I'm by myself, I'm not living in solitude. There are countless other lives out there happening simultaneously. Someone's in the back of the taxi heading home from the best first date of their life while someone else is catching the subway home after learning they were fired. It's the perfect portrayal of the human experience, and I've grown quite fond of it.

"Who's West? You know what? Never mind. I've entered full panic mode trying to find something to wear to the release party tonight. I don't have time to think about your boyfriend of the week."

"Hey," she sulks. "Wait, are you asking me for fashion help? If so, I'll circle back to that less-than-flattering take on my dating life later."

"Yes, I am. Do you have anything I can wear? I need to make a good impression. There are going to be a lot of important people at this party, and I want to look good."

She holds her pointer finger up at me, grabs her phone, and begins jabbing rapidly at the screen. I stand there, hands on my hips, impatiently waiting for whatever could possibly be more important than my current clothing emergency.

"There, done."

I draw my brows together in confusion. "What's done?"

"I canceled my date with West. We're going shopping." She applies the last of her mascara before springing up and grabbing her purse off her bed in a flash.

I whine, immediately turned off by the idea of trying clothes on. I've accumulated a new wardrobe since the move, but most of it was purchased online during late-night, stress-induced retail therapy sprees. Dressing rooms are the bane of my existence. I'm already pitting out, thinking about how I'm going to do my hair. Now, I have yet another reason to stress.

"Why would you cancel a date? Can't I just borrow something from your closet? It would make life so much easier. Plus, you'd be able to hang out with a hot guy."

"West is hot, but I'm not sure I see it working out." Before I can reply, she puts a hand up, shutting me up immediately. "I don't want to hear it. And no, you can't just borrow something I've worn before. An event like this calls for a new outfit. Text Scarlett and tell her to meet us in SoHo."

The two have never met, but I've droned on and on about how much I love Scarlett to Amelia. The two are surprisingly similar in many ways, and if there's one thing they share–aside from their fear of commitment–it's a love for fashion. I reluctantly text Scarlett before being whisked away by a terribly eager Amelia.

✻ ✻ ✻ ✻ ✻

I COME out of the dressing room wearing a god-awful sand-colored maxi dress with a deep cowl neckline that shows *way* too much cleavage. Amelia and Scarlett, who have been acting as my personal stylists for the past two hours, are waiting outside, armed with overpriced coffees.

I anxiously chugged mine as we went from store to store, and now I'm dealing with the consequences of my own actions. My stomach is gurgling, and I'm painfully bloated. I feel and look like I'm approximately six months pregnant, which is the last thing you want when you're putting clothes on and off. I've already worked up a sweat, and I've actively avoided looking in the mirror as much as possible.

"Holy shit, you look incredible!" Amelia claps, nudging Scarlett to grab her attention. When her eyes land on me, she lets out a low whistle.

I look down at the dress, screwing myself into a twisted position to avoid getting sweat stains on it. The beige coloring is unforgiving, and one wrong move would show how damp I've become.

"I look like I'm about to go to the club. There's no way I can wear this around professionals."

"You're not wrong," Scarlett harrumphs. "*But* Parker would lose his ever-loving mind if you wore this." Her brows raise expectantly.

"I'm not choosing an outfit just because Parker would like me in it. I don't care what he thinks. Besides, how many times do I have to tell you? He has a girlfriend. Why would I try to impress a taken man?"

I head back into the dressing room, carefully sliding the gown off. I hang it back up and grab the last one in the room, sending up a wordless plea that this is the last one I have to try on. I don't know how much more of this I can take.

I step into the black, asymmetrical-hemmed halter dress. The sweetheart neckline compliments my chest perfectly, and the ruching creates a slimming effect. I hate to admit it, but l love it. I blow out a breath, hopeful that Amelia and Scarlett feel the same way.

As soon as I step outside, both of their jaws fall to the floor. A bit more dramatic than I was expecting, but I'll take it.

"Holy shit, your tits look amazing in that," Amelia says as she looks down at her petite frame and pouts. "Maybe I do need to go buy a pair of those after all."

"I'd say you can have mine, but I actually very much enjoy them." I cup and push my boobs up closer to my chin. I do a quick spin, showcasing every angle of the dress. "I think this is the one."

"Uh yeah, duh. That's obvious." Scarlett laughs, jaw still ajar. "Even I want to fuck you in that. Parker is going to have an absolute heart attack when he sees you."

I click my tongue in disapproval before going back to change. I don't even want to entertain that thought. Although, I'd be lying if I said that there wasn't a small part of me that was thrilled about the idea of Parker seeing me in this dress.

"She's right. Twenty bucks, he proposes on the spot," Amelia agrees.

"You two are giving this dress far too much power." I push through the heavy curtain and hang up all the dresses that didn't work before heading to the cash register to pay. After checking out, I walk outside, basking in the light breeze. I've never been more thankful that New York is having a chillier spring as I feel my body temperature drop rapidly.

The door closes behind me, Scarlett and Amelia on my heels. "We're not giving the dress too much power. We're giving *you* that power. Any man would be an absolute lunatic not to fawn over you at any given point. Let alone when you're wearing stuff like that." Amelia points to the bag filled with my newest purchase.

"Well, I can always count on the two of you to hype me up, that's for sure."

Scarlett throws her arm around my shoulders and leads me toward the subway. "Oh, we're just getting started. Now it's time for hair and makeup."

"Don't you need to go home and get ready? I'm not the only

one going to this party, you know. You're both invited, in case you've forgotten."

Scarlett lifts her expensive, sizeable tote and gives it a pat. "I've got my outfit and supplies in here." She juts her chin out at Amelia. "And that one has already volunteered herself for the job."

"You two are my canvases tonight. I'm just the artist." Amelia bats her lashes. "Now let's get our asses home. I've got my work cut out for me."

✳ ✳ ✳ ✳ ✳

"Are you two almost ready?" I yell at Scarlett and Amelia from my bedroom. I'm sitting on my bed, attempting to buckle up the sky-high black stilettos that Amelia let me borrow. After a minute of struggling, I stand, nearly twisting my ankle in the process. I'll be genuinely shocked if I can get through this night without breaking a bone.

I glance at my reflection in the mirror and find myself radiating with pure confidence. Apart from a couple of weddings I've attended, I've never had an excuse to dress up like this.

Amelia has styled my hair into voluptuous, loose curls reminiscent of styles worn in the 1920s. One side rests behind my back while the other elegantly drapes over my shoulder. She paired the hair with a matte neutral eye shadow, a winged liner so sharp it could cut glass, and a bold, wine-red lip. My breath catches in my throat, and I push down the rush of emotions threatening to surface over the fact that I've never felt this beautiful in my life. Now's not the time to dwell on that.

I wobble toward the kitchen and sit down on a bar stool to limit the amount of movement I have to do before I have to be on my feet all night.

"We're ready!" Amelia and Scarlett come rushing out of the bathroom, both dressed to the nines.

Amelia's wearing a bright fuchsia pink, one-shouldered maxi dress with a slit that hits her upper thigh. She's carrying a small cream clutch, which matches the platform heels she's wearing perfectly. Scarlett, on the other hand, is dressed in a strapless burgundy dress with rosettes embellished on the slit that, too, rests on her upper leg. They're breathtaking. I motion for them to twirl, and they humor me, giggling as they spin.

"Oh my god. You guys look stunning."

"We do clean up nicely, don't we?" Scarlett's smile is contagious, and I take a moment to soak it all up.

No one talks about how difficult it is to make friends in your late twenties. Everyone is so wrapped up in their jobs and relationships that they neglect to spend time on their existing friendships, let alone make new ones.

Yet, here I am with two people who have altered my life in a way I don't think they will ever fully understand. I'm not sure how I got so lucky or what I did to deserve them, but I'll never take them for granted.

I take a quick selfie of the three of us, tuck my phone away, and grab my clutch off the counter.

"Let's go break some hearts."

20

DYLAN

The rooftop bar has been completely transformed in a way I never thought possible. I push my shoulders back and sit a little taller as I take in all of my hard work. String lights have been hung over the lounge area, where sleek black couches have been placed. There's a DJ nestled in the corner playing all of the latest hits, and the bar is already packed with people waiting to order a drink.

Before I grab a drink and socialize, I stop to study the sky, which is splashed in hues of rose, tangerine, and lavender as the sun dips behind the skyscrapers. It's as if Mother Nature has grabbed a paintbrush and spent her sweet time creating a spellbinding masterpiece full of wispy brushstrokes. It's enchanting.

"Pretty breathtaking, isn't it?" a gravelly voice calls from behind me.

I blink back into focus, the party around me suddenly becoming clear again. I turn to find Amelia and Scarlett–who made their way to the bar–have been replaced by Parker. My breath catches, and a flutter of anticipation twists in my chest. He's always been beautiful in my eyes, but tonight, there's something there that I've never seen before. Yet I can't place my finger on it.

His fitted midnight black suit jacket matches his slim trousers impeccably. I know if he turned around, I would find the pants sculpting his ass beautifully, and I gulp down the thought of staring at his butt. Under the jacket, he's wearing a black button-down, free of a tie. He's left the last few top buttons undone, and my eyes catch on the ink peeking through. My mind flashes back to his arm tattoo on the plane, and I discreetly fan myself over the thought that there's more hiding underneath his clothes.

I bring my gaze back up to his face and notice he's let his stubble grow out more. His loose dark hair has grown out, and tendrils fall in front of his face. The youthful look it gives him contradicts the ruggedness of the five o'clock shadow. His lips are turned up into a genuine smile as his eyes rake down my figure.

"New York's sunsets definitely rival Woodland Heights', and that's hard to do," I say, suddenly breathless.

"They do. But I wasn't talking about the sunset."

I roll my eyes, but my face flushes with heat. I wish I had gotten a drink before this interaction. I'd kill to cool myself off with an ice cube or two right about now. "That was bad, even for you."

He chuckles and walks past me, relaxing his arms on the glass wall that separates us from a thousand-foot drop. My stomach involuntarily cramps at the blasé gesture, and I reach out for his sleeve, tugging him backward, closer to me, without processing what I'm doing.

I've been scared of heights since I was a child, and the irrational fear of him falling plays in my mind, frame by frame. He must notice my discomfort because he takes yet another step back and places a hand on my lower back. The small gesture sends a bolt of electricity through me, and my body hums at the contact.

"Still not a fan of heights, huh?"

I let go of the breath I was unaware I was holding now that he's put some distance between him and the ledge. "Unfortunately not."

"Hosting a release party on top of a skyscraper was a bold move for someone who can't even handle the stairs of a waterslide."

"It's New York. It was the only option." I reply roughly.

As much as I want to joke around with him, my pulse is throbbing, and there's a rush of blood in my ears. I'm almost certain it has nothing to do with the scare he just gave me and everything to do with the hand that's sitting rather close to my ass.

He shakes his head, his grin still on full display. "Why don't we get you a drink? Take that edge off a little?"

I nod wordlessly, and he grabs my hand, leading me through the crowd. I lock eyes with Scarlett and Amelia, who both mouth "OMG" as they notice my hand locked with his. I avert my gaze back to the bar. I know damn well that if I entertain them, my poker face will crumble, and I don't need Parker knowing that he has that effect on me.

"What would you like?"

We saddle up to the bar, and his hand goes from my own to my hip. I glance down at his hand, his fingers splayed firmly against my clothed skin. The grip is possessive, and as much as I want to hate it, my body longs to be explored more.

"Dylan?" his deep, rumbling voice calls for me.

I look up to the bartender, who's staring at Parker longer than I'm comfortable with. A kernel of jealousy plants itself in my gut. *Fuck.* "Oh, I'll take a tequila soda with lime, please."

"Make that two, please."

When I bring my attention back to Parker, he's already

looking at me, his eyes darkened with hunger. Without breaking eye contact, he places cash in the tip jar, grabs the drinks once they're finished, and hands me my glass.

"Thank you." I take a sip, letting the refreshingly strong drink wash over me. The liquid courage warms my belly, and before I can process what's happening, Parker is dragging me over to an empty couch. I sit across from him, our knees inches away from one another.

"Cheers to putting together one hell of a release party. This turned out better than I could've even imagined it. And it's all thanks to you." Parker lifts his glass, and I hit it with my own.

I take another sip before setting it down and looking around, taking it all in again. It exceeded my expectations, too. "You can thank the party planners I hired, not me."

"Don't do that," he commands.

"Do what?" I question.

"Discredit yourself. They may have brought it all to life, but it was your vision they were working with. You were the one who thought out every meticulous detail, down to the napkins."

To be fair, it *was* my idea to include some of my favorite quotes on the cocktail napkins to help garnish interest. The drink stirrers were also topped with moons and stars to tie in some of the book's elements.

"Well, thank you," I say quietly. I've never been comfortable with flattery in any capacity, and it took me months of dating Parker to shake off the habit of arguing with him whenever he complimented me. I never felt worthy of the praise. It's something I'm still working on, and I fear I may be working on it for the rest of my life. I file that thought away to bring to next week's therapy session as I take another drink.

"Of course." He cups my chin and lifts it so we're eye-to-eye. He sweeps his thumb across my jawline, and I swear my heart falls straight into my ass at the tender touch. "Now relax. You've made it this far. You've done an incredible job. Enjoy the fruits of your labor for once. Can you do that for me?"

I dip my head in agreement, careful not to be too abrupt to keep his hand in place. I'm not sure what's in the air tonight, but the physical contact has me ready to combust. I mentally run through my calendar, trying to place the last time I saw any action. It's been *far* too long. No wonder I'm going feral.

"I can do that," I whisper.

"Good girl. Now dance with me."

Despite being terrible at accepting praise, the velvety tone that envelope the words "good girl" makes my body ache. Parker stands and reaches his hand out in support. I neglect my drink on a nearby table, forgetting about it entirely, as an electric current surges from my head to my toes at the idea of dancing with Parker the way we did once upon a time. It's a small gesture that's so well-known yet so alien, thanks to the time we've spent apart.

I take his hand, and he leads me to the dance floor, where a small handful of attendees are swaying to the newest love song on the charts. My brain can't process a single lyric playing as Parker and I come face to face. It's like my mind has tunnel vision, only capable of focusing on the man in front of me.

He wraps an arm around my waist and grabs my free hand, leaving me to hold onto his shoulder and stare into his cerulean blue eyes. There's always been a height difference between us, but I had forgotten what it feels like to crane my neck to get a better view of his statuesque face.

As we rock gently together to the melody of the music, Parker refuses to take his eyes off me, and I have to remind myself not to cower from the ferocity. His stare bounces from my own gaze down to my lips, and the temptation to stand on the balls of my feet to press my lips to his burns through me like a wildfire, but I bite it back, unwilling to be the one to cross that line.

"You've gotten better. You haven't stepped on my toes once. I think that might be a new record," he teases.

I bury my face into his chest, hiding my embarrassment–and the giant grin that's engulfed my face. With a deep inhale, I catch a whiff of sweet smoke like a blazing campfire in the woods. It's the cologne he's worn in all the years I've known him, and it makes my head foggy. "Be careful what you wish for. We're just getting started." There's a trace of laughter in my voice, but it's muffled by the silky folds of his shirt.

"Are you saying you'll do me the honor of dancing with me all night?" I can hear the smile in his voice, and it makes my heart hammer against my ribs.

"If you're lucky," I grumble against his torso.

"Something tells me I will be," Parker mutters into the top of my hair, pulling me closer to him. I'm not sure where this confidence has come from, but being pressed up against him makes my judgment go haywire, so I don't question it.

Instead, I let myself revel in the thought that maybe, just maybe, the universe did bring us back together for a second chance.

※ ※ ※ ※ ※

THE NIGHT IS WRAPPING, most of the party has left, and I'm buzzing with energy and alcohol. I wipe my forehead with the back of my hand, clearing it of the sweat I've worked up from dancing. It felt so freeing to take a step back and not worry about work for once. Though it was technically a work event, after I gave my speech thanking everyone for coming, I got to let loose and just be me. I hadn't realized how badly I needed it until now. It helped that Parker refused to leave my side the entire night.

It felt like we were falling back into old routines, and a twinge of wistfulness settled into my soul. It felt like the days before my dad passed away. I felt young again.

Amelia and Scarlett prance up to me, arms linked. Seeing my two favorite people becoming so close fills me with a profound sense of love. I've found my circle. I've found my footing.

"We're about to head out. You ready to go?" Amelia slurs. It looks like I'm not the only one feeling the effects of the open bar.

"Yeah, let me just find my purse."

"Actually, ladies, do you mind if I walk her home?" Parker swaggers up to my side, placing his arm around my waist. Despite being hot, a chill courses through me. Scarlett wiggles her eyebrows at me, and Amelia bursts out into a fit of giggles.

"Of course, we don't mind. Get her home safely, Parker. Or else I have to kick your ass. And I'm a purple belt." Scarlett creates a v-shape with her pointer and middle fingers and points them in Parker's direction in an "I'm watching you" motion. On any given day, I'd take Scarlett's threats seriously, but with a few drinks in her system, she's closer to resembling a harmless chihuahua.

"You have my word." Parker bows at the waist, sending me into a hysterical outburst. Scarlett and Amelia skip toward the door, leaving me and Parker alone, aside from a few stragglers. He grabs my bag from behind his back and hands it to me. "I believe you were looking for this."

"Thank you. How gentlemanly of you," I reply with a hiccup.

The minute I place the clutch's chain on my shoulder, Parker's hand finds its way back to my back. He gently ushers me toward the elevator, both of us swaying slightly as we can't seem to break the laughing spell. As soon as the doors open, we step onto the empty elevator.

I stand pressed against the back wall, unsure of what to say or do now that it's just the two of us in such close proximity. Before I can process what he's about to do, Parker presses the emergency stop button of the elevator, causing the entire thing to jolt.

"What are you doing?" I collect myself after jerking forward at the sudden movement.

"We need to talk."

21

PARKER

Dylan is staring at me like I've got three heads. It was not my intention to stop the elevator and have this conversation with her tonight, but with just enough tequila flowing through me, I have no choice. We spent all night dancing closer than "friends" typically dance with each other, so now feels like as good a time as ever.

I'm tired of walking on eggshells. And I'm especially tired of her believing something that's not true.

"Talk about what?" She crosses her arms over her chest, pushing her breasts together in a way that accentuates them more than they've already been highlighted in that dress.

"God, you're beautiful," I sigh.

Her eyes follow my line of sight, and she rolls her eyes but keeps her arms where they are. "Thank you. But I'm guessing that's not what you wanted to talk about."

I clear my throat and force my gaze up to hers. "No, it's not. There's something I haven't been completely honest about."

She narrows her eyes, staying silent. She points her chin down and raises her brows, expecting me to continue. The look is deadly, and I instantly feel ten times smaller. Lying these past few months has been completely and utterly painful, and it's taken everything in me not to tell her the truth.

"Olivia and I aren't together. We haven't been for months. I'm very much single."

Confusion flickers across her face as she processes what I'm saying. I swallow a feeling of relief that she doesn't seem mad, but I don't allow myself to get too comfortable with the feeling. I fidget my fingers behind my back, awaiting her response.

"I'm confused." She cocks her head.

I power on, ready for the truth to be on the table. "I let you think I was in a relationship because Blake convinced me it was a good idea. I know now that I was an idiot for listening to him. He has no idea what he's talking about. He said that being in a relationship would make you want me more. But he's a dickhead that has no leg to stand on when it comes to relationship advice. It's been killing me not to tell you the truth these past couple of months. Especially after seeing how upset you were with me."

Her eyes fill with tears, and I exhale, emptying my lungs of any air. Fuck, this is going *so* much worse than I thought it would. I expected anger, rage, yelling–not sadness. The last thing I wanted to do was disappoint her.

"Why would you lie to me?" Her voice breaks. She looks like a porcelain doll, so fragile and breakable, and it feels like a punch to the gut.

"Why do you think?" I throw my hands up, exasperated. She flinches, and I run a palm down my face. I wasn't expecting to do the *whole* confession tonight, but there's no going back now. I need to tell her the entire truth, or else I risk losing her forever. I've already done that once before. I'm not willing to do it again.

"I don't know," she whispers.

"Because I'm still in love with you, Dyl! Because walking away from you on your porch five years ago was, and still is, the biggest regret of my life. I was a shell of a man for years after I ended things. There are no excuses for my mistake, and I can't take back what I did. It's something that I'm going to have to live with for the rest of my life, but I've dreamed of the day I could tell you how I really feel. I never thought I'd get the chance to apologize for the pain that I caused you, but here we are. I hope you know how sorry I am. How sorry I always will be.

"But I'm so afraid that I'm going to hurt you again. That *I'm* going to end up hurt again. I couldn't live with myself knowing I broke you again. I wouldn't make it out alive."

With my words, the final tether that's been holding us together all night is snapped. Without uttering a word, she rushes over to me and crashes her lips into mine as she snakes her arms around my neck. I groan into her mouth and wrap my arms around her petite waist, sliding my hands down to the top of her heart-shaped ass.

Her tongue slides into my mouth with force, and I tangle it up with mine. The lip gloss she reapplied tastes like strawberry and vanilla, and I get drunk off the flavor. The taste is delectable, and it makes my cock strain against my pants. She grinds her hips into mine while I harden under her even more. I didn't know that was physically possible, but it's painful.

I know she can feel how hard I am for her when she breaks the kiss to smirk against my lips. I take the opportunity to mumble against her lips, "Hold on tight."

I need her closer.

Dylan's grip tightens, and I lift her dress up to her hips to give me easier access. With one quick move, I sweep her up into my arms. Her legs immediately wrap up around my waist, and I flip us around so her back is pressed against the cool metal wall.

"God, I've missed this," she breathes.

She presses her forehead to mine, and I take a moment to

look into her eyes, her cheeks fully reddened, her luscious lips swollen, her hair unkempt. She looks frenzied, and I can't get enough.

"Baby, you can't say stuff like that. I don't have much control right now." I'm fully panting, and I use my free hand to explore her body, wandering up to her breasts. They've been teasing me all night, and I want nothing more than to have them in my mouth. I glance up at her for permission, and with a tight nod, she grants me access. I pull down the dress, her perky pink nipples peeking out for me.

"I don't want you to be controlled." She rolls her head back as I take her breast into my mouth, sucking on it gently. She runs her hands through my hair, and I push myself into her further while I begin to nibble at her chest. I use my hips to hold her into place, taking my other hand to her second erect nipple. I give it a pinch, and the moan she lets out turns me into an animal.

I break free with one last kiss to the center of her chest. "If I were to stick my fingers in those panties of yours right now, how wet would I find you, baby?"

I place her back down on the ground and lift the dress further up, exposing the black sheer g-string she's wearing. I run a feather-light finger up her thigh, teasing her with the touch I know she's dying to have right now.

"Soaked," she whimpers.

I move my touch further up her thigh, stopping when I hit the heat between her legs. As I swipe my finger over her pussy, I feel just how wet she truly is. My restraint is bursting at the seams as I speak through gritted teeth, "You weren't lying. You're drenched."

Dylan bites her bottom lip, looks up at me with her large, unblinking eyes, and nods innocently. "Just for you."

I run my finger, now wet with her arousal, against her

bottom lip. She follows the motion with her tongue, gliding it across the path I've made.

My self-control is no longer existent, and I reach down, giving myself a rub through my trousers. The thin material does little to hide the bulge she's given me, and I don't miss the way her eyes lock on my erection.

As much as I enjoy seeing her watch me through hooded lids, I stop touching myself to lift her chin back up to me. I'm desperate for her touch, but I want this moment to be about her.

"I want to taste you. Is that alright?"

"Yes," she squeaks.

I kneel down in front of her, the movement drawing a hushed gasp from her. I hook my fingers into the strings of her underwear and slowly draw them down her legs, helping her step out of them. I toss them to the side before placing gentle kisses up her legs where my finger lingered earlier. Her hands slide back in my hair, and she gives it a small yank, which winds me up more.

I alternate between kissing and licking as I get closer to the apex between her thighs, which is glistening, begging to be licked. My mouth salivates at the sight, and I run a finger across her lips. She bucks at the initial contact, and I clutch the swell of her hip, holding her firmly in place.

I replace my finger with my mouth, running my tongue up her folds painfully slow. I moan into her, "Oh baby. You taste so good."

"Fuck."

She slams back as I spread her lips open with my fingers. I work my way to the top to find the small bundle of nerves swollen and waiting for me and give it a flick of my tongue. She squirms under my touch, and I use both hands to pin her to the wall, rendering her completely helpless.

As I continue to bury my face into her, she succumbs to the

pleasure. I sweep my tongue quickly across her clit as her moans grow louder and louder, her taut muscles going lax with pleasure.

I begrudgingly pull myself off of her, letting go of one of her hips. "I want you to come for me, okay? But I need you to be quiet. Just because the elevator is stopped doesn't mean someone can't hear you," I beg.

Before she can reply, I slide a finger into her slickness, twisting it as I flick my tongue against her sweet spot once again. She slaps a hand over her mouth, and I continue to work, adding a second finger while I lap her up like the dessert she is.

Her walls begin to tighten around me, her legs growing tense. I smirk as she approaches her climax, knowing that I can still read her body like a book. Years may have come between us, but what she likes, what she needs, will forever be ingrained in my mind. I'd spend the rest of my life pleasuring her if she'd let me.

"That's it, you're so close for me," I murmur.

"Don't stop. I'm going to come."

As she throws her head back, I ready myself for the full-body trembling that accompanies her orgasms. She continues to clench around me, seconds away from tumbling over the edge, until a sudden robotic voice fills the small elevator.

"9-1-1, what's your emergency?"

Her eyes go wide, and we both look over at the emergency button that she unknowingly pressed amid her build-up. I slide my fingers out of her, making a show of licking them clean. Her face goes red-hot while I savor her taste. I love it when she gets shy.

The fire department calling has all but ruined the moment, and I need to try to keep everything under control before she gets too embarrassed.

"Hi there. I'm so sorry about that. I accidentally hit the

emergency button in the elevator," I call back, still on my knees in front of her. My eyes don't leave hers, and although a bucket of ice water has all but extinguished the moment, I can see the lust lingering in the way she's sucking in her bottom lip. In the way her chest is covered with angry red splotches.

It takes everything in me not to return to what I was doing. I need her to come more than I need air right now, but I shove my desire down, urging my dick to get the memo.

"Everyone's alright?" the deep but muffled voice asks.

"Yes, thank you so much for checking. I apologize again." I reply politely, the line going dead.

I stand up, pulling her dress down in the process. I flatten her unruly hair, wipe away a smear of mascara from under her eye, and hand her the underwear thrown on the elevator floor with a laugh. The tension melts away as soon as I see her breaking down into hysterics.

"So good you called the cops on me, huh? That's a first," I snicker.

She playfully hits me across the chest, making a show of fixing the top of her dress and tucking herself back in. I feel my cock twitch against my zipper, knowing that just moments ago, she was going wild for me.

"Shut up. You and I both know that your head is big enough as is. We don't need that ego of yours getting any bigger."

"If we weren't in an elevator, you would've been screaming my name. I'd say that's cause to have an ego."

She blushes but doesn't argue and smacks the emergency stop button again, resuming our trip down to the lobby.

"We should probably-"

"Soo..." I start at the same time. I cut myself off, let out a low chuckle, and gesture for her to resume her thought. "Go ahead." The elevator ding marking our arrival interrupts her yet again.

As we walk off together, I naturally gravitate toward her,

wanting to touch her in some capacity. Now that we've crossed over the boundary of physical touch, I know I'm going to be craving it every chance I get.

"Do you want me to walk you home? Finish this conversation on the way?"

"Actually, I'd like to be alone for a little, if you don't mind." Her eyes move from the ground in front of her up to me, and she gives me a sad smile. I notice the small step she takes away from me. It's as if a switch has been flipped, and the sudden change in attitude makes my head throb. I stumble back, trying to help her feel at ease, dipping my chin.

"Sure.... Can you at least text me when you get home so I know you're safe? And take my jacket so that I know you stay warm?" I hesitate. I'm uncomfortable with the idea, but the mood has shifted, and I don't want to make things weirder than they've already become in the last sixty seconds.

"I don't want to take your jacket. You need it."

"I don't. Besides, it gives me an excuse to see you again."

She huffs out a small laugh. "I don't think you have to worry about that. We do work together and everything."

"You can never be too sure." I offer a cheeky grin, trying to lighten the mood as I see her mind running a mile a minute. This girl has been an overthinker since the minute I met her, and I know that she's in her head right now. Unfortunately, I can't talk her off the ledge like I once did–especially since I know I'm the reason she's lost in her thoughts.

"Alright."

I shrug off my suit jacket and wrap it around her shoulders, pulling it tight. I catch her staring at my chest and arms, and in spite of the terrible timing, I bask in the idea that she's checking me out. The look she's giving me makes my skin prickle, and I do my best to shake off the never-ending burn of desire. It's useless, though, because I will always be insatiable with Dylan.

"Promise me you'll text me as soon as you're home," I demand.

"I promise."

Ignoring her aloof demeanor, I gently grab her wrist and pull her tightly into my chest. She wraps her arms around my waist, and we stand in the deserted lobby, holding one another. I bury my face in her hair, inhaling the subtle rich spices and vanilla of her perfume.

It's the smell that has lived in my dreams for the past year–the one that stops me in the streets whenever I smell something similar. The one that made me do a double take every time I walked past it in California, knowing damn well that the girl who wears it was nowhere near, but still hoping anyways.

The hug lingers far longer than I expected, and I make no move to break free from the hold. Her grip relaxes on my waist, and I have to force myself to pull away, even though my mind is screaming to never let go.

"I'll see you later." She gives me a halfhearted wave and walks into the dark New York streets. I'm immediately met with a spasm of guilt, knowing I should've fought harder to ensure she got home safely. I just poured my heart out to her and tasted her (and will be dreaming of doing so for the foreseeable future), and I have no idea if she feels the same way, and now she's walking home alone. *Fucking idiot,* I scold myself.

As I step out onto the bustling sidewalk, I contemplate whether or not I just made the second biggest mistake of my life.

22

DYLAN

As soon as I walk inside, I'm met with loud music blasting from a speaker in the living room. Amelia and Scarlett have changed into pajamas, and bottles of wine are strewn all over the kitchen counter and coffee table. It looks like the party didn't stop when they got home, exactly as I expected.

"DYLAN!" the two shout as they dance around the living room. I press my back to the front door as soon as it's closed and slide down it into a sitting position on the floor. I bring my knees to my chest and wrap my arms around my legs, resting my forehead on my forearms. Scarlett and Amelia read my mood, turn down the music, and rush over to me.

"Who died?" Amelia asks while Scarlett simultaneously asks me what's wrong. I groan in response and point to the closest full bottle of wine on the counter. Scarlett grabs the pinot noir, brings it to me, and I take a swig straight from the bottle.

"That bad, huh?"

"Parker and I made out," I say under my breath.

"About damn time," Amelia replies. I blink slowly, stunned.

The baffled look on my face must be apparent because she continues, giving me no time to respond.

"Don't kill me, but you're one of my best friends, and if you saw the way that you were glowing every time you were around Parker, you'd feel the same way. I love you, and I know you're afraid of getting hurt, but I also know how happy he makes you, no matter how hard you try to fight it."

I pass over Amelia's words of wisdom, knowing that I'm not quite ready to acknowledge those feelings head-on. My head is already spinning from everything that happened tonight; the last thing I need is to bring my feelings into this and what it could mean for my future.

I had every intention of walking home with Parker, but after the nightmare that was the 911 call, it felt like the walls of the elevator were caving in–my anxiety getting the best of me. I felt like I was choking.

His love confession has been playing on repeat in my head for the past hour. I spent my early twenties desperately hoping he'd come running back, admitting that he messed up. As each year passed, my hope dwindled until I accepted the idea that it was never going to happen. I had become okay with the outcome–alright, mostly okay.

"That's not all," I keep going. "He may or may not have confessed his love to me and eaten me out in the elevator in what I can only describe as the hottest sexual experience of my life."

Scarlett lets out a piercing squeal so loud I have to cover my ears. Amelia runs to the coffee table, grabs her wine glass, and pours herself a hefty glass from one of the nearby open bottles before sitting next to me, hand cupped around her ear in a way that tells me she's ready for every dirty detail.

"Care to explain how you went from pretending you hated this man to getting off in an elevator?" she pushes.

"For starters, I didn't get off."

"Oooh.." Scarlett pulls a face, lips pressed tight in disappointment. "So he's not good in bed? I always took him as the kind of guy who knew what he was doing."

I ignore that comment, not wanting to remotely think about one of my best friends dreaming about what the man I love is like in bed.

Shit, the man I love? I push that thought aside. I'll unpack that later, along with everything else that is crumbling in my life.

"No, I accidentally pressed the emergency call button right as I was about to come. It will forever go down as the most embarrassing moment of my life. Secondly, you guys should have heard his confession. He gave this whole speech about how he's still in love with me but is afraid to get hurt again and worries that he'll do something to mess it up between us. He also admitted to omitting the truth about having a girlfriend because Blake told him to."

I notice Scarlett's brows draw together in repugnance, and if I had the mental capacity to dissect that right now, I would. I know I've been in my own bubble lately, but I would have to be an absolute fool not to notice how she and Blake have been with one another lately. It'd explain why she's constantly on her phone and always shutting me down when I question who she's texting.

Rather than judging me, I'm met with looks of sympathy. Both of their eyes soften, and Scarlett joins Amelia on the floor, resting a soothing hand on my own. I place the wine bottle I've been white-knuckling onto the ground and close my eyes, pushing away the tears that are threatening to fall.

My mind has never been more fucked, and the surge of emotions rising in me has made my feelings go berserk. This is why I've been so standoffish these past couple of months. I knew that if I let myself get comfortable, I'd end up more confused than ever. Little did I know just how emotional I'd really feel.

"And how does that make you feel?" Scarlett asks in a low voice. She's doing everything she can to make me feel better and break down the mountain of information I just forced on her. They both are. I let out a shaky exhale as Amelia's hand slides into mine, giving me a small squeeze of encouragement.

All of the playfulness has been suctioned out of the room like a vacuum, and the fact that I'm responsible for it only makes me feel worse. The two were having such a great time before I got home, and now we're sitting on the floor while I try to verbalize just how messed up I am now.

The first tear falls down my cheek, and before I can stop it from reaching my chin, a gentle finger wipes it away. I lock eyes with Amelia, and she offers me a feeble smile.

"Don't cry. It's all going to be okay. And if it's not, we're going to be right here beside you," she whispers. Scarlett begins rubbing her thumb slowly over my hand, a motion so small but so full of love that I feel like I could burst.

"I don't know what to think. I'm scared. I don't want to get my heart broken again," I croak, my voice scratchy.

"You're human. I think anyone in your shoes would feel the same way. You don't have to make any decisions tonight. Why don't you sleep on it, and we can talk about it some more tomorrow when we're all a little more sober and you've had some time to think?" Scarlett consoles.

"Ooh, I have just the thing to help!" Amelia hops up and runs for the kitchen, her figure hidden behind the counter. I can't see her, but I hear the fridge open, followed by one of our drawers. The rattling of silverware is barely audible over the pop music that continues to play out of the speaker.

She jogs back, a pint of ice cream, along with three spoons, in hand. For the first time in hours, I let out a weak laugh. She discards the lid, passes out the spoons, and shoves the pint into my hands.

"Ben and Jerry's has been medically proven to be the best cure for sadness–particularly any sadness related to men."

I take a scoop of the cookie dough and brownie bite-filled ice cream and let out a faint groan of delight. As someone with a chronic sweet tooth, they weren't kidding when they said that a sweet treat can solve all your problems.

"Thank you, guys. I don't know where I'd be without you."

I set the ice cream down, and they pull me into a tight three-way hug.

"You'd probably be at some slimy dive bar, letting ugly men buy you drinks until you go home alone to cry yourself to sleep," Scarlett jokes. "At least that's my preferred way to cope."

"I can't tell if you're kidding, but if you're not, we need to put a pin in this and come back to it when I'm a little less fucked in the head."

"Pfft, of course I am." She grabs the pint, and I happily hand it over to her. It sounds like she may need it more than me right now.

"The upside is that the party was a raging success." Amelia changes the subject, and Scarlett looks grateful for it. "There's no way Katherine can keep walking all over you after seeing how well it went."

She's right. Everyone in attendance was thrilled about Evelyn's book. At some point in the evening, Evelyn came to me with happy tears in her eyes. She went on about how she couldn't believe the party was all for her, and I felt fuzzy inside, knowing that I put together a party for one of the most deserving people in the world.

I didn't speak a word to Katherine, but from the glances I caught throughout the night, she looked like she was having a good time. At one point, there was even a smile on her face. I about collapsed at the sight. Between that and the elevator debacle, I'm having a hard time believing hell hasn't frozen over.

"It did go really well, didn't it?" I gush.

"Of course it did. We knew it would! Celebrate your accomplishments every once in a while. You deserve it. You've been working your ass off, and Amelia and I are so proud of you." Amelia nods in agreement.

"Thank you," I whisper before I take one last bite of ice cream and slowly stand up, still feeling shaky on my legs. "I need to go to bed. Tomorrow, I'll be more in the mood to celebrate, I promise."

"Fine, but we'll hold you to that. I'm taking us all out to a celebratory brunch." Amelia steadies me on my feet, wrapping her arm around my shoulders, and kisses me on the forehead. The gesture makes me feel like a child–reminding me of the days when my mom and dad would tuck me into bed together after reading me a story–and it gives me more comfort than expected.

"Deal. Thank you. I'll see you guys in the morning."

I drag myself to the bedroom before they can respond and begin peeling off my dress. As I lift it over my head, I catch a whiff of the burning wood and clove of Parker's cologne again. The smell takes me back to nights spent sitting around a bonfire in the autumn when the red and gold leaves were weeks away from falling and winter threatened to envelop us in snow. It's a scent deep-seated in my memory, and with it, pressure builds behind my eyes. I desperately need sleep before I become an emotional wreck yet again.

Get your shit together, Dylan, I admonish myself.

As soon as I change into my pajamas, my phone's vibration brings me back down to earth. I look down at the caller ID—my mom. She never calls me this late, and my mind runs a mile a minute, immediately going to the worst-case scenario.

I study my room, looking for five things I can see, four

things I can touch, three things I can hear, two things I can smell, and one thing I can taste to alleviate myself from the anxiety that's rising. I fail miserably, only making it halfway through the grounding technique before answering in a panic, "Hello? Is everything okay?"

Her cheerful laugh seeps into my bones and wraps around me like my childhood blanket. "Hi, honey. Everything is okay. I just wanted to check in and see how everything is going. I don't know how to explain it, but I just felt the need to call you tonight."

I've always heard about a mother's intuition, but my mom's clairvoyance has never led her astray. She often knows what I need most before I can identify needing it myself. It's as if there were an unbreakable, invisible string attached to us from the minute of my birth. Any time I'm sad, angry, frustrated, heartbroken, she knows. It's because of her that I believe in unconditional love.

With her words, the dam breaks, and the tears begin again. I sniffle, trying to keep them at bay.

"Hey, hey," she soothes. "What's wrong?"

I wipe my face, clearing it of the stray drops as I will as much air into my lungs as possible. I've got to be starting my period soon. There's no other way to explain the basket case behavior I've been displaying today.

"I'm so confused," I speak lowly, collapsing into bed.

"About what, honey? Does this have anything to do with a certain ex-boyfriend of yours?"

I haven't seen my mom since moving to New York, but we FaceTime or text at least once a day. I like having the peace of mind knowing that she's still doing alright after going through everything she's gone through. I don't expect her to fall back into old patterns, but I still feel responsible for her wellbeing. I want to see her happy.

"Maybe."

"Why don't you tell me all about it tomorrow when I see you?" Her voice drips with excitement.

"What?" I jerk upright in bed, gripping my phone tightly. A rush of energy fills my veins, and I push out of bed, unable to sit still. I bounce from foot to foot, all exhaustion weighing heavily on me, seeming to momentarily evaporate.

"I booked a flight out there. I hope that's alright. I had this gut feeling that I needed to see you, and I bought the tickets before I could second guess it. I probably should've asked first, but–"

"Mom, I'd love that." I cut her rambling off.

There's nothing I need more right now than my mom. I love my life in New York, but I've grown a little homesick, and there's no better cure than a visit from the woman who means the most to me. No matter how old I grow to be, I will always need my mom when times get tough. She's my rock. My refuge.

"Thank goodness. I was worried you were going to be upset with me."

"Mom, I love you," I yawn, trying to dispel her concerns.

"I love you too, Ducky. You sound exhausted. Why don't you get some sleep? I'll text you my flight information."

I lie back down and pull my comforter up around me, burying myself into a tight cocoon. The weight of the blankets offers me further solace. As soon as my head hits the pillow, my eyes grow heavy. I've been go, go, go all day. I didn't realize just how tired I was until I stopped.

"Okay. Can't wait to see you."

"Me too. Goodnight, sweetheart."

"Goodnight, Mom."

I end the call, text Parker letting him know I'm safe, and let the phone drop onto the bed beside me. I may not know what's going to happen, but I know, deep down, that everything is going to be okay. And it's that thought that rocks me to sleep in a matter of minutes.

23

DYLAN

My morning started with the much-needed brunch that Amelia dragged us to. Between the crying and the tequila sodas, I woke up with a splitting headache. Thankfully, the omelet soaked it right up and made me feel like a functioning member of society again.

It was going to be a while before I drank again. My liver and mental state needed a break, and I hated how dependent I was becoming on alcohol to solve all of my problems. I knew better. I had seen the destruction it could cause, and I'm not willing to go down that path myself.

Now, my mom and I are sitting on the couch, eating homemade cupcakes and watching Sex and the City. We started baking when she was going through her recovery. She needed a distraction, and once she stopped drinking, she craved sweets, so we spent almost every weekend trying out new recipes and watching Samantha, Carrie, Charlotte, and Miranda navigate dating in the city. Little did I know that one day, I would be living a very similar life.

I hadn't noticed how badly I missed it until it was no longer a part of my weekly routine. Now that I had it back in my life, I was going to make it a priority to continue it, even after she left. Although I'm feeling much better today, I can't stomach the idea of my mom leaving–despite her just getting here–so I rid myself of that thought before it can bring my mood down.

She respected my space while we whipped up the French vanilla cupcakes with buttercream frosting–which made the apartment smell heavenly–but I could tell she was getting antsy waiting for me to divulge what was going on.

I grab the remote and turn the TV down after finishing my second cupcake. I don't care how bad they are for you; I will always go for seconds and thirds of my mom's cupcakes. They're a small slice of home.

"I guess we should talk about it."

"Whatever do you mean? What's there to talk about?" She plays dumb, and a grin breaks out on my face. I rest my head on her shoulder and sit in silence for a second, committing this moment to memory.

"Parker's back."

"Back in what way?" she coaxes.

I left out the very large storyline, which is my feelings, during our calls. I'm not sure why, but I was already having a hard enough time processing it myself. I thought I was old enough to sort through it without my mom's help, but here I am, uneasiness eating away at me because I didn't tell the one person who's been there for me my entire life what's been going on.

"Well, you know we've been working together.."

"Yes. From the sounds of it, it's been going fairly well." She mindlessly strokes my hair, not pushing me to share anything I'm uncomfortable with.

"It has. Evelyn seems really happy with the work we've been doing. Katherine has even seemed to back off a little."

"Then what's the problem?" she asks, sounding genuinely perplexed.

"Yesterday, after the release party, Parker admitted he was still in love with me. He and Olivia aren't together. It was all a ruse to make me jealous."

"That's a terrible idea. I swear to god, men are so simple-minded sometimes," she barks, and a laugh bubbles from my chest. "How did you react to the news?"

"I kissed him... and let's just say that escalated."

She pulls away from me, lips puckered in suspicion. "Escalated how?"

Most people shy away from telling their mom the nitty gritty details of their sexual escapades, but I never have. After everything that happened with my dad, we spent every waking second together trying to get her in a better place. She became my built-in best friend, and the boundaries most people have with their parents seemingly disappeared. Now, one could make the argument that we're too close.

I shield my face with my hands, peeking out at her face in between my fingers as I drop the bomb. "He went down on me in the elevator."

Yup, *definitely* too close.

Her body shakes with laughter, and I playfully punch her arm. I groan, wishing the furniture could swallow me whole so I wouldn't have to face the consequences of my actions–and my mother's reactions to them.

"Well, that's certainly one way to cope. So I'm guessing you're now confused about where to go from here."

"Never been more confused," I confess.

She shifts on the couch, pulling away to sit cross-legged next to me. She's dressed comfortably in leggings and a black hoodie, now smeared with flour. Her hair is tied back in a ponytail on the top of her head, and when I take the time to look at her, it hits me just how beautiful she is. I've always known she's been stunning, but when she spent sun up to sun down drinking, her skin was lackluster, and new wrinkles were forming at an alarming rate. Her eyes had lost the sparkle that I remember when I was younger.

She rarely ate, and every time I hugged her, I was afraid of snapping her in half. Her frailness was at the forefront of my mind, and it's a big part of why I can now cook. I would try to whip up every recipe imaginable to find something she could stomach. It never worked—not until she began attending meetings.

Eventually, her color returned, and she no longer struggled to get out of bed. The days spent wasting away inside turned into days spent outdoors. It started with small walks around the neighborhood, then gradually became hikes. Fortunately, living in the mountains meant there was a vast array of hikes within a thirty-mile radius.

She made new friends in AA, and they started attending yoga, getting monthly facials, and gardening. She found a core group that understood what she was going through better than I ever could. A couple of them were also widows, and I now viewed them as family as much as those who shared my blood.

That was the only way I could stomach leaving her. Had she never healed, I'm not sure I would have ever left. I know she wouldn't have wanted that life for me, but I couldn't let her hurt alone.

Now, looking at her, she looked youthful. Free-spirited. I massage softly at my heart as hope blossoms in my chest. I may have lost my dad young, but she turned her life around, and she wasn't going anywhere anytime soon.

"Can I tell you a story about me and your dad?"

I perk up, always in the mood for stories about their relationship. They had what I consider a fairy tale love. The two met right out of college. It was a blind date, and they both swore it was love at first sight. At least, my dad always did. My mom jokes that it took her a couple of dates to be convinced, but he eventually charmed his way into her heart. He had the personality for that.

As cliche as it sounds, he lit up a room. He was the life of the party, always trying to make everyone feel comfortable. He would've given a stranger the shirt off his back, even if he had nothing himself. Luckily, he did well for himself. So much so that my mom didn't have to work while I was growing up. She was the one who took me on all the school field trips, packed my lunches every morning, and chaperoned all of the sleepovers.

"Of course." I sit up, matching her position.

"I know your father and I looked perfect from the outside, but we ran into some problems before we got married." She scoops up my hand and unconsciously brushes her thumb over my skin.

I snort. "Yeah, right."

"I'm serious. Your grandmother hated your dad when she first met him. She was a tough ass, though, so I was hardly surprised. No one was ever going to be good enough for me in her eyes."

I never met my grandmother, but I had heard stories about how she was a nightmare to be around. They mostly came from my dad, but he always talked about his problems with her lightheartedly, so I never thought much of it. I never got to see how exaggerated his stories were because she passed away when I was one.

"She banned me from seeing him. We tried to make it work, but I was still living under her roof to help save money, and eventually, it got so bad that we ended things."

My jaw drops in surprise. "Why am I just now hearing about this?"

Her eyes crease, and her laugh lines grow heavier as she puffs out a small chuckle. "It was before we were married.

Before you were even an idea. There was no point in telling you."

"How long were you guys broken up?"

"Technically, three months. That didn't stop us from sneaking around, though." She wiggles her eyebrows wickedly, and the idea of her rebelling from her mom for the sake of love makes me love her that much more.

"You were sleeping with him even though your mom hated him? You hussy!" I place a hand on my chest in mock disbelief.

She rubs her temples at my outburst, but I catch the way her lips twitch in amusement. She continues, "I'll have you know it was more than sex."

I stick my tongue out and mime a finger down my throat in disgust. I'm a hopeless romantic as much as the next person, but I don't need to hear about my parents getting it on. It's not lost on me that I'm telling her about Parker, but it's not a double standard because she's my *mom*.

She fully ignores me. "Anyways, he showed up on your grandma's doorstep one night and demanded that she give him a chance. He whipped up a whole dinner. It was spaghetti, and it was absolutely disgusting, but it made me fall in love with him even more. He was so hell-bent on getting her approval.

"While we ate, he told her that while he respected her opinion, he was going to marry me one day anyway. To this day, it was one of the most romantic things anyone has ever done for me. She appreciated his determination and won her over that day."

Unknowingly, the familiar burn of tears prickles at the corner of my eyes. I look up at the ceiling, attempting to blink them away. I'm beginning to think that this is a serious medical problem because who the hell cries this much? Is there a doctor I can see about this? Maybe it's overactive tear glands.

"The reason I'm telling you this is because there are going to be times when life pulls you apart from the person you love the most. But if you're meant to be together, you'll find your way back to one another. You both were so young when you started dating, and you had so much going on then. More than any early twenty-something should have to deal with. And that's something that I will forever regret. I'm your mom. I'm supposed to make your life easier, not more difficult." She drives away the thought with a snap of her hand and gets back on track.

"Sometimes you just need a little space from one another to realize what you truly want. It might be in your control, and in other instances, it's not. Either way, it doesn't matter. What matters is that life is bringing you back to give you a second chance. If you want it, that is."

"What if I get hurt again? You saw me last time things ended between us. I'm not sure I'd make it through that again," I choke.

"Of course you would. You can make it through a lot more than you realize, sweetheart. I struggled with addiction for three years after your dad passed. There were days that I prayed I wouldn't wake up. I didn't want to spend another day here without him. But here I am, and I'm so happy I'm still around. I've had a front-row seat watching you become the incredible woman you are today, and I wouldn't trade that for the world. I know for a fact that you are so much stronger than you give yourself credit for."

She wipes away a lone tear that escaped down my cheek and then cups my face gently into her hands. "Do you love him?" I silently nod, unable to mutter the words out loud. The minute I do so, the more real it becomes.

"Then I think you know what you need to do."

"I know. Thank you. I love you, and I'm so happy you're here."

"I love you too, Ducky. I'll hop on a plane anytime you need me, okay? Just don't be afraid to come visit little ol' me every now and then, too."

I curl up against her side, wishing I were as small as I was as a child so I could fit into the crook of her arm as I did in the past. Although I may have grown too big for this, she still wraps both of her arms around me and pulls me into a tight embrace, the warmth encompassing me like a cozy sweater pulled over my shoulders on a chilly morning.

I push down my regret for not visiting her since moving here and my fear of telling Parker my true feelings. For now, I want to soak up every minute I can with my mom. Everything else can wait.

"Ooh, turn it up. Carrie's about to meet Aidan for the first time." I break free from her arms, point to the remote that's resting on the arm of the couch next to her, and grab another cupcake. "They should have ended up together," I babble with a mouthful of cake.

"Big was never good enough for her," she agrees. And as we sit there all afternoon, I feel weightless for the first time in months.

24

PARKER

It's been four days since the release party. Four agonizing days. It's not like I was expecting Dylan to profess her love for me back or for us to get together right off the bat. But we've gone four days without contact. My body physically vibrates with the need to text her and see how she's doing, but I stop myself.

We're only a week out from the book tour, which means we'll have to talk about it at some point, but it'd be better for me mentally if that were sooner rather than later. I can't stomach spending two weeks together and having her avoid me at all costs.

I told Blake everything. Of course, he was disappointed that I told her the truth, but he ultimately supported my decision. Especially after I told him that I had gone down on her in the elevator. Let's just say that I was met with some back pats and "atta boys." It was exactly the reaction I'd expect out of him, which is why I wasn't holding my breath in the first place.

"I can help who's next!"

The barista's voice pulls me out of my drifting thoughts. I blink a couple of times, bringing my focus back to her face.

She's looking at me impatiently with her hands on her hips, and a flood of embarrassment runs through me. I mutter an apology, put in an order for a drip coffee, and miraculously find a seat in the packed coffee shop.

When my name is called, I go to grab my drink, only to be stopped by dainty fingers wrapping around my wrist. When I look over to the owner of the hand, my breath catches in my throat, and I immediately grow hot. It's a face that I was never expecting to see again.

"M-Mrs. Jenkins?" I stammer. I thought seeing Dylan walk onto that plane was unbelievable, but seeing Dylan's mom in the city is like seeing the ghost of my failed relationship's past.

"Hi, honey. How many times have I told you to call me Abigail?" Her gaze blinks down at her hand still around my wrists, and she immediately removes it. "Sorry, I just can't believe it's you."

She pulls me into a tight squeeze, and I feel some of the tension I've been holding over these past few days slowly unwind like a thread. Because my parents constantly fought and my mom remarried when I was in high school, I felt invisible most of the time–like a phantom of a person in my own home.

When Dylan and I started dating, we spent a lot of time around her parents–barbecues, camping trips, fishing on the lake, you name it. I knew that my family life was broken, but I hadn't realized just how fractured it had been until I saw what a healthy family looked like.

James and Abigail became like second parents to me, and I mourned the loss of Dylan's dad as if he were my own. I had never had that male father figure in my life once my dad left, and losing the closest thing I'd ever had hit me harder than I had ever expected. I never told her, though. I wanted to be strong enough for both of us.

When I lost Dylan, I also lost a piece of my family that I had grown to love and care about. I entered a world where I had no one, and although it made me the man I am today, I've spent innumerable hours wondering what my life would look like if I had chosen to stay.

I pull away from Mrs. Jenkins, and a wistful comfort washes over me. It's reminiscent of the quietness of an early morning before the city wakes up, peaceful and grounding.

She looks good. No, she looks better than good. She's put some weight on, and I don't feel like I'm hugging a whisper of a soul anymore. She seems revitalized. Full of life. And being near her seems to fill me up with that same rejuvenation that I didn't know I so desperately needed.

"You look amazing. Do you have time to chat for a second?" I ask hopefully.

She glances down at her watch while I fully ignore mine. I don't care if I'm already running behind today. I don't care that Blake's probably going to rip me a new one. I'll take the day off if I have to. Call in sick.

She hesitates, and my stomach nosedives. "I have to catch my flight in a couple of hours, and Dylan took the morning off to spend a little more time together, but I snuck out to grab a coffee. I don't know how you guys sleep in the city. It's so loud." I snort. You could say that again. "But she was asleep when I left, so I've probably got a little time before she notices I'm gone."

Relief settles into my bones, and I gesture at the table where my stuff is resting. "Let's grab a seat." I set my coffee on the table and sit as she does the same across from me. She looks up at me with her emerald eyes and a soft smile that brings me back to my roots, and I almost break down.

"Just in town visiting Dylan?"

"Well, my daughter has done a pretty terrible job of keeping up with me, so I had to take things into my own hands." She takes a sip from her coffee, but I pick up on the twinkle in her eyes that makes them shine brighter.

I huff out a laugh, yet I can't ignore the queasiness that rolls through my gut. Did Dylan tell her what happened? The two have always been closer than any mother and daughter I've seen, so the chances are high. I fiddle with the sleeve of my coffee cup at the thought.

She cocks her head to the side, knitting her brows together. "If you're wondering if she told me what happened last week, the answer is yes." She reads me like a book, and I curse under my breath. Damn, she's good.

She takes another swig of her drink and then sets it down, placing a hand on one of my own in a nurturing manner. "Look, you two are adults. I'm not here to tell you what you should and should not do. I'm also not going to betray my daughter's trust and tell you how she's feeling. What I will tell you, though, is what I told her." The thrum of the coffee shop chatter goes silent in my mind as I concentrate on the woman in front of me.

"James was the love of my life, and my time with him ended far earlier than I had ever hoped. If it were up to me, he'd still be alive and we'd be living out our forever together. But I wasn't that fortunate. And if there's one thing his death taught me, it's that life's short. We only get one shot, and we don't know when our time is up. If you have feelings for someone, you owe it to both of you to make those feelings clear," she remarks quietly.

"If they're reciprocated," she gives me an elusive wink before schooling her face back into a tender yet neutral expression, "do something about it. Don't waste time questioning whether or not it's right or wrong. Follow your heart."

I sit at a loss for words, trying to process her advice. Instead of responding like a normal person, all that comes out is, "How did you become so wise?"

She grins triumphantly. "I've seen some shit in my years.

You don't go through what I've gone through without learning a thing or two."

"I could use this guidance more often. I might fuck up a lot less."

"Unfortunately, fucking up is an essential human experience. Look, you know you're like a son to me. I have so much love for you, and I want to see you and Dylan happy. Whether that's together or not is entirely up to you two. But I know this will work out exactly the way that it's supposed to. You both just need to be honest with yourselves."

She pats me on the arm once again and looks at her watch. "I should probably get going. I don't want Dylan to notice that I'm missing. Plus, her coffee's going to get watered down." She motions to Dylan's iced coffee–an iced vanilla latte, half sweet, I presume–before picking it up along with her own and standing to leave.

"This may make me a traitor, but don't be a stranger, okay?" She stands, tucking her chair into the table, and extends her arms out to me.

"I won't." I accept the hug, holding onto her as tight as I can. The embrace is a safe haven, and I try not to let my jealousy manifest. I'm grateful for how my life turned out, but running into her is a reminder of the absence of a strong family foundation.

While I could have let it turn me bitter, I like to think that I'm using it to fuel my fire and create something strong for myself later in life. That's why I've avoided dating and why the breakup with Olivia hit me harder than expected.

I didn't experience a strong relationship growing up, but Abigail and James changed my perspective. They were proof that not every relationship had to end in a hideous divorce, and you didn't have to scream at your kids to get your point across. They were loving, affectionate, and attentive. I aspired to have a family like theirs one day. I could only hope that Dylan would be there, too.

"Good to see you." She grins and heads toward the door. I sit back down and stare at my coffee, lost in my head.

She's right. Life's too short. I may not be able to make Dylan love me, but I sure as hell can show her just how much she means to me, and I hope that it's enough.

25

DYLAN

Ever since my mom left, all I can do is replay her advice in my head. I know that she's right. I've been lying to myself about my feelings for Parker, and if there was a time to run into it full force, it would be now. Especially now that I know he feels the same. Yet I can't bring myself to say the three words back to him. In fact, I've done an excellent job of avoiding him.

Until today.

We leave for the book tour tomorrow, and I know we need to have a conversation before we go, so I invited him over. Which is why I am now pacing through my apartment like a mad woman. I've already had to change my shirt and reapply deodorant three times.

I ended up in an oversized vintage band tee that I've had for years and leggings. The clothes are casual, but that didn't stop me from doing my hair and putting on a full face of makeup. I didn't want to look like I was trying too hard, but I also didn't want to look like a bum. Girlhood at its finest.

Amelia is out grabbing a drink with the man of the week, so I have the apartment to myself, thank god. The last thing I need is her adding to my stress. I know I'd never hear the end of it if she saw just how nervous I am right now. She's been asking me about Parker at least twice a week, and I can only distract her for so long.

I glance around the apartment, making sure nothing is out of place. I may or may not have spent the last three hours deep cleaning every inch. Candles are burning, quiet background music is playing, and I saged the place earlier. I'm not taking any chances–I need all the good energy I can get.

I pace up and down the living room, feeling jittery. I know some (okay, most) of it has to do with seeing Parker, but that third cup of coffee I had this morning definitely isn't helping either. I close my eyes, take a deep inhale, and try to talk myself off a ledge.

You've been working with him for months. This is no different.

There's a knock at the door, and my heart lurches in my chest at the sound. I give myself a couple of gentle slaps on the face to pull it together. It's not like we have the entire apartment to ourselves. Oh, that's right. We do. And we clearly have some unfinished business. The thought of the elevator makes the room feel like a sauna, and I curse myself for not opening a window to get better airflow in here.

I plaster a smile on my face, open the door, and have to clutch it tightly when I see Parker looking undeniably delectable on the other side. He's dressed casually in a black sweatshirt and matching black sweatpants, socks, and Birkenstock clogs. That's not what makes my breath catch, though.

It's the distressed baseball hat he's finished the outfit off with. His hair, which is the longest I've seen it, is peeking out at the bottom. The length has brought out his natural curls, and my fingers twitch with the urge to run a hand through them.

"Hi," I whisper when I stop drooling.

"Hi," He replies in a hushed tone, a grin pulling on his lips.

"Come on in."

I move out of the doorway and gesture inside. As soon as he walks past, I mouth a quick "oh my god" to myself before I make my way into the kitchen. "Can I get you anything to drink? Water? Tea? Coffee? I also have snacks if you're hungry. I just went grocery shopping yesterday, so I've got a little bit of everything..." my voice falters. I nibble on the inside of my cheek to quiet my nervous rambling.

His lips tremble with the urge to laugh, clearly entertained by my prattling. "Coffee would be great if you don't mind."

He sits down at one of our bar stools, watching me intently.

"Black with a splash of creamer?"

Yes, I still remember his order. I know a person can change, but if I had to take a stab in the dark, he's still drinking the same thing he always did. Parker's a man who appreciates a routine. Whenever we went out to eat, I knew his order before he did. He'd contemplate switching it up but never would, no matter how much time he spent studying the menu. He liked what he liked, and I couldn't fault him for it. I found it endearing.

"Am I that predictable?"

He lets out a rugged chuckle, and it's like a shot of espresso straight to the heart. The sound energizes me far more than the coffee I consumed earlier, and all I can think about is how I want to do everything I can to keep him laughing.

"Some things just never change."

I load the ground coffee beans into my machine and grab the creamer from my fridge while it brews. Meanwhile, I can feel his eyes burning holes into my back the entire time. I fight the need to turn around and make eye contact with him. The more natural I act, the less weird this will be, I remind myself.

I know that we're going to have to talk about the release party, but bringing attention to it makes it real, and that terrifies me. But I know that not mentioning it will only make things more difficult between us–especially now that we're about to be on the road together for a couple of weeks.

I add a splash of creamer to the coffee and slide the mug in his direction.

"Look-"

"We should probably-" I start.

We both speak over one another, and there's something about it that unfurls the ball of anxiety at my chest. He may have a tough exterior, but there's a good chance he's feeling the same way I am, and that brings me a sense of comfort.

"You go ahead," I push on as I start making a coffee for myself. I need something to do with my hands before I spontaneously combust. We're just going to pretend that the other cups that I had this morning don't count and pray that I don't go into cardiac arrest–from both the caffeine and this conversation.

"We should talk about it," he encourages gently, his hands cupped around his mug. It's the beginning of May, and although I'd do anything to wear my sundresses and soak up afternoons strolling in the park, today is gloomy. The cold rain that's been on and off all morning matches the chill currently running down my spine.

I let the warmth of my coffee heat up my insides as I try to keep my hands steady. I lean back against the kitchen counter and watch Parker as he runs a finger up and down the handle of the cup. The movement is slight, yet I can't tear my eyes away from his hands while he does it. I dream about being on the receiving end of those soft touches. How would he touch me if I were to take him to the bedroom right now?

"If we have to," I joke, trying to keep the mood light. I need a distraction, or I'm going to pounce on him in about five seconds.

He doesn't take the bait.

"How are you feeling?"

"Confused. Scared. Unsure," I answer honestly.

"If it makes you feel any better, I feel the same way." He pushes out of his chair and saunters over to me. "Can I hold you, Dyl?" His voice is barely detectable, and I forget about my now hardly-touched mug sitting on the counter. I answer with a small tuck of my chin.

In an instant, his arms are around me, pulling me into his chest. Just like the day of the photoshoot, his closeness feels like stepping back into a dream I never want to wake up from. I close my eyes and take a deep inhale. The combination of coffee and musk from his cologne mixes together, and I get carried away by the intoxicating smell.

"I never got the chance to apologize. I'm sorry that I lied, I'm sorry that I listened to Blake, and I'm sorry that I didn't tell you how I was feeling sooner. I wanted to give you space, but I knew that if I didn't tell you soon, I would lose my mind." He begins to trace small circles on my lower back under my shirt. "Drunk off tequila wasn't exactly how I envisioned that conversation going." He whispers into my hair, and my skin breaks out into gooseflesh.

It takes all of my willpower to pull away enough to look up at him. His typical calm gaze has been replaced with a wariness that tugs at my heartstrings. These past couple of weeks have left me more confused than ever, but I know his intentions were pure, and seeing him unsure of how to react around me makes me nauseous.

We've gone from being the loves of one another's lives to strangers to a place of the unknown, tip-toeing around each other.

Before I can respond to his apology, his eyes fall down to my shirt. "Did you wear that on purpose?" The lump of his Adam's apple is visible, and his voice is strained.

I look down at my worn, ratty Neil Young shirt, and it hits me like a ton of bricks. *Shit.* How could I have possibly forgotten? I didn't even think about it when I got dressed this morning. It would explain why it was shoved into the back corner of my closet shelf. I just figured it had gotten wadded up back there over the past few months.

It used to be his.

He gave it to me after declaring that *Harvest Moon* was our song. I know it sounds cliche, but that memory is one that I'll always cherish... or it was. In all of the chaos that has been going on lately, I had completely forgotten about that night.

We had been dating for eight months, and we had spent all of our summer nights sitting on the dock on the lake. The dock was a short ten-minute walk from my backyard, and we'd sneak away there every night to get some alone time and stargaze. It became our unofficial make-out spot. On one or two occasions, there may have also been more than making out, but I don't need to go down that road of thought right now.

We had just finished making s'mores over a bonfire when we walked to the dock to watch a meteor shower that was supposed to be visible that night. We lied facing the sky, with my phone playing music quietly as the stars danced in the sky.

Parker grabbed my phone unbeknownst to me, put on Neil Young, and grabbed my hand, pulling me up against him. Under the country moon, which stained the night a shade of crimson, we swayed wordlessly to the music. It was something out of a romance movie, and I'll never forget the butterflies that fluttered in my gut.

We didn't want the moment to end, so we put the song on repeat and stayed out there for over an hour, the meteor shower completely forgotten. Around midnight, when we finally pulled ourselves away from one another, he took his shirt–the very one I'm currently wearing–off and handed it to me. Something to always remember him by, he told me.

I haven't listened to the song since. Whenever it came on the radio, my instinct was to change it or run the risk of crying.

I've even run out of a store a time or two shortly after the breakup because it was playing, and I couldn't escape it.

I yank myself out of the memory and his arms and clear my throat. "No, I'm sorry. I didn't even realize it. I found it in my closet and realized I hadn't worn it in a while. I just wanted to be comfortable."

He lifts my chin with his thumb, his touch pensive as he outlines the shape of my jaw. "Still love the way that it looks on you."

I step back and beeline it to the couch, forcing myself to put some distance between us. We need to finish the conversation we started, and if I let him keep his hands on me, there's no telling what I'd do.

He lingers in the kitchen, stunned for a beat. I fuss with the fringe of a throw blanket, waiting to see what his next move is. Though I keep my eyes locked on the frayed fabric, I feel his presence sit down on the chair situated parallel to the couch.

"I love you, Parker. I don't think I ever stopped." I shift my gaze out the living room window, knowing damn well that I'll fall apart if I look at him as I say the words that I've been too scared to admit to myself all of these years out loud. "And I don't know what that means for us, but I do know one thing."

I finally gather enough courage to look at him, and he's hiding a smile behind a closed fist. No matter how hard he tries to look serious, I can see the corners of his lips lifting, and he looks brighter than I've seen him look in the months we've been back in each other's lives. I feel that same weight off my shoulders now that everything is on the table.

"What's that?"

"I don't want to do anything to jeopardize this job. We leave tomorrow for the tour, and we've got three more weeks until this project is over. As much as I would love to explore what the future holds for us, I need us to stay professional until it's over."

"I completely understand and respect your decision. I don't

want us to rush into anything. This is a lot to process for both of us," he agrees.

"It is." I pull my knees up to my chest and wrap my arms around my legs. This is going far better than I was expecting.

"I will stay as professional as you need on two conditions."

His demand captures my attention, and my curiosity sends a thrill through my bloodstream. "Yes?"

"The first condition is that you have to go out on a date with me as soon as the book tour is over. We'll have some loose ends to tie up when we're back, but that's a technicality. Your time on Evelyn's campaign will be up. If Katherine tries to assign you any more busy work, you'll let me know immediately, and I will get you taken off it. I've been waiting months to take you out, and I will not be waiting any longer than I have to."

It's my turn to hide my mouth behind my arm, trying not to let him see the goofy grin threatening to take over my face. When I feel like I can control my emotions enough, I put my hands back down on my lap and nod, keeping my lips pursed as if deep in thought. Little does he know this is one of the easiest yeses of my life.

"Deal. What's the second condition?"

"Take off your shirt." He leans forward in the chair and rests his elbows on his knees. The power in his command makes me clench my thighs together, yet the request throws me off kilter.

"Excuse me?" I sputter.

"If you're going to make me wait, I'd like my shirt back," he prods.

"Oh," I stumble over my words, wholly puzzled by where this is coming from. I'm taken aback by the abruptness, but a bigger part of me is dying to undress for him. I can see the longing in his stare, and I thirst to find out what he would do if I let him have his way with me.

"I can go change into something if you'll give me a second."

I point to my bedroom door behind him. He doesn't break his focus on me.

"No, I'd like it right now."

My cheeks heat, and a pool of desire builds in my core. I know what game he's trying to get at–we have always loved games. And I'm not going to let him win this one. He thinks I don't have the balls to change in front of him, but I'll take any opportunity I can get to see him come undone. And I know that stripping down will do just that.

Without saying another word, I grab the bottom of my–or should I say his–shirt and lift it over my head, very grateful that I wore one of my cute bras today. I'm left standing in my lace black bra that makes the girls look great, if I say so myself, as I toss it over to him. It lands on his lap, and he quickly looks down to where it landed before his eyes whip back over to me.

His gaze skims down my body, and despite being across the room, the intensity of his look feels as if he were up against me, roaming his hands over my bare torso. I put on a strong face and place a hand on my hip.

"Happy?"

"Very." He smirks and stands, throwing the t-shirt over his shoulder. His eyes remain trained on my body, but I don't allow myself to shy away.

I find myself being pulled toward him like a magnet, and I have to remind myself to keep my feet planted firmly right where I am before I do something about the sexual tension that's making the hair on my arms stand up.

"Glad that we had this conversation. Now that I know where you stand, I need to pack. We have an early flight tomorrow."

"You're such an ass sometimes."

"An ass that you love." He winks and strides toward the front door. "I'll see you at the airport!"

And with that, he's gone, leaving me topless and fuming in my living room.

26

DYLAN

The first half of the tour has exceeded my expectations. After reading Evelyn's book for the first time, there was no doubt in my mind that she's extremely talented. But seeing the turnout thanks to the marketing that we've done so far has been incredible.

Although it's not the biggest book tour known to man, the audience that Evelyn charmed on social media has been enough to sell out of the copies that we brought along with us every night. Her fans have genuinely felt like her friends, and I've already connected with many of them on social media.

It's nights like those that make me thankful for what I do. I know that marketing isn't a life-saving career. Social media gets a bad rap because we're always so connected all the time, but I'm watching someone's dream come to life right before my eyes because of it, and that's something that I'll never get over. Where else can you connect with people from all over the world?

In a world so big, it makes me feel like I'm a part of something worthwhile–even if it is just creating content calendars and scheduling posts. They have a much bigger effect on people like Evelyn, who are trying to chase the dreams they've always envisioned for themselves.

Parker's also a man of his word and has been the definition of a gentleman the entire time we've been out. Of course, there have been stolen glances and the brushing of hands every now and then, but he's kept his hands and lips to himself the entire time.

That hasn't stopped me from touching myself at the thought of what it would be like to sneak into his hotel room every single night. To save some money, we've been staying in some two to three-star hotels, and the lack of warm water has been a saving grace for my hormones. I need a cold shower every time I'm around him, and it's getting progressively harder to keep my own word.

I swear, every time my head hits my pillow, all I can think about is him coaxing me through my almost orgasm on that elevator. And when I'm not thinking about that, I'm daydreaming about how he ordered me to take my shirt off shortly after I finally admitted that I loved him back. I should've been appalled, yet I'm not sure I've ever been more turned on in my life. I'm so wound up that I feel like I'm going to snap any second.

Luckily, we had two days off of the tour, and our last stop before our small break was New Jersey, so I got to spend time at home and take a much-needed break from the tension.

I spent the past two days sleeping, trying to unwind as best as I could before we had to leave again. Although book tours might not seem like a high-stakes event, I've been going nonstop for the past week. Between that and the horny stupor I've been in, I haven't gotten a full-night's rest since we left.

Now, I'm gearing up to get back on the road and head to the airport to do it all over again.

I run through a mental checklist, making sure I have everything I need for another week of living out of a suitcase.

Clothes, check. Pajamas, check. Toothbrush, check. Vibrator, without a doubt, check.

"You all set to go?" Amelia pops her head out of her bedroom, leaning on the frame of her door. I rummage through my purse to make sure my license, wallet, and phone are in there. I don't know what it is, but every single time I travel, I feel like I'm forgetting something. I know I'm not. I have a checklist on my phone that I run through every time I go out. My type A personality would never let me just raw dog it.

"I think so!" I push my bag onto my shoulder, suddenly hit with a ripple of déjà vu as I think about the flight out here when I was forced to sit next to Parker after years of no contact. Little did I know that my life was about to completely change in more ways than I could've ever imagined.

Amelia prances over and wraps her arms around my shoulders, pulling me in for a hug. "Have fun. Be safe. Be sure to wear a condom!" She pulls away with a knowing sneer on her face.

"I'm not going to be sleeping with him, Mia," I protest, although I'm not even sure I'm convinced that's true.

"Whatever you say. I expect a full report when you get back! Tally up the orgasms, and leave no detail untouched, please, and thank you."

I don't dignify that with a response. Instead, I give her one last squeeze and call a car to take me to the airport.

❋ ❋ ❋ ❋ ❋

As I'm in line for TSA with Parker, my phone vibrates with a call. It's an unknown number, and although I don't typically answer those, an unknown part of me feels like this could be important, so I pick it up anyway.

I eye the line for security, feeling confident that I can get this call over with before I have to put all of my electronics in a bin. Yes, I know. It's the twenty-first century, and I don't have TSA precheck. I really need to pony up and get it, especially now that I'm traveling from time to time for work. I want to be as efficient as possible. Parker, being the saint he is, waits with me in the treacherously long lines despite having it himself.

"Hello?" I pick up.

"Hi, is Miss Jenkins there?" The voice on the other end of the line is sugary sweet, as if it belongs to a teenage girl.

"This is she. How can I help you?" I hold the phone to my ear with my shoulder while I unpack my laptop from my backpack.

"Hello, this is Sophia from Love and Lit."

Love and Lit, a small family-owned bookstore in Charleston, is our first stop on this second leg of the tour. I've never seen it in person, but the minute I saw photos on Instagram, I knew I wanted to see if I could make it happen for this tour. The shop's facade is baby pink, and the interior is filled with floor-to-ceiling shelves full of romance books. There's even an attached cafe that features coffee drinks named after famous books and characters.

It's my paradise, and if I wasn't working, I'd be spending too much time and money there.

"Hi Sophia, what can I do for you?"

"I'm calling because there seems to be some kind of mix-up. We received the stock from Blue Bird, and it appears we're short on books. We only have about half of what we ordered." Her voice is timid, like she's afraid to break the bad news to me.

I pull the phone away from my ear so she can't hear me mutter "fuck" a little too loudly. At any other airport, this slip-up would earn me stares from other airport goers, but in New York City, everyone is so wrapped up in their own world that no one bats an eye, which I'm very grateful for at this moment.

"Thank you so much for bringing this to my attention," I say calmly, commanding my voice to stay as steady as possible. I don't want to alarm this poor girl. "Do you mind if I talk with her publishers and call you back once I've got this sorted?"

"Of course! I'll talk with you soon."

I hang up and look over to Parker, who's been quizzically staring at me with an arched brow since my outburst.

"Everything okay?"

"No. We don't have enough stock for the signing tomorrow. They only have about half of the books that were promised, and the tickets to the event are already sold out." Panic claws at my throat, and I struggle to keep it at bay. I knew this tour had been too good to be true. It was only a matter of time before something went wrong.

"Shit, okay. Don't panic. We can fix this."

"How are we going to fix this? As soon as Katherine finds out, my head is going to be on the chopping block! And the worst part is it's not even my fault." My vision grows blurry around the edges, and the lump in my throat makes breathing normally a challenging task. I rush out of line and find the nearest bench to sit down to get my bearings together.

I lean forward and place my hands on my knees, my head in between my legs, trying to get control of my breathing. I haven't had an anxiety attack in years, and the oncoming fit does little to soothe my mind.

Once started, it feels impossible to slow my brain down from thinking about the worst-case scenarios. Katherine's been waiting for a reason to fire me. All it takes is one fuck up, and I'm out of a job.

Without looking up from between my legs, I feel a whisper of a touch on my lower back. The heat of Parker sitting next to me has me on high alert, and it does wonders to distract me from the anxiety that's tearing through me like a serrated knife.

I focus on his towering form, paying extra close attention to his sneakers–counting each one of his laces over and over, giving my brain something else to focus on other than the impending doom of Katherine's wrath. I close my eyes, leaning into Parker's hands, which are tracing doodles on my back. As my breathing steadies, his touch remains, and I stay down for a beat longer than needed, cherishing the contact as much as possible.

"That's it. It's all going to be okay. Take one more deep breath for me, Lucky." His voice is compassionate, but it's the nickname he lets slip that stops me in my tracks, sidetracking me entirely. I come up for air, brushing a damp piece of hair off my sweaty face. He's looking at me so earnestly that my breath catches in my throat for an entirely different reason.

He doesn't give me time to question him about the blunder before he carries on, "I think we have some extra copies at the office. I can swing by and pick them up. Nobody has to know."

I check my watch for the time. Our flight boards in forty minutes.

As someone who's typically at the airport at least two hours early–yet another trait of my type A personality–I was already nervous about being here this late in the first place. Parker was the one who insisted it was no big deal. Look at where that got us.

"We don't have time to go get them. We board soon. You'll miss your flight." I look at him disbelievingly. My minor anxiety attack set us back fifteen minutes, and we have no time to spare, contrary to his indifference.

He nonchalantly shrugs, and despite my growing concern that we're absolutely screwed, I admire the way he can stay calm under pressure. I, on the other hand, feel like I'm seconds away from losing my fucking mind....again.

"I can get a rental car and meet you there. I'll just drive through the night."

"I'm not letting you do a twelve-hour drive by yourself. That sounds like my own personal nightmare."

"You know how much I love road trips. I'll be fine. But I appreciate the concern." He winks at me and stands. He reaches his hand out to me to help me up, and I reluctantly take it. I grab my backpack that I tossed onto the floor mid-panic and throw it back over my shoulder, the weight dulling the loss of Parker's hand.

"I don't care how much you love it. It's dangerous. At this rate, you won't get there until at least 2 AM." I reply frankly.

"Is this your way of saying you care about me and my safety?" he dares.

The haughtiness of his question drives me crazy, but unfortunately, he's not wrong. I do care, and I'll do anything to get some uninterrupted time with him. Not that he needs to know that.

"Don't read into it too much. I just don't want you to be alone. Besides, you're saving my ass by doing this." I grab my suitcase and roll it closer to me. "Even though this is your fault in the first place," I mutter under my breath.

He holds a hand up to his ear as if he didn't hear what I said. "What was that?"

"Nothing. Let's just go get this rental car," I concede.

He's beaming as he takes my suitcase from me and pushes it alongside his. Why does he have to be so damn considerate? I brush aside the way it makes me weak in the knees. I'll deal with that when I'm at the hotel and can access the toys I brought.

"If you say so. Dibs on the music choice!" Parker calls out as he skips down the airport hallway.

27

PARKER

I look down at the clock of our rented minivan–the only car available at such short notice—which reads 12:30. The numbers look cloudy, and the drive is finally weighing down on me. According to the maps, we're only a little over an hour away from the hotel, and I thank any and all deities that this is almost over.

We stopped at a gas station a few hours ago to use the restroom, and I indulged in some cheap, sickeningly sweet coffee in hopes that it would help keep me up, but the effects of the caffeine weren't as potent as I was hoping, and I'm fading fast. I lean over the steering wheel, stretching out my lower back, which is now cramping up. It does little to alleviate me from the pain, but it's better than nothing.

I'd love to blast music to help keep me awake while we drive down the nearly empty highway, but I keep it at a low hum so I don't disturb Dylan, who's been sleeping in the passenger seat for the past half an hour. After her anxiety attack this morning at the airport, I want her to get all of the rest she can get.

I did allow her to drive this morning because I knew if I put up too much of a fight, we were never going to get anywhere.

We're both too stubborn for our own good, and my number one priority was getting us there in one piece–even if it meant reluctantly letting her shoulder some of the burden of driving. I'd rather her drive during the daytime than fight off sleep this late at night, anyway.

The passing towns, which are few and far between, fill the car with a soft glow, and I take advantage of the light to cast glances at Dylan. I've always found her magnificent, but there's something about watching her serenely sleep after such a difficult day. Seeing her find enough peace to shut her mind off, even if it's just for a short stint.

Throughout college, Dylan was always the strong one in our relationship. Although my parents separated at a fairly young age, the repercussions of their divorce took a toll on me far more than I'd ever imagined. I was on the receiving end of countless calls from my mom, trying to coerce me into having a relationship with my stepfather after years of failure. She'd beg me to come home when I didn't have class, and although the guilt ate me alive, I couldn't bring myself to visit.

I tried to play my part in the "big, happy family" image she painted to the outside world as a teenager. But the constant comparison to my step-siblings from him was more than I could manage. Once I left for college, I felt like I could catch my breath. I didn't have to pretend anymore.

Unsurprisingly, the phone calls with my mom always ended in fights, and I struggled to cope with the never-ending quarreling. Eventually, we stopped speaking altogether. She was tired of me not fitting into the mold that she had made, and I was tired of feeling like I wasn't good enough even though I had so much going for myself.

That's when Dylan became my safe space.

It wasn't until James passed away that she became the one that grappled with anxiety. I remember the first time she had a breakdown like it was yesterday. My fighter had become so troubled right before my eyes, and I didn't know how to handle it. I knew from then on that I was going to do everything I could to ease the pain I knew she was feeling.

I've never told her this, but after her first episode, I went to our college library and began researching what to do to help ease anxiety attacks. I spent hours reading and scouring the internet to find anything and everything I could to help. It was at that moment that I knew I needed to become the strong one for us.

Even though I had to swallow my own pain, I don't regret a thing. Being there for Dylan in any capacity made me feel like I had a purpose in life. I was no longer the man who wouldn't live up to my parent's high expectations. I was the man who would do anything to see the love of his life thrive.

The minute I saw her fall to pieces at the airport, I was taken back to the days she broke down in my arms. It served as a reminder that, even in all of those years apart, she still struggles. It made me feel hopeless–like I had abandoned her all those years ago. All I wanted to do was pull her into my arms and comfort her the way I used to.

Of course, I just had to let the old nickname slip. I caught the way her eyes flared when I said it. It wasn't intentional—just an old habit. I had been so careful not to use it since she's come back into my life, but now that it was out there, it felt so damn good. It felt like the most natural thing in the world. Like I was born with the sole purpose to utter the name.

As strong as I pretended to be through the entire thing, I wasn't secure enough to hear her response, so I kept speaking so she couldn't get a word in. It's easier for me to act like nothing happened than to hear her tell me she never wants to hear that nickname again. We've both admitted that we're still in love with one another, but I can't dive off the deep end right away. I need to have some semblance of patience, which is proving to be much easier said than done.

I look at her again, and her eyelashes flutter slightly as she sleeps, and I wonder what she's dreaming about. A small part of me hopes it's about us—the possibility of a future for us together.

Does she think about me the way I think about her? I don't have the courage to admit it, but she consumes my every waking thought, and I never want it to stop. I let the thought devour me as the quiet beat of *Harvest Moon* (which has been playing on repeat since the minute I knew she was asleep) acts as the background soundtrack of my pathetic hopes and wishes.

We have a few more days left of this tour, and I'm eagerly awaiting the day when I can make her mine again–for good this time. I already know exactly how I'm going to ask her to be my girlfriend again. Fuck, even the term girlfriend doesn't seem like enough. I want more. I want it all. Marriage. Babies. Traveling the world together. Sunday morning coffee dates. Game nights. Trips to the neighborhood wine bar. I want everything I can get with her.

I never thought I'd get the chance to ask her to be mine again, but I always dreamed of it anyway in case life threw me a bone. I guess some of my hopes and dreams weren't too pitiful.

I keep my eyes on the road as I reach over and softly tuck a flyaway strand of hair behind her ear. It's purely selfish, allowing me to see the radiance of her pale skin while she sleeps.

I don't realize how far my mind has wandered until we turn into the hotel parking lot in what feels like a split second, and Dylan shifts, slowly blinking the sleep out of her eyes as she comes to.

"Are we here?" Her voice is raspy, and I hate how my body responds. I shift in my seat, begging my dick to stand down until I can make it to my room. I'm exhausted, but I'm also restless and in need of a release before I can fall asleep. That's been the case every single night of this tour. Little does Dylan know, thanks to the paper-thin walls of the low-cost hotels we've been crashing at, I can hear her also chasing her release every night. My self-discipline is virtually non-existent.

I pull the car up near the lobby and put it into park.

"Yeah. Have a nice nap?"

She stretches, reaching her arms out to touch the roof of the car. Her shirt slides up her body, and I force myself to look out the window to avoid getting a hard-on. Just a little longer.

One week, I remind myself. Only one more week until I can act on my feelings. My patience is wearing thin.

28

DYLAN

We pull into the hotel around 1:45 in the morning, and I'm so tired that I'm delirious. I feel the exhaustion threatening to pull me down, and my legs feel like cinder blocks. Despite my short nap, I'm feeling the decision to drive deep in my bones.

I was in charge of the first half of the drive in spite of my resistance. I was always planning on driving, but I didn't want Parker to drive the later shift. I've been a night owl for as long as I can remember, and there's something about driving late at night that I've always found therapeutic.

Driving on vacant highways, not a car in sight, the stars and moon acting as the only illumination. It's a reminder that we're a part of something much bigger than our minds will ever be able to understand.

After living in the city for months, the late-night drive felt like returning to my roots in Woodland Heights, where I'd always take the family truck out late at night to clear my head–especially after losing my dad.

Parker refused, saying, and I quote, "Your safety is my top priority. I'd feel a lot better making that drive." How was I supposed to argue when he was being so damn cute and protective? I'm just a girl, and I will never turn down chivalry.

I grab Parker's bag and hand it to him before closing the trunk. Just the idea of rolling this bag the short distance from the parking lot into the lobby makes my knees nearly buckle. I need to be horizontal ASAP.

"Got everything?" I ask.

Parker is visually worn down, his typically bright eyes accompanied by dark bags. However, his signature grin is still plastered on his face, albeit a little weary.

"Yes. Let's check in and get to bed already," he begs.

I salute him in agreement, lock the car, and head into the hotel lobby. By the time we get our room keys and we're on the elevator, I'm barely standing. I use the walls to help hold me up, though it doesn't take much because my mind runs a mile a minute thinking about the last time we were in a confined space like this, and I suddenly feel a burst of energy cut through my fatigue.

My pulse pounds under my skin, and a buzzing current fills the air. It's so electrically charged that I can practically taste it on my tongue. I stare at the ceiling, unable to make eye contact with him on the off chance that he's also thinking back to our last elevator experience together.

"I'll meet you in the lobby around 10?" I question.

"Why don't we plan for 9:30. Give us enough time to find some coffee. I have a feeling we're going to need it after today."

I snort out a small giggle and nod as the elevator doors open. He goes to leave but turns to face me at the last second, holding onto the elevator frame to prevent the doors from crushing him.

"Thank you for driving with me. You were right. That drive would've been miserable without you. I'll see you in the morning. Hope you sleep well," he says groggily.

"Of course. Sleep well," I reply sweetly, desperate to escape this metal death box. If I have to stay in here any longer, I think I may explode.

When the doors close, I let out a deep exhale, the room immediately feeling lighter now that I'm free from the sexual tension crushing me with its heavy foot. I just have to get through one more week, and then I can jump his bones the way I've been dreaming about since the release party.

I know that I'm the one who said I wanted to keep things professional, but my self-control is scarcely hanging on. We've been sharing hotel room walls for the past week, and it's taken everything in me not to go next door to succumb to my needs. I can only imagine he's heard me taking things into my own hands, thanks to the thinness.

The close proximity of the elevator ride up now has me wide awake, and I internally groan to myself, knowing damn well that I'm going to have to...let off some steam (again) before I can finally sleep for the night.

I get off the elevator and find my room. Once I enter, I place my stuff down, collapse into bed, and throw my arms over my face. Laying down in an uncomfortable hotel bed has never felt better. Rather than unpacking, I grab my laptop out of my backpack. I kickstart it and try to pull up the internet, but I realize the front desk receptionist never gave us the WiFi password.

As much as I want to go to sleep, I know that no matter how hard I try, I'm not going to be able to pass out without a movie on. Yes, I am one of those people who needs background noise to fall asleep. No, I don't need to hear about how unhealthy of a habit it is.

I would watch something on the TV, except our rooms don't have televisions. I curse the company for being so cheap.

I heave myself out of the bed, swiftly run downstairs, and find it written on a poorly printed, faded piece of paper. Thank god I don't have to socialize with the new front desk receptionist, who has just started her shift and clearly has no interest in helping me, considering she doesn't even glance in my direction as I approach the desk.

I return to my room, finally ready to unwind for the night. Except for when I go to unlock the door, the keypad flashes red. I sigh and try again. And again. And again. Only to be met with the same red lights acting as a blinking reminder that I'm so close to being in a bed, yet not close enough.

I drag myself back toward the elevator one last time. This is the last thing I need after spending my entire day pent up in the car with the love of my life who I can't show my feelings for. Okay, I put those restrictions on myself, but that's neither here nor there.

I press the button down to the lobby and slouch against the elevator walls. It's going to be a while before I can get on one of these things again without thinking about the way that Parker guided me through the...experience.

When I get to the lobby, it's still eerily quiet, though considering it's the middle of the night when most sane humans are sleeping, this doesn't come as a surprise. The unbothered front desk receptionist is still scrolling on her phone and barely glances up in my direction when I get to the desk.

I clear my throat, trying to get her attention without being too pushy. When she doesn't look at me, I cough a little louder. This time, she peeks up, a distinct look of contempt on her face. It's apparent she's annoyed that I'm here. *You and me both, honey.*

"Can I help you?" she drones.

"Sorry to bother you. I came down a second ago to get the WiFi password, and when I went back up and tried to get into my room, my room key didn't seem to be working." I place it gently on the counter, giving her the softest smile I can muster. I've worked enough customer service roles to know I need her on my side to solve this as soon as possible.

She takes it off the counter without a word and scans it. Her eyebrows knit together in confusion, and I brace myself for the bad news I already know is on the way because that's just how my luck seems to be swaying these days.

"The key is programmed correctly."

She doesn't continue, leaving me unable to articulate a single thought. At this point, I'm about to sleep on the dated, lumpy hotel lobby couch. I don't have the energy to fight her, so I stand there silently, willing her to keep talking.

She eventually says, "It must be an issue with the door. We're going to have to send a technician up there to take a look at it."

I sag against the front desk in relief and press my palms to my eyes. Okay, it could be worse. Sure, it's annoying that it will be a minute before I can climb into bed, but I'm just happy they can fix it.

"Unfortunately, maintenance is gone for the night, so you'll have to wait until the morning." She pops a bubble with her gum, and I grind my molars at the sound.

She's entirely unfazed that I'm shit out of luck after one of the longest days of my life–not that she knows the hell I've been through. I don't expect much, but *some* sympathy would be nice.

"Is there another room I can use for the night while I wait? I'd really love to get some sleep. I've been driving all day and just need a bed." I plead. Maybe giving her a little back story will stir up the compassion that she must have–even if it is buried very, *very* deep.

She purses her lips, visually uninterested in my pleas. "No, I'm sorry. We're completely booked up for the night."

I'm seconds away from snapping, but I take a couple of deep breaths and remind myself to do some mental meditations. It's not like it's this–very uncooperative–girl's fault that I can't get into my room. My yelling at her will only make her even more unhelpful, so I wolf down the urge to lay into her. I need to be productive.

"Would you be able to call surrounding hotels to see if they have any availability?" I ask kindly.

"No, sorry. You're more than welcome to, though."

Without giving me another second, she looks back down to her phone, clearly scrolling through social media right in front of my face. I refuse to let some early twenty-something-year-old get to me.

I clench my fists, count to twenty, and then head back toward the elevator. I'm not about to spend hours calling nearby hotels, which leaves me only one option.

After a nerve-wracking elevator ride to the third floor, I silently rap on room 305's door with a wince.

The door swings open seconds later to reveal a very disheveled Parker, wearing nothing but a plain white t-shirt and boxer briefs. I keep my eyes latched on his face, not trusting myself to look any further south. I just calmed down. I don't need to be getting riled up when I have to share a room with him. That leads to poor decisions.

"Dylan?" He looks at me through squinted eyes.

Here goes nothing.

29

DYLAN

I give him a pathetic little wave. "Hi, I'm so sorry to wake you up. Is it alright if I come in for a second?" My voice comes out more timid than expected, and I force my shoulder blades together and stand with confidence.

"Yeah, of course."

He moves to the side, holding the door open for me. I glance around the room, noting that he wasted no time unpacking. It's one of the many differences we have. I will forever live out of a suitcase and take two weeks to do laundry once a trip is over while he unpacks, washes his clothes, and steam presses them as soon as he's back. I typically try to keep my opinions to myself, but it's honestly crazy behavior.

"Everything okay?" he asks, sitting on the edge of his unmade bed.

"Yeah." I rub the back of my neck, bracing myself while I rock back and forth on my heels to ease the tingling in my legs. "I went down to the lobby to get the WiFi password, but when I came back, my key card wasn't working. Maintenance can't come fix it until the morning, so I'm kind of stranded."

"Fuck, I'm sorry. What time is it?"

I look down at my phone, which I thankfully brought with me. The battery is also full, thanks to being charged for twelve hours on the drive. It's a small win that I can celebrate when I'm not about to ask Parker to share a room with me.

"Two thirty. I'm so sorry to bother you. I didn't know where else to go. The hotel is full, and I didn't want to spend the rest of my night calling around trying to find somewhere else with occupancy."

"Don't apologize. Of course you can stay in here. I'll sleep on the pull-out couch. You take the bed."

"No, I don't want to put you out. I'm the one coming in and disrupting everything. I'll take the couch. You keep the bed and pretend I'm not even here," I reply meekly.

"As much as I'd like to, that's impossible. You're taking the bed. I'm taking the couch. End of discussion." His voice is firm, and I hate the way my body betrays me at the sound of it. I discreetly cross one leg over the other and clasp my hands behind my back.

He glances down at my outfit. For whatever reason, I chose today, of all days, to wear jeans and a sweater. In my defense, our flight was only supposed to be a couple of hours. Plus, while it may be impractical, I enjoy dressing cute for flights. That way, I can step off the plane and hit the town (and by, that I mean find the closest local coffee shop and bookstore).

"You need another one of my shirts?" His lips twitch up into a smirk.

Under the scrutiny of his gaze, my skin prickles. I'm fully covered, but I might as well be naked. The boundaries of being professional together are about to get blurred *big* time.

"No, that's okay. I can just sleep in this."

"Be serious, Dyl. Nothing about that looks comfortable. Let me give you something to wear."

"Fine, but you're not allowed to look," I mumble, suddenly

self-conscious about changing in front of the man who I've undressed in front of hundreds of times.

He holds his hand out to me for a firm handshake as a symbol of his promise. "You have my word." I look at his extended palm and roll my eyes, biting back the smile that's fighting to overtake my face.

Without warning, he pulls his shirt over his head and holds it out in my direction. I freeze, letting it fall to the ground. I'm unable to peel my eyes away from his bare torso. Thanks to the colder spring the city has been having, I have yet to see him shirtless after all these years.

He's muscular without looking like he tries too hard. My gaze snags on his arm first. His biceps are lined with corded muscles and sprinkled with sporadically placed tattoos, short-circuiting my thoughts. Just as I had imagined, there are countless that have been hiding, and I didn't realize how attractive I found tattoos until right this moment.

My eyes continue to travel over his body, catching on the deep lines that sit right above the top of his boxers. There's a trail of hair following the planes of his lower stomach, and I gulp, thinking about where it leads.

I force my eyes back up, stopping at his stomach momentarily. The subtle ridges of his abs make my mouth go dry. It's the physique earned through light physical activity and a balanced diet rather than hours spent at the gym. It's natural. Effortless. Unfair.

But his toned, undeniably delicious figure isn't what makes me unsteady. It's the small tattoo on his chest, right where his heart is.

There's no way that's what I think it is. It has to be a coincidence.

Without thinking, I point to it. "Is that…" My voice is ragged, and I can't finish the question.

He looks down at the tattoo, and his posture becomes rigid,

obviously apprehensive about the attention. He runs a hand through his hair and lets out a small nervous laugh.

"Yeah, I wasn't expecting you to see it before I could explain." His voice cracks and the vulnerability in it makes me take a step toward him.

The small, intricately inked four-leaf clover tattoo stares back at me, and my already heavily beating heart ramps up. If it gets any faster, I'll be dangerously close to a heart attack.

I'm profusely sweating, and I want to rip my clothes off right now to cool myself down in any way that I can, but I feel like I'm stuck in quicksand that's dragging me below the surface centimeters at a time.

"After we broke up, I got this tattoo. I know that sounds crazy, but it's something I spent a lot of time thinking about. I've always called you my good luck charm, and this clover is a reminder of that. It's a reminder of you and the way you made me feel like I had a little bit of magic in my life."

He pauses, letting the words sink in. "Even though I was the one who walked away, this tattoo is a reminder of the beautiful life that we shared. It's a reminder of my mistakes, but it also serves as a reminder that I have to believe in myself the way you always believed in me. You're still my good luck charm. You always have been."

By the time he's done speaking, his voice is barely louder than a whisper. I bridge the gap between us, instinctively running a soft finger over the outline of the tattoo. My eyes burn with tears that I'm trying to stave off. I blink rapidly, trying to relieve myself from the cocktail of emotions rushing through me. Sadness. Regret. Elation. Adoration. Nostalgia.

Parker's carried this symbol of us for the past five years. Meanwhile, I thought that he moved on. When I saw that he was in a new relationship after we ended things, I had all but given up hope.

"I didn't know..." my voice trembles as I try to find the right words. The weight of what we had lost and what there's still time to regain is almost too much to bear.

Without thinking, I lean in for a kiss, pressing my lips gently to his. Fuck being professional. This is the man I've been in love with for the past five years, no matter how hard I tried to shake the feelings. We lost so much time, and I'm not willing to lose anymore for a job that I'm not even sure I want anymore.

He immediately kisses back, gripping the sides of my face in his hands as I run my tongue across his lips, begging for entrance. He opens his mouth further, letting me inside, and I wrap my tongue up with his. He tastes like spearmint, and the freshness is intoxicating. It goes straight to my head, and it feels like a fire has been ignited in my chest. I'm rising higher and higher, leaving me unsure if I'm still touching the ground.

Parker pushes me back toward the window, sliding his hands down to my hips. He pins me against the window, and I let out a breathy moan into his mouth. I run a hand through his loose, damp curls and catch a whiff of his shampoo. He clearly just showered, and the scent of cedar and mint fill my senses. I want to bottle it up and carry it with me everywhere I go.

"I love you," I profess against his mouth. All fucks are officially out the window as a result of his confessions and the way his body feels pressed up against mine. His fingers dig deeper into my pelvis, and the pressure sends me spiraling.

I need *more*. So much more.

"I love you too," he replies frantically in between kisses. I don't think I'll ever tire of hearing those three words out of his mouth.

He pulls away just long enough to pull my sweater up and over my head, leaving us both shirtless. He reclaims my lips, and feeling his skin against mine is enough to make me shudder with desire.

I lift my chin toward the ceiling as his lips move from mine down to my neck. He presses tender kisses down my neck, and

I squeeze my eyes shut, soaking in the gentleness of his movements. Before I can get too comfortable, he begins nipping and sucking at my skin, leaving small marks up and down the base of my throat.

He presses himself up against me, positioning his erection against my stomach, and the thinness of his underwear allows me to feel everything. He's fully hard, and the feel of it makes me whimper. I have never needed to get someone naked faster than I do right now. I want to get down on my knees and show him the same pleasure that he showed me in the elevator all of those weeks ago.

"Turn around." His voice is hoarse, and the possessiveness in it has me doing as I'm told without batting an eye.

I lean up against the window, and I notice some stragglers crossing the street after a night out. I briefly wonder what they think about us, but all my thoughts vanish as Parker grabs my wrists with one hand and presses them above my head against the window.

I'm completely and utterly at his disposal, and it makes the insistent heat in between my legs grow hotter. I'm not sure I've ever been this horny, and I don't know what to do about it. All I know is that I need him to fuck me.

Before I can beg, he finds the button on my jeans and flicks them open with one quick flick of his wrist.

"I think it's time we finish what we started."

I nod, speechless for a second time tonight. He takes his time planting kisses down my spine as he slowly pushes my jeans to my ankles. I feel a soft hand wrap around my calf as he lifts my legs one by one, helping me step out of my pants.

I'm left standing almost completely nude, in nothing but my black bra and underwear. The set may not be the sexiest I own–I was planning on being on a plane and very single–but at least they match.

"You drive me wild, Lucky," he groans, and the use of my

nickname I hadn't heard in years up until today makes me feverish. I swear if we're quiet enough, he could hear my heart hammering. The air seems thicker, charged with a crackling tension that makes it impossible to think clearly.

"There are people down there. They can see what we're doing." I barely manage to get the words out. I'm met with a husky laugh that makes me quiver.

"Good, let them watch. I want them to see just how beautiful you are. Just how lucky I am to be the one to worship you."

Suddenly, the air grows cold as I feel the loss of his body pressed against mine. The ghost of his touch lingers, and I would do anything to feel it again. As if Parker hears my silent prayers, I feel his body up against mine within seconds. Except now, there is no underwear getting in the way of feeling just how turned on he is. His length is pressed against my backside, and I'm dizzy with lust.

I've never been one to sleep around, but I dabbled when Parker and I were broken up. Every time, I was met with disappointment. When I feel just how big he is–the perfect size, not too big, not too small–I'm transported back to the days we slept together. He was the first guy to make me come, and he read my body like a map. He knew all of the right buttons to push to make me come apart underneath him without fail.

My body throbs at the thought of him doing it again.

Parker gets on his knees behind me and pulls my panties down and off, and my core aches for his touch.

"I need you to come for me this time, okay? I don't care what it takes. I want to feel you fall apart under my tongue. Can you do that for me, baby?"

I bow my head once in agreement. Words don't feel like enough. Hell, I don't trust myself to speak. I'm a marionette at his mercy. He's pulling the strings, and I'm no longer in control of my own will. He could ask anything of me, and I'd give in without a single question.

His mouth traces up my legs, and I ignore the gooseflesh breaking out at the feeling. He pays extra attention to my ass, spanking me with the perfect amount of pressure. It's enough to send a wave of pleasure through me, yet the sting reverberates through my body. The combination of pain and pleasure is tantalizing.

Without uttering a word, Parker licks unhurriedly up my center, and I writhe under the feel of his tongue. He doesn't let me revel in the pleasure for too long, though, because he reverts to teasing me slowly by licking up the back of each of my thighs. I wriggle, desperate for him to continue.

He tightens his hold on my thighs, holding me in place, tired of my squirming. He continues licking, and when his tongue reaches my inner thighs, he takes an agonizingly long time licking up each one of my lips until his mouth finds my small bundle of nerves.

"Bend forward for me, baby."

The small audience we had earlier has dispersed, and I'm thankful as I reach back, undo my bra, and lean forward, pushing my torso against the window. The bite of the cold glass makes my nipples peak, and I reach up and pinch one with a free hand.

As I roll my nipple in between my fingers, Parker laps up my clit, alternating between sucking and licking, and it takes everything in me not to scream his name at the sensation. He slides a finger inside of me and curls it just the right way. I buck my hips involuntarily, and he holds me in place, leaving me very little room to move.

"Fuck," I gasp. My walls are already tightening around his fingers, and I know that I'm only seconds away from tumbling over the edge. This has been building up for weeks, and all I want to do is show him just how good he makes me feel.

"That's it, baby. I can feel how close you are. I want you to come for me," he growls against me. The licking and sucking become small nibbles, pulling my clit in between his teeth, and he adds yet another finger inside of me. The feeling of him filling me up is enough to send me toppling over.

I see stars as my peak shatters, my body tremoring under his touch. Parker doesn't ease up as I ride the wave, moaning loudly without a care who can hear us. He doesn't release me from his touch until I've come down from space and I'm standing on shaky legs.

He stands up behind me, turns me around, licking his lips and fingers just like he did on the elevator. The view of him savoring the taste is enough to make me lean against the window for support. He's unashamedly relishing in my pleasure, and there's nothing sexier.

When I find the strength, I push him forward and slide down to my knees, ready to repay the favor, but he stops me with a tight hold around my elbow before I can sink down to the ground.

"Not right now. We can get to that later. I need to feel that cum on my cock." His plea fuels my desire further, which I didn't think was possible.

I stand, unable to tear my eyes away from his hard length, standing at attention for me. I salivate at the sight. I'm dying to take him in my mouth, but who am I to argue?

He lifts my chin with a hook of his finger, and I'm met with a smug smirk. "I'm up here." A rosiness flushes up to my cheeks, knowing I just got caught gawking at his dick. I push away the humiliation and give him a cheeky grin in return.

"What can I say? I like what I see." Without responding, he whirls me back around toward the window.

"Don't move," he instructs.

Although I can't see what he's doing, I hear him shuffling through his suitcase. My palms become damp, and I release shallow, uneven breaths, unsure of what to expect.

Like lightning, he's back behind me and brings my wrists

together behind my back in a flash. I feel a soft fabric wrap around my wrists, restricting my movements.

"What's that?"

"If you're going to wear my shirts, you need to earn them," he purrs into my ear, his hot breath making my skin break out in goosebumps. I peek behind my back, and sure enough, my wrists are bound with the Neil Young shirt he took from me last week.

Holy shit.

Parker and I always had fun in the bedroom, but it seems like the years apart have made him even more adventurous. A delicious coil of tension is already building in my gut again. Neither of us has touched the thermostat, yet the room suddenly feels exponentially warmer.

I hear the rustling of foil from behind me.

"I'm on birth control. And I haven't slept with anyone since I last got tested," I interrupt, starving to feel him with nothing in between us. I don't mention the sad fact that not a single soul has touched me in over a year.

"I got tested right before I came out here, too. I'm clean. You want me to fuck you bare?" He runs a silky-soft finger down my spine to the aching center in between my legs.

"Yes, yes. Please. Just fuck me."

"I love it when you beg for me, Lucky." He tosses the condom to the side and clutches my hip as he lines himself up with my entrance. Slowly, he sinks into me, and I inhale sharply at the feeling. It's so familiar yet so foreign.

When he's fully situated inside of me, he wraps a steady hand around my throat and pulls me up so my back is pressed against his chest. He begins thrusting painfully slow, hitting my sweet spot with every unhurried movement.

"I need more," I mewl.

He cusses under his breath into my neck as he picks up the pace. The tightening of my center grows rigid, and I know it's not going to take much for me to come apart all over him for a second time. I'm as taut as a tightrope, and I'm moments away from snapping.

"You have no idea how much I've missed this." His guttural voice makes my pussy clench around his cock. "Fuck, I can feel you tightening around me already."

He removes his hand from my throat and trails it down my torso, resting it in between my legs. I spread my legs further, giving him easier access, which he happily takes. He continues to pound into me, his thrusts greedy and deliberate. I swallow the feeling of my impending climax, trying to make this last as long as possible. I'm not ready for it to end.

Unfortunately, Parker has other ideas. He massages my swollen, sensitive clit in slow yet sure circles, and it's enough to make me combust.

"I'm going to come," I cry.

"Good girl. Come for me."

My body shudders under his touch as white-hot pleasure explodes behind my eyes like lightning bolts. The crescendo of pleasure flows through me like a symphony as I convulse.

Parker continues to slam into me, and the force is enough to make my knees collapse. He wraps an arm around my waist and holds me up, never wavering in his tempo. As my orgasm crests, Parker finds his own release, his cock twitching as he fills me up with his load. The only sounds filling the room are his low grunts and my panting. There's something about hearing him lose control that riles me back up, but neither of us makes an effort to move.

As our breathing evens out, Parker slowly pulls out of me, unties me, and drags me over to the bed, my body no longer physically capable of staying upright. I curl into his arms, feeling smaller and more protected than I have in years. His skin is slick with sweat, and I relish the feeling of the heat radiating off of him despite my own stickiness.

As I shut my eyes, trying to memorize every detail of today, I feel his fingers curling in my hair, slowly twisting strands. His fingers fall from my scalp down to my neck, landing on the curve of my spine. His touch washes me out into the sea of sleep, and right before I fade to black, I hear a soft "I love you" whispered against the shell of my ear.

30

PARKER

Last night was unbelievable. Actually, that might be the understatement of the century. We slept for a whopping two hours because I kept waking up with my hands all over her. I couldn't help myself. Once the dam was broken, there was no going back. Dylan's a drug that I want to inject into my system, and I'm not sure I'll ever get enough.

There's something about coming back together with someone from your past. It's so easy to slip back into the way things were. Touching her, kissing her, exploring her body with my hands–it all felt instinctual.

As I scan the room with sleep crusted in the corner of my eyes, I see just how big of a mess we made. The comforter is no longer on the bed, half of the cushions of the worn-down pull-out couch are on the ground, and I can make out a smudge on the window in the shape of a handprint. I smirk to myself thinking about all of the trouble we got into.

Not only did we fuck, but we made love. And as much as I enjoyed ravaging her in every way possible, it was the moments of slow, sensual sex that would be replaying in my head for weeks on end. Seeing her with her guard down in those moments made the past few months worth every second. She'd never understand just how ravishing I think she is.

Dylan stirs next to me, and I plant a small kiss on her forehead. The fact that I'm holding her in my arms right now feels surreal, and if I had a free hand, I'd pinch myself to remind myself that this is real life.

"What time is it?" Dylan's scratchy morning voice calls out for me. She's lying on her stomach, facing me, her eyes still shut tight as she tries to avoid the sun that's peeking out from behind the blackout curtains. I glance over at the clock on the nightstand.

"Nine."

She lets out a groan and pulls the sheets over her head, bringing a chuckle out of me. She was never a morning person, and it doesn't look like that has changed.

"Want to get some breakfast? My treat." I pull the sheet down from her face, and she blinks up at me, still in the process of waking up. I trace my finger down her back like I did last night when she first fell asleep, and she leans into my touch. The sight of her naked in bed, though I can't currently see anything too revealing, makes my dick twitch. I guess he didn't get the memo after the multiple rounds last night. I think if I tried to touch her again, he'd fall right off.

"What kind of breakfast?"

I laugh again, knowing I have her in the palm of my hand at the mention of food while giving her back rubs.

"Whatever you want, Lucky. Our options are limitless."

She ponders for a second. "I could go for some pancakes right about now."

"Then pancakes you shall get. Join me in the shower?"

"Fine, but you better keep your hands to yourself. I don't know if I can physically handle another round."

I haul myself out of bed and pull the sheets down, leaving

her completely exposed in front of me. I can't wait to have that view for the rest of my life. "I can't make any promises."

She rolls her eyes, but I don't miss the playful glint. It's enough to tell me that as soon as we're in that shower, we're going to be all over one another yet again. And with that unspoken promise, I'm running toward the bathroom.

✹ ✹ ✹ ✹ ✹

The table we're situated at is full of pancakes topped with berry compote, avocado toast, omelets, coffees (which have already been refilled multiple times), and a smorgasbord of other breakfast foods. At first glance, you'd think we were feeding an entire family, and yet the small two-person table sitting on the porch of Park and Grove is only occupied by me and Dylan.

Apparently, a full night of physical activities has left us with the appetites of wild animals. As Dylan looks down at all of the options, trying to decide what she wants to start with, I'm overcome with joy. She looks happier and freer than I've seen her in weeks. Her eyes are shimmering as if made from the stars themselves, and the look makes me want to live in a world of perpetual dusk.

"Careful, or else you're going to give yourself decision fatigue."

She jokingly wipes the corner of her mouth free of any slobber. "It all just looks so incredible. I don't know where to start."

She mulls over it for a few more seconds before snagging the plate of pancakes toward her and digging in. I take a moment to observe her, and it makes me forget about the feast in front of me. As she lets out a moan of content at the first bite, I can't stop the large grin that consumes my face.

She peeks up and notices I have yet to touch a plate. "You going to eat?"

I pick up my fork and dig into the homemade cinnamon roll sitting nearby, trying to play cool. "Uh yeah. How are the pancakes?"

"Orgasmic." She shovels another bite of food into her mouth.

"Better than me?" I wink at her as I take my first bite. *Fuck, that's good.* She's right. The food really is a burst of pleasure to my taste buds.

"It's neck and neck," she jokes.

I pretend to be wounded, but I know that the multiple orgasms I gave her last night are enough to put me far beyond a great pair of hotcakes.

I take a sip of my coffee, and we settle into a comfortable silence as we continue to eat. I know deep down that we need to talk about last night and what it means for our future, but I'm worried that if I bring it up, it's going to scare her away–but fuck it. I'm not willing to wait any longer. I want to make her mine for the rest of my life, and I'm not willing to take no for an answer. Especially after everything that transpired in the last twenty-four hours.

"So, we should talk about last night," Dylan says, vocalizing my same inner thoughts. The sentence, though the least bit threatening, makes my stomach bottom out. My throat closes up, and I'm unable to respond, so I offer a nod, waiting for her to take the lead.

"How are you feeling about everything?" she asks.

Well, change of plans. This is my chance to take the lead. Put my last cards on the table.

"I love you, and now that I have you... if I do have you, I should say, I don't want to let you go again. My life is exponentially better with you in it, Lucky. And I'm sorry if that's scary to hear. The last thing I want to do is force you into anything, and I know this all feels like it's happening quickly. I want you to feel confident in us. But I'd rather spend the rest of my life alone than spend another day without you."

By the time I finish my speech, she's rested her fork on the edge of her plate, and she's looking up at me with flushed cheeks and oversized pupils.

"I do," Dylan replies in a hushed tone.

"Do what?" I raise a brow in confusion.

"Feel confident in you. In us. I can't imagine my life without you, Parker. I spent so many years telling myself that I didn't want to get into another relationship because I was afraid of getting hurt again. And while that was true to some extent, I was more worried about finding someone else who would compare to you. It's you. It's *always* been you."

The way she enunciates 'always' makes my heart soar. I have to bring a hand to my mouth to stifle the smile that breaks out on my face.

"I do have one request, though," she continues.

"Of course." I'll give her anything she wants.

"I want us to give this a fighting chance again. But we need to keep this on the down low. I don't want Katherine to find out. It'd be the ammo she needs to fire me once and for all."

I flop back in my chair, unaware that my posture had grown stiff, and wipe a small bead of sweat that has gathered on my forehead. I can work with that.

"How diligent of you." I simper. "You have my word. Does this mean I'm not allowed to kiss you anymore? Because that would be a damn shame."

"Kisses are allowed. In private only."

"If we're alone, does this mean we can do more?" I wet my bottom lip with a swipe of my tongue, and I notice her gaze catching on motion. She swallows, then pulls herself out of the lust-filled daze we've both been living in the past twenty-four hours with a small giggle.

"Maybe. If you're lucky."

"Well, you *are* my good luck charm, so I have a good feeling about it."

"You're so corny sometimes, you know that?" The bite of her words falls flat when I glimpse the grin she's wearing. I don't have time to respond to what she deems is a harmless insult because she whispers, "I missed it."

I reach across the table, doing my best to dodge the plates that have filled the table, and grab her hand.

"I missed you," I reply.

Her smile grows bigger, and the beaming look on her face is enough to make me want to ignore the responsibilities of the rest of the book tour and travel around the cities with her, soaking up as much time together as possible.

I look down at my watch with my free hand and swear under my breath. Time to bring myself back down to Earth and make sure the last couple of dates on this tour go well.

"We should get going. We've gotta be at Love and Lit in half an hour to help set everything up."

I take out my wallet, throw down some cash to pay for our meal, which we scarfed down with no leftovers, and stand, reaching my hand out for hers. She interlocks her fingers in mine and stands, and all I can think about is if I died today, I'd die the happiest man alive. I've got my luck back.

31

DYLAN

After a whirlwind day of driving, a night full of raunchy trysts that will stay with me forever, and a brunch that solidified everything I had been feeling, the event at Love and Lit went off without a hitch. We had the perfect amount of books, the audience loved meeting Evelyn, and no one had a single clue what we had gone through twenty-four hours before the signing.

As happy as I am that it was successful, the events that took place between me and Parker are what make me feel like I'm drifting through life untethered as I walk into our hotel. Although the seedy hotel we had initially been booked at had its quirks, Parker and I decided to celebrate by booking a night at the Wentworth Mansion, a historic five-star inn in the heart of downtown Charleston.

The minute you step into the lobby, it feels as if you've been transported to Europe in the nineteenth century. The original wood floors display intricate designs, the ceilings are decorated with ornate crown moldings and ceiling medallions, and the grand furniture in the sitting room rests in front of built-in bookshelves stacked with books and a traditional wood-burning fireplace. It's grander than anything I've experienced before, and I feel out of place.

"This is way nicer than I was expecting," I hiss to Parker, who's standing pressed to my side, his hand interlocked with mine. He respected my wishes and kept the PDA to a minimum when we were working, but ever since wrapping up, he's been glued to my side. It's funny how normal it feels–as if it's nothing new, just another day spent with my boyfriend.

When we decided to splurge on a night at a different hotel, this was not what I had in mind. I lingered with Evelyn while the signing wrapped up and left Parker in charge of booking a room at the hotel of his choice, so I had no idea where he'd ended up until now.

"I know, but I figured we deserved a little treat. There's a lot we need to celebrate."

He leaves me no time to question how much this must have cost before dragging me to the hotel's restaurant, Circa 1886. I peek inside and immediately feel outrageously underdressed. Thank god I opted for a dress today instead of the jeans I was eyeing, but it still doesn't feel like enough for the fine dining room.

"Parker, this is way too much. I'm not dressed for this," I groan.

"Don't worry. We're just going to grab a drink at the bar before we get cheap fast food for dinner because I can't afford to eat for the next month after booking this place," he jokes.

"That's not funny." Guilt rolls through me that he booked this all on his own. I'm not rolling in money in any sense of the word, but I still want to contribute to getaways like this.

"It's a joke. Don't worry. I'm not joking about the food thing, though. I think I saw a Taco Bell around the corner."

My ears perk up, and my mouth salivates over the idea of engorging myself with tacos galore. I haven't eaten anything thing since our brunch this morning, but considering the amount of food we managed to take down, I didn't have much of an appetite until the mention of dinner. My stomach grumbles, and I drag us over to the bar, ready to get this drink over with so I can get something to eat.

"Slow down there, tiger." A low, amused sound escapes Parker. "I'll feed you soon. I know how you get when you're hungry."

He pulls out the barstool for me, and I slide into it, reddening at his gallantry. Parker takes a seat on the stool next to me and rests his right hand on my thigh, which is now exposed thanks to my dress sliding up. The contact of his warm palm on the cold skin of my leg sends a chill sweeping through my bones, which swiftly turns into a surge of heat. The contradiction of the sensations is maddening.

As if he can sense my lust, he sweeps his hand further up my thigh until he's inches away from the spot where I'm dying to be touched. I whip my head around to see if anyone is nearby to see his antics. Because it's not quite dinner time yet, the bar and restaurant are nearly empty. When I turn my attention back to Parker, he's not paying any mind to me. Instead, he's talking to the bartender, who must've moseyed up while he was teasing me.

My eyes lock on his hand, and I'm unable to tear them away from the veins that are protruding with his possessive grip on my upper thigh. There's something about seeing his fingers, covered in silver rings, curled around my skin that makes my primal instincts act up.

"Earth to Dylan," Parker's voice snaps me back into focus, and when I look up, the simper he's wearing tells me he knows damn well what he's doing to me. He juts out his chin toward the two glasses of wine now sitting in front of us, brows raised. "I think we need to make a toast."

I don't give him the satisfaction of reacting to his smugness, which evidently riles him up because he lets out a throaty growl that only stokes the fire in my belly. He pushes my legs apart further, swiping a finger, so light it barely registers, up my center before grabbing his wine glass and lifting it in the air. I bite my bottom lip to keep my moans to myself, and, with a pout, I bring my glass to his.

Parker leans forward, his voice a soft murmur against my ear. "Make it through this glass of wine, and I promise I'll take care of you in our room." He taps his glass against mine, takes a small sip, and then returns to me for one last whispered remark. "Until you can't stand anymore."

I gulp and try to wash away my desire with a sip of wine, but when the notes of black currant and vanilla hit my tongue, I groan for an entirely different reason. I'd recognize this Cabernet anywhere.

I might not have been a big drinker growing up, but Parker and I adopted a tradition where we'd splurge on a bottle of wine every year on our anniversary. We'd go to our local supermarket, pick out an expensive bottle of wine–not knowing a damn thing about what we were choosing–and drink it under the stars. We'd tried multiple bottles before we found this one, which quickly became one of our favorites. We didn't drink it often, so when we did, it was a treat.

"Is this what I think it is?"

"Yes, it is. When I was here earlier, I had them put a bottle aside for us. I figured it's been a while since we've had anything to celebrate together, and this seemed like a good enough cause."

The thoughtfulness of the gesture makes me take a breathless pause. I take another sip, close my eyes, and savor the taste and the flashbacks it brings. I think back to the first time we shared this bottle–it was our third anniversary.

We picked up the bottle on a whim and drove to a lookout near Parker's house. The long, windy road up the mountain spits you out at a clearing that overlooks all of Woodland

Heights. It was our best-kept secret. When we reached the top, I discovered that Parker had set up a small table with candles and flowers. He even packed a picnic of takeout from our favorite local Italian restaurant. It must've taken him half the day to get everything put together.

We ate pasta, drank wine, and laughed until our stomachs ached for hours. When it came time to end the night, he surprised me with pillows and blankets hiding in his trunk. We made a fort in the back of his car, made love, and fell asleep just as the sun peeked over the horizon. I don't think I slept more than two hours that night, and when I woke up that morning, thanks to the blinding sun coming in through the car's windows, I was dead tired. But it didn't matter because it was one of the most romantic things anyone had ever done for me.

"This is perfect. Thank you," I gush.

"Of course. I just wanted to say thank you for all of your hard work. None of this," he gestures to the hotel bar, "would've happened without you. I've tried to find the words to express how much your effort and heart have meant to both me and Evelyn on this tour, but nothing feels like enough. I hope you understand how much I admire you. And how much I love you–more than I ever have. I plan on spending every waking second reminding you in case you don't. So here's to you kicking ass and taking me back." He lifts his glass one more time with a wink.

I raise my glass to his silently, but I don't take a drink. I keep my gaze locked on him, studying him like I'm taking a photograph. His sharp jaw, his blue eyes, the haphazard curls falling in front of his face, the tattoo I now know is hiding underneath his plain black t-shirt–all of it is mine.

Rather than reply with something eloquent, I nod toward the bottle that the bartender placed in front of us while I was deep in my thoughts. "Why don't we cork that and bring it back to the room?"

"Oh? What for?" He asks coyly.

"I want to show you just how much I love *you* and how happy I am we're getting a second chance." The wine warms me up as I take another sip. And another. By the time I'm to the bottom of the glass, my body is buzzing, though I'm not entirely sure the wine's to blame.

"What did you have in mind?" His brow arches in question. I'm not sure what it is, but I love his need for me to vocalize what I want to do to him. It only spurs me on further.

"I never got to return the favor last night."

With that, he leans over the bar and flags down the bartender. "We'll take that check whenever you're ready!"

32

DYLAN

The rest of the week with Parker has felt like a fever dream. The last few dates of the tour went swimmingly, and now we're spending a day in Boston, the last stop, before the official end of the tour. Everyone has been loving meeting Evelyn, and it's going to be a little bittersweet walking away from this.

Parker, Evelyn, and I spent almost every single night together exploring new cities, trying new restaurants, and visiting the tourist traps. From days spent wandering around the Ben & Jerry's flavor graveyard (RIP Turtle Soup) in Vermont to Lucy the Elephant in Jersey, these are memories that I'm going to hold dear forever.

We've formed a true friendship, one that I would have never expected, but now that I have it, I know it will stick around. I never imagined my small circle growing the way it has, but I'm so grateful for it. The people in my life showed me that I deserve to be put first–that no matter how alone I feel, there's a light at the end of the tunnel.

Then there's Parker. I know I made him promise to keep things between us for the remainder of the project, but I can't keep my hands off him. Any time we're alone, I'm clawing at his clothes. I don't know what's gotten into me, but I have no intentions of stopping it.

After we broke up, I took the time to learn one of life's hardest lessons. You don't need someone else to complete you; you're whole on your own. I was forced to learn to love myself and enjoy my own company. It was not an easy feeling to sit with, and I'm not afraid to admit that I spent countless nights alone blasting sad music and crying in my childhood bedroom. Eventually, it got easier.

But now that I have Parker back in my life, I feel complete. Of course, I still love who I am down to my core, but with him in it, life feels more meaningful. Brighter. He's a beautiful part of my life's mosaic, but not the entire picture. His added pieces make the portrait more exquisite than I could've ever imagined.

"Dyl?" Parker's voice jerks me back to the present–I really have reverted back to a middle schooler with a crush.

"Yeah?" I look over to him and notice that we're stopped in front of Beacon Hill Books where Evelyn has her signing later tonight. My gaze must grow bemused because he snorts. Without offering any explanation, he pulls me into the store.

"I just need to do something really quick. Would you mind waiting here? It should only take a second."

"Um, sure," I reply. He hands me his coffee and leaves me standing in the front by myself. I take a moment to look around and find myself immediately at ease. We've seen our fair share of bookstores on this tour, but I think this one is my favorite.

It's designed like a home, with mismatched floral furniture throughout the space, perfect for cozying up with a book. The pale green bookshelves, complete with elegant crown molding that looks antique, are built into the walls, stocked to the brim with colorful books of all genres. There's even a working fireplace that is unfortunately not on because we've made it to late spring, and the sun is shining.

It makes me miss the colder months, and I can't help but dream about how magical this place would be in the heart of winter, decked out for Christmas. I envision lit wreaths placed on the old windows, Christmas trees tucked into various corners, the fireplace adorned with garland that makes the store smell of fresh pine and citrus, and a layer of fresh snow falling outside.

Younger Dylan would've loved it. I still would. There's something about the winter that makes my soul feel at peace.

I make a note to come back later this year.

As I'm meandering the bookshelves, practicing my best self-control (yes, I do deserve a trophy for this) because I don't have any room in my suitcase, Parker walks up with a brown paper bag stuffed with tissue paper.

"Ready?"

I eye the bag suspiciously but keep my mouth shut. If he wanted to tell me what was inside, he would. However, as someone who's extremely nosy, I'm dying to know. I take the high road, bite my tongue, and hand him his coffee.

"Yeah, let's go."

He opens the door for me, and we walk out into the cool air. The storm that kept me up all night has dissipated, and there's a slight chill thanks to a small breeze. I close my eyes briefly, savoring the feeling of the wind tickling my skin.

As I'm soaking in the weather, I feel Parker's fingers interlock with mine and tug me. When I open my eyes, he's looking at me with a soft smile. I blindly follow him, unsure of where we're going, but not caring because I would follow this man anywhere in life.

"Let's take a walk."

I nod and lean closer to him. He feels warm and sturdy next to me, and it takes everything in me not to rest my head on his shoulder as we go. As we walk in comfortable silence, he squeezes my hand, a small gesture that makes my heart flip. I let out a sigh of contentment and run my thumb up and down his in return. It's these small moments that mean more to me than any grand gesture.

After what feels like only seconds–I blame the love fog I was in–we arrive at Fiedler Field. My confusion from the bookstore only grows, but I still can't bring myself to ask what we're doing or what he's planning.

"I think this is the quietest I've ever seen you. I know you don't like surprises, yet you've taken this exceptionally well for once. What's going on in that pretty head of yours, Lucky?"

Parker gestures to a bench overlooking the Charles River. I take a seat, folding my hands in my lap and watching the small waves of the water, losing myself in my thoughts. He sits next to me, placing the mysterious shopping bag in between us.

"I'm just taking it all in. I think I'm still processing everything. I wake up every morning, and I have to remind myself that this is all real. I'm working the job I always dreamed of. I moved to the city that I've always envisioned for myself. And now you're here with me. It doesn't feel real."

When I glance at him, he's studying me with soft eyes. The gaze is so full of adoration that it sends my heart into a tizzy.

"Do I need to pinch you? Because I will. I'd be happy to do it naked, too, if that will help. I don't mind," he jests.

"You're so stupid," I mumble, but my lips hook up in the corners. My cheeks have never hurt more than they have this past week, and it's a happiness that I hope stays with me for the rest of my life.

He nudges the bag close to me. "Open it."

"It's for me?"

"Of course it is. Did you think I just went to a bookstore for myself?"

I narrow my eyes and place my pointer finger and thumb on my chin in a musing manner. "That's very true. For someone who works in publishing, I'm not sure I've ever seen you pick up a book."

"You're so full of shit. I read all the time, and you know it." He lets out a gruff laugh, and it's music to my ears.

"I know. I just really love any opportunity I get to make fun of you. It's almost as fun as kissing you."

"As long as that's first."

"Actually, there's something else that trumps it, but we're in public, and I don't need you getting excited." His eyes flare with excitement, and I pat his head like a puppy as I let out a small giggle. "Down, boy."

Before we get too distracted, I grab the bag and place it on my lap. I gently take out the tissue paper until the present is easy to grasp. I pull it out to discover my favorite romance novel. It's one that I've reread at least five times (okay, more like ten, but who's counting) since college. I also already own a copy, and there's no way he doesn't already know this.

I look over at him with a lifted eyebrow. "What's this?"

"Your favorite book," he replies proudly.

"Well, yes, I know that. I love it, I really do. But I've had the same beat-up copy for the last eight years…" I trail off, trying not to sound unappreciative. It's still a very thoughtful gesture.

He lets out a small laugh and runs an anxious hand through his hair.

"I didn't forget, don't worry. Flip through this one."

Now, I'm more confused than ever. I flip to the front of the book to find a message written on the title page.

"LUCKY, *our story is still unfolding, just like the stories in your favorite books. Flip through to see a message I've hidden for you for our next chapter.*"

. . .

I FEEL my hands shake as I start leafing through the pages. "It may be harder to find, so take it slow. I promise it's worth it." His voice wavers, and it takes everything in me not to look up and comfort his nerves.

I continue to flip through the book until I hit the halfway mark, and I see two small words highlighted in blue. They're so subtle that I almost miss them, but when I catch them, my palms grow sweaty, and I gasp. *Be mine.* I reread the words over and over, trying to process what they mean.

I know this scene like the back of my hand, and it's one of my favorite moments throughout the entire book. It's the grand gesture that you dream of having yourself. The one that makes real-life men seem that much more unappealing.

The fact that it's highlighted sends butterflies fluttering in my stomach, and I find it suddenly hard to breathe. Does this mean what I think it means?

Before I can question him, Parker gently grabs the book and places it back between us. He takes my hands into his, and the boyish grin he's wearing is infectious.

"I know you said you wanted to remain professional, and I promise to be when others are around. But I can't wait any longer. I lost you once, and I'm not willing to do it again. I've loved every second of the past week and want to spend the rest of my life with you by my side, Lucky. Be my girlfriend."

I bite my lip, trying to contain my excitement, but I fail, and a grin so large it overtakes all of my features breaks out on my face. My cheeks are spread so wide it feels like my face is going to split in two.

"This is the most thoughtful gesture anyone has ever done for me."

"You deserve it." We sit in silence as my brain seemingly forgets how to function. "So, no pressure, but is that a yes?" he asks after the quietness stretches for a little *too* long.

"Yes. One hundred percent yes."

He makes a show of acting relieved by placing a hand on his chest. "Thank god. You scared me there for a second."

He stands, pulls me up, and picks me up in his arms so my feet are no longer touching the ground. He spins me around just like the romance novels I know and love. Except this love story is real life, and the man I've always dreamed of is standing in front of me.

He presses his lips to mine, and I no longer feel like I'm on this planet. The kiss is so slow and gentle that I feel like I'm floating up to the sky–and I never want to come back down.

Suddenly overcome with need, I bite his lip gently, which pulls a guttural growl from his throat. The sound only goads my desire more as I wrap my legs around his waist and grind my hips into his. I stand no chance of breaking the kiss to see the scene we're causing, so I can only hope that the park is still relatively empty before we scare anyone away.

His hands slide down to my ass, and he gives it a squeeze, exploring my mouth with his tongue while he does so. Before we get too carried away, he pulls his lips away from mine, and the loss leaves me pouting. He sets me down, wrapping his arm around my shoulder.

"Why don't we take this back to the hotel? I'm not done celebrating you yet, and the last thing we need is to get arrested for public indecency."

The heat already gathered at my core grows hotter, and my face flushes red at the thought. I lick my lips and nod, letting him lead the way back to the hotel to ravage me in every way he knows how.

33

PARKER

Now that we're back in the city, all I can think about is the fact that in two short days, our contract with Thrive is officially up, which means I can scream that Dylan is my girlfriend from the rooftops. We've been texting from sun up to sun down, and we've done a good enough job of keeping this whole thing under wraps that Katherine doesn't expect a thing, which means she can't make Dylan's life a living hell–more than she already has.

I kickstart my computer for the day and immediately open my emails because today is one of the biggest days of my career so far since moving to New York. Not only did the book tour go incredibly well, but the last I heard, Evelyn's books were flying off the shelves.

I see an email at the top of my inbox from our contact at The New York Times with the subject "IMPORTANT" bolded in all caps. I've been waiting for this email every day this week, and the anticipation makes me fidgety. I click a nearby pen repeatedly, needing to do something with my hands. If this email says what I think it says, my career is about to change for good.

I hesitantly click open the email and scan it as quickly as possible. Sure enough, it's exactly what I was expecting. Evelyn made it on the New York Times's Best Seller list. With nearly 15,000 copies sold within the first week of release, we did it. We fucking did it.

I push myself out of my chair, not bothering to close my laptop, and run briskly to Blake's office. I shove the door open, unconcerned if he's busy, and find him on the phone, feet up, ankles crossed on his desk–his usual stance.

His eyes flick up to mine, and I mouth, "Hang up."

"Hey Ryan, something important just came across my desk. Do you mind if I give you a call back later this afternoon?" He pauses for the person on the other end of the line to speak. "Sounds great. Talk soon."

He hangs up the phone and sets it down on his desk.

"What's so important?"

"Check your email." I shuffle from foot to foot in excitement, knowing I get to be here when he sees the news. He clicks through his computer, and I can see his eyes scanning the words in front of him. When he looks back in my direction, there's a gleam in his gaze.

"You fucking did it, man."

He stands up from his chair, strides over to me, and wraps me in a hug, patting me on the back. Because I was never close with my parents or siblings, Blake's opinion has always mattered to me more than anyone else's. We're close in age, but all I've ever wanted to do was make him proud the same way you would an older brother.

He may have his flaws, but he has a good head on his shoulders–especially when it comes to business. He took a chance on me in California, and he's the reason I have this job here in New York, so I owe him more than I'll probably ever be able to repay him.

"I'm proud of you." He pulls away with a genuine grin,

telling me he means every word of his praise. I return the smile, unable to stop the expression as I hear the words I've desperately wanted to hear for most of my life.

"Thanks, man. Feels pretty damn good."

"I'm sure it does. You know what this means." His face morphs into a mischievous smirk, and I dread the second half of that sentence. Any time he gets that look, I know that there's going to be far too much alcohol involved, and I will be paying the price tomorrow.

"Do I?" I groan. Deep down, this is one of the few times that I can't wait to go celebrate and have a couple of beers. I've worked hard these past couple of months, and it feels good to know that it all paid off. Not to mention the fact that now I no longer have to hide being with Dylan…which reminds me that I need to tell Blake the news of our relationship.

I've been dying to tell him, but I wanted to do it in person to see his reaction. I imagine there's going to be a "happy for you, man" and "so, did you fuck her yet?" involved.

I love Blake and value our friendship immensely, but I can't wait to call Dylan and tell her the good news. There's something about knowing that I get to talk to the woman I love about the good things that happen in my life that make them that much more worthwhile. Sharing your triumphs with someone who matters to you is far better than experiencing them alone.

"Of course you do. We're taking the day off, and we're getting drunk."

And there it is.

"I don't know how you do it." I shake my head in disbelief.

"Do what?"

"Work so damn hard and still manage to party like you're in college." I mockingly look around the room. "How are we going to manage to get out of work early without drawing too much attention to me?"

"Have you forgotten who I am? I practically run this place. Besides, it's not going to matter soon anyway." Blake's retort is cocky yet vague, and I don't miss how his body straightens at the mention of work. There's something he's not telling me, but I leave it alone for the time being. I'm not letting anything bring the mood down.

"That's exactly what I mean," I mutter under my breath, ignoring the shift in the mood.

He shuts his laptop from across his desk, grabs his phone, shoves it in his pocket, and throws an arm around my shoulders. "Sean's?"

After being out of the office for the past couple of weeks, I have about fifty emails to respond to, but my mouth waters at the idea of grabbing a Guinness and fish n' chips from our favorite local Irish pub.

"Is there any other option?" I quip.

"That's what I like to hear."

With that, we're gone without a single person lifting their head in our direction as we go.

❋ ❋ ❋ ❋ ❋

WITH MY THIRD pint of beer in front of me and basketball on the TV, I've never been happier to be out of the office. I love what I do, don't get me wrong, but what more could you ask for on a Wednesday afternoon? Especially when you just finished up with your biggest client to date.

I take a long drink of my beer, and the delicious, ice-cold drink, which has made my brain a bit fuzzy, makes me temporarily forget all that Blake and I have to talk about. My phone vibrates in my pocket, and I know without looking that it's Dylan finally getting back to me. I didn't want to break the news to her over text, so I texted her as soon as I was walking out of the office, letting her know that I had some exciting news to share with her over dinner tomorrow.

I glance over at Blake, sitting beside me at the nearly empty bar. He's on his fourth beer, and I swallow my concern over the alarming rate he's throwing them back. In the years we've been friends, I've seen him hammered more than I can count. But he's also not the kind of guy to toss back beer after beer in the middle of a workday.

"I have something to tell you," I announce.

He tears his eyes away from the television and rests his head on his hand, which he's got propped up with his elbow on the bar.

"Lay it on me."

He takes another large gulp, and I wince. When he sets the glass down, I do my best to discreetly pull it toward me, away from his grasp. If he notices, he doesn't mention it.

"I asked Dylan to be my girlfriend on tour."

"Hell yeah! I'm so happy for you, man." His eyes are glazed, but there's a trace of enthusiasm. "So Operation-Get-Dylan-Back is officially complete then, huh?"

I stare down at the brown and black spotted marble counter of the bar and wipe my thumbs across the condensation of my glass. I smile to myself like an idiot.

"Yeah, it is. I've never been happier."

"I bet. I know how much this girl drove you crazy for years. I hope you guys have a long, happy, healthy life together."

I raise my brows at his authenticity. Unfortunately, the moment doesn't last too long before he asks, "So does this mean that you guys fucked?"

I sigh and chuckle to myself at how spot-on my prediction of his response was. My laughter trails off when I think about just how right I was. Thinking about how he views women as objects leaves me feeling deflated. As if the only reason a man would get into a relationship in the first place was so that he could sleep with her any time he wanted.

"I don't kiss and tell," I reply, taking a swig of the last dreg of my beer.

He rolls his eyes and swiftly grabs for his, leaving me no time to stop him. He downs the last of it and wipes his mouth. "That means yes, but if you don't want to talk about it, I'll respect it." He throws his hands up in an act of surrender, and I'm thankful he doesn't push me on the subject.

I'll tell him almost everything, but the days of talking about my bedroom activities like they're conquests are long gone.

"What did you mean when you said that it's not going to matter that you're leaving work in the middle of the day earlier?" I grill him, changing the subject and putting the spotlight on him before he can ask me any more questions that will make me question our friendship.

He chews on his lower lip and runs a hand through his hair. He doesn't break eye contact with the TV hanging above the bar, but I can see him mentally bracing to drop whatever bomb he's been withholding from me. I inhale deeply, steeling myself for the conversation that I know is going to put a damper on the entire day.

"I'm leaving Blue Bird. I put my notice in with the higher-ups yesterday."

"What do you mean? You've only been here for a little over a year, and you're one of the top editors." My head is swimming at the news, though the beer isn't helping either. I've been here for months and am just now finding my rhythm. One of the reasons I moved to New York was because I knew we'd get to work together. What was the point if he left me before I could make my mark with the company?

"I know. That's why I'm starting my own company, and I want you to come with me as my second in command."

I whip my head toward him. "What?!"

"Between the work I did in California and the connections I've made here in the city, I've got enough work that will follow me once I go. I'm tired of being someone's bitch. It's time to work for myself, and there's no better time than the present." He smiles boastfully, and the offer sobers me up in seconds.

I desperately wish I had another beer right now, but I need to stay clear-headed. I turn in my chair to face him, and I can tell by his expression that there is no convincing him otherwise. The decision has been made, and now the ball's in my court. I am in no way, shape, or form in the headspace to make a choice this big right now.

"Can I take a couple of days to think about it?"

He slaps his hand across my back, and I do my best to hide my slight flinch at the pain. With the drinks in his system, he underestimated his own strength, and that hurt like hell.

"Of course, but I hope you make the right choice."

I grimace at his words, and suddenly, all I can think about is texting Dylan. So much for having a great day.

34

DYLAN

Today is officially the last day working on Evelyn's account, and we're ending it with a meeting to go over all the campaign numbers. No matter what Katherine has to say, she can't bring me down because I know that this project went well. It went better than well–I crushed it, and even if she doesn't give me the proper recognition, I know the numbers speak for themselves.

Evelyn has gained thousands more followers over the past few weeks, the ARC readers Parker and I chose have been making viral content, and every date on the book tour was completely sold out. If that doesn't appease Katherine, nothing ever will.

As if she's been summoned, Katherine peeks her head around my cubicle. "Dylan, can you come to my office please?" I grit my teeth at the sound of her voice, the sound all too similar to nails on a chalkboard. She gives me no time to respond as she disappears back into her office.

I look down at my watch. It's only eleven, and our meeting isn't until one-thirty, which is never a good sign. I run a hand down my face and take a deep breath before dragging myself out of my chair.

If I had been in this position a few months ago, I would've feared that my time at Thrive was over. Now, I know that I'm an asset that the company can't afford to lose, and I stride toward her office with my chin held high.

While I'm walking toward her office, my phone vibrates. I take it out of my trouser pockets to find a text from Parker telling me he's got good news and wants to celebrate with dinner tomorrow.

All of the concerns about this conversation with Katherine promptly leave my head, and I feel a sense of peace from the short text alone. Parker grounds me, and no matter what I face in life, I know I can handle it with him by my side.

I open the closed door to Katherine's office–which she intentionally closed, knowing damn well I was right behind her–and step inside.

"Close the door behind you, please." She doesn't bother looking up from her computer, and I flare my nostrils in annoyance as I do as I'm asked. I turn around with a fake smile on my face and take a seat in the chair across from her.

I sit in silence, my hands clasped in my lap, and I grow restless as the time slowly passes. She still hasn't looked in my direction, and she's typing away on her computer, doing a mighty fine job ignoring me. The clacking of the keyboard grates my nerves, and I have to clench my teeth to keep myself at ease. I clear my throat, trying to draw her attention away from her screen.

"One moment."

One minute goes by, not a peep. Two minutes pass, and I'm tapping my fingers on the arm of the chair while I shake my leg. The confidence I had when I walked in is beginning to falter, and if she doesn't start speaking, I'm afraid I'm going to lose it completely.

"Thanks for waiting." She pulls her large, red, rectangular glasses off her face and places them down in front of her as she brings her eyes to mine. I don't offer a response, letting her sit in the same silence that she made me stew in. Disappointingly, she doesn't seem to care and continues.

"I know we have the meeting with Evelyn in an hour and a half, but I wanted to talk to you before one-on-one."

My stomach does a somersault, and I rest my hands back in my lap so I can give myself a little pat of encouragement. My conviction may have grown shakier while I sat in silence, but I know damn well that no matter what she says, I've proven myself, and I've never been more proud.

I give myself a small mental pep talk and tilt my head toward the ceiling, straightening my posture. I'll fake it until I make it through this entire meeting if I have to.

"I've been looking over the numbers, and I must admit I'm impressed." My hand flies to my mouth as I take in a sudden audible breath. I quickly pull it shut, hopeful that she didn't hear my gasp.

Was that a…compliment?

"You've taken everything that I've given you with no complaints, and Evelyn sent me a detailed email this morning about how happy she was working with you in particular." She interlocks her fingers in a steeple in front of her and leans on her elbows to bring her body closer to mine from across her desk. "I'd like to offer you the role of Marketing Coordinator."

My eyebrows shoot up to my hairline, and I'm certain my eyes are the size of saucers. The initial tension I felt in my shoulders vanishes and is replaced with a calmness that I haven't felt in Katherine's presence since starting here. I keep my posture straight, indisposed to show her my true feelings.

"The role has a few more responsibilities. You'd be working under Scarlett, as I just promoted her to Marketing Director this morning. And you'd receive a ten percent raise." The words sound pained coming from her mouth, but I don't mind it because I'm finally getting the recognition I deserve–even if the raise is less than ideal.

A sudden rush of pride bubbles up inside me as I think about Scarlett getting the credit she deserves. I can't think of a more worthy person.

"Thank you so much for this opportunity. I appreciate your confidence in my abilities, and I will do everything to show you that this is the right decision to make."

"Mhmm," She replies curtly. "You can go now." And with that, she sends me away with a wave of her hand. Typically, I'd be hurt by the blatant dismissal, but I'm on cloud nine, and there's nothing that could bring me back down.

I skip out of the office and immediately pull my phone out of my pocket. I text Parker quickly and let him know that I also have something worth celebrating, then stuff it back in my pocket.

I let out a small squeal and find Scarlett at her desk, who's already waiting for me, with a grin on her face. Without saying a word, she leaps up and pulls me into a hug, which leads to us jumping in circles in giddiness.

I can feel the stares of my coworkers, but I'm too wrapped up in the moment to give it a second thought.

"Hi, boss." I pull away and wink at her.

"I'm about to make your life a living hell," she jokes, and I let out a small giggle.

"Can't be any worse than what I've gotten from Katherine these past few months."

I sit down on the edge of her desk and release a breath. Although some people may hate working closely under one of their best friends, there's nothing I'd love more. Scarlett is incredible at what she does, and I know that anything I can learn from her will only help me become better at what I do.

She relaxes back down in her chair and crosses her ankles.

"All of your hard work paid off, Dyl. Just like I knew it would."

"Me? Your hard work paid off! You're one step closer to taking Katherine's job." I nudge her shoulder with my fingers, and she lets out a snort.

"Yeah, we'll see. Dinner tonight to celebrate? On me."

"Let's do it!" I agree.

"How does Italian sound?" She pulls out her phone and looks at me expectantly.

"I'll never turn down a bowl of pasta."

"I was hoping you'd say that. I'll text my friend who works at Ammazzacaffeè and see if she can get us a last-minute reservation." She starts typing away, and my mouth waters at the thought.

I look down at my phone—two hours until our meeting.

"Perfect. Keep me posted. I'm going to get some work done before our meeting. Ooh, do you think this means I can move to that empty desk?" I point to the vacant desk that's been sitting untouched for months right next to Scarlett's. "I may need your help with clients, after all."

"I'll talk to Katherine and see what I can do." She playfully smirks, and I reluctantly head back to my desk.

In a few short hours, I'll be enjoying a heaping bowl of Bolognese and celebratory wine with one of my best friends. And tomorrow, I get to break the news to my *boyfriend*. Life is perfect.

35

PARKER

The steaks are sitting on my kitchen counter, seasoned and ready to be cooked. The wine is poured, and my favorite jazz playlist is playing throughout my apartment on my speaker. I've got candles lit and even invested in a room spray so that Dylan won't think that my apartment is the typical bachelor's pad. It is, but anything helps.

We've only been in town for a few days since the end of the tour, which means she's not gotten the chance to come over yet. Her seeing where I spend a lot of my free time makes me anxious for some unknown reason. Probably because the last time we dated, I was a naive college student whose idea of decorating was music posters and navy plaid sheets. I've come a long way since then.

There's a soft tap on my front door, and the sound brings a grin to my face. I grab the bouquet I picked up at the flower stand on my way home and hide it behind my back before opening the door.

Dylan's standing on the other side, looking as beautiful as ever. She's wearing a light pink floral slip dress and a denim jacket. The neckline gives the perfect peek of cleavage, and I push my need to claim her aside. There's time for that later.

"Hi," she whispers, her cheeks pinched, eyes wrinkled from her million-dollar smile that stops my heart every time I see it.

I pull the arrangement of wildflowers from behind my back as I whisper "hello" back. The grin that she's wearing grows, and she throws her arms around my neck, causing me to lose my balance. I grip the door frame with my free hand, catching myself from falling. When I'm steady again, I wrap both of my arms around her waist and pull her to me. I take a deep inhale, savoring her signature sweet yet spicy scent.

I take a step back, usher her in, and hand her the flowers. She brings them to her nose to smell and hums joyfully to herself. Once the door is closed, I turn around and find her studying my apartment in wonder.

"Welcome home," I say as I help her out of her jacket. I place it on one of the barstools that sit up against my kitchen counter and make my way back to the stove. As she's making herself comfortable in the same seat, I stare at her, waiting in agony to see what she thinks. All I've ever wanted to do in life is impress this girl–now more than ever.

"This place is beautiful. You've really come a long way, haven't you?" She closes her eyes and inhales deeply. "It even smells incredible. Who are you, and what have you done with the Parker I knew five years ago?"

I chuckle and throw my kitchen towel over my shoulder.

"He grew up. And thank god for that because I needed to." I'm brimming with satisfaction as I place the flowers in a vase with water–yes, I even went and bought a fucking vase for the girl–and pour her a glass of wine. "You alright with steak for dinner? I've got Parmesan-crusted potatoes and asparagus to go with it." Her brows fly up in surprise, causing me to snort out another laugh. "What?"

"You can cook now, too? Maybe all those years apart weren't

such a bad thing after all." She lifts her now full glass of wine up for a toast and takes a sip. I halfheartedly roll my eyes at her and throw butter into the piping hot cast iron skillet I've had heating up on my stove. Once it melts, I place the two steaks down.

After a few minutes, I flip them and, with a quick glance at my watch, pull the potatoes and asparagus out of the oven. Dylan is watching me in silence, and I bathe in the way her undivided attention makes me feel.

"How was your day?" I ask, cutting the silence.

"It was great. You're not the only one with exciting news to share." She takes another sip of her wine, trying and failing to be as nonchalant as possible. I can tell she's practically bursting at the seams, and her excitement is contagious.

"Oh, is that so?" I question as I baste rosemary-infused butter over the steaks and take them off the heat to rest.

"Yes! But I want to hear yours first." She's wiggling in her seat, so I hurry to plate our food in a way that I'm damn proud of. All of those episodes of Chopped I binged paid off.

I plant a kiss on her cheek and bring the food and flowers over to my kitchen table.

The long, gray, concrete table is set with silverware and more candles. I place the flowers in the middle as a centerpiece and take a moment to admire my work. It may just be dinner, and she deserves far more than something this simple, but I put a lot of thought into it. When I look up, she's still sitting at the bar, watching me with soft eyes and a hand to her chest.

"This is so romantic," she coos. She glides over to me and wraps her arms around my waist, holding me from behind. "Thank you for all of this. It's beautiful."

I turn to face her and take her jaw into my palms, rubbing my thumb across her silky skin. "You deserve it. You deserve more than this, actually. But this is just the beginning." I lift her chin up to me and press one more kiss to her nose. As much as

I want to get lost in her tonight, I pull away. "Let's eat before the food gets cold."

She lets out a small grumble of disappointment, which pulls a chuckle from my chest. I shake my head and pull her chair out for her. After getting her situated, I take my place across from her and pick up my wine glass one last time. "Cheers to us, Lucky. We're just getting started." We gently hit our glasses together with a *clink* and take a small sip.

"I love you so much." She jumps in before I can get a word out, clapping her hands together. "Now tell me what the good news is. The suspense is killing me."

I take a bite of steak and chew slowly, reveling in the explosion of flavor in my mouth with my eyes closed. I did good–I did *so* good.

I peep an eye open, and she's shaking her head at me, clearly annoyed. I love riling her up. "Parker! I'm serious! What's the news?"

I make a show of swallowing and wiping the corners of my mouth with my napkin. I wash the bite down with some water and finally give in.

"Evelyn made the New York Times Best Seller list."

Dylan lets out a high-pitched shriek, and I cover my ears to keep my eardrums intact. "You did it!" she crows.

"We did it," I correct her. "I just helped make sure the book was ready to hit shelves. Your marketing helped garnish interest. You're the one who helped put together the book tour and brought in those audiences every single day."

"We make a good team, don't we?" She rests her chin on her knuckle, tilting her head. The twinkle in her eyes, paired with that question, makes the urge to ditch dinner and make love to her almost unbearable. The quiet rumble of my hungry stomach stops me, which means I need to hurry so I can show her *how* much better we are together.

"We do. Your turn. What's this good news you've had

waiting for me?" I throw her question back at her, and she shifts to sit taller.

"I got promoted. My new title is officially Marketing Coordinator, and I'm going to be working under Scarlett."

I push out of my chair, abandoning my food, and run to her side. I pull her up and out of her chair and into my arms, spinning her around. Her arms wrap snugly around my neck, and she lets out a melody of laughter that will forever remain ingrained in my mind. I set her down and rest my forehead against hers, cupping the back of her head.

"Congratulations, Lucky. I don't know anyone more deserving." I croon, brushing my nose against hers. Her hot breath hits my lips, and my gaze falls down to hers. They're perfectly plump and only inches away from my own.

"Thank you," she utters breathlessly. My breath hitches when she licks her lips, and I succumb to the temptation, closing the distance between us.

She lets out a small moan into my mouth, and I greedily swallow the sound that makes my entire body buzz. Her hands go from my neck up into my hair, and she gives it a light tug. A groan escapes from me against her lips, and I latch onto her hips, pulling her tighter against me so she can feel the growing bulge hiding beneath my jeans.

She breaks us apart, leaving me winded, my chest heaving. My eyes rest on her swollen lips, then trail down to her chest. Her dress shifted while we got carried away, giving me a better view of her supple cleavage. She follows my stare and grins, fixing herself. "That's dessert. The quicker you can eat, the sooner you can have it."

With a pat on my chest, she sits back in her chair, and I rush back over to mine. I'm ready to down this food as quickly as possible so we can resume *that*.

We sit in silence, both with stupid smiles on our faces that we simply can't seem to shake.

Once we're both finished, Dylan leans back in her chair and rests a hand on her stomach. "That was incredible. Looks like you're going to be doing all of the cooking in our relationship from here on forward."

I mimic her stance and cross one leg over the other, folding my arms over my chest. "Oh, is that so? What do I get out of it?"

"Unlimited dessert." The wicked flare in her eyes is a reminder of what we stopped only moments ago, and my cock twitches at the sight.

"You drive a hard bargain, but you've got yourself a deal."

I stand and stack our plates. As I'm heading to the kitchen sink, I catch Dylan sneaking off toward my bedroom out of the corner of my eye. "Where do you think you're going?"

"I think it's time for dessert, don't you?"

I drop the plates in the sink and race after her. The dishes can wait until the morning.

36

DYLAN

I'm lying in Parker's bed, wrapped up in his sheets, trying to catch my breath. That may have been one of the best desserts I've ever had–and I'm not talking about the whipped cream that may or may not have been involved.

Parker slithers his way up my bare stomach, planting small kisses up to my collarbones.

"I should take a shower. I'm all sticky." I replay all of our... activities in my mind, and my cheeks heat up. "Want to join me?" He mumbles into the crook of my neck.

My skin breaks out in gooseflesh at the feeling of his hot breath against my skin, and I give him a small shove with a giggle. If he's not careful, I'm going to have to go back for seconds, and I'm not sure either of us can handle that right now.

"Yeah, I'll be right behind you."

He pecks me on the lips and walks to the bathroom, his bare ass just asking to be gawked at. With a tilt of my head, I take a mental snapshot of the view and lay back down on the bed to get myself together.

After a few seconds, I sit up, wrap the sheet around me, and shuffle the sheets in search of my phone. Between the cooking, dinner, and escapades after, I have no idea what time it is. When I can't find anything on the bed, I stand up and start looking around the room until I find an iPhone face up on the floor.

I bend down and pick it up, clicking the power button. The screen illuminates, reading almost ten p.m. One glimpse at the wallpaper–a photo of the New York skyline–tells me this isn't my phone, but before I can set it down to find my own, my eyes snag on an email notification.

Although I can't see the entire email, the small blurb that is visible appears to be from Thames & Type, a publishing company in London. I don't know much about the business, but when my eyes scan across the words, "We'd love to talk further about the job opportunity we previously discussed," my stomach plummets.

A job opportunity in England? Why hasn't Parker said a word about this?

My eyes sting as tears build, and I take an uneven breath, trying to give myself a moment to process this. I'm sure there's a reasonable explanation if I just asked, but my brain is shutting down. The room feels like it's caving in on me, and I'm not in the right head space to have that conversation. What am I supposed to say anyway? Hey, I was snooping through your phone and saw this email?

My vision begins to grow spotty around the edges, and I sit on the edge of the bed with my head in between my legs, just like I did at the airport. I focus on inhaling and exhaling slowly and deeply, but my mind won't slow down. All I can think about is what it was like to lose him all those years ago and how devastated I was. It felt like the life had been drained out of me, and I'm not ready to go through that same pain again.

We just got back together, for fuck's sake. If he couldn't handle a long-distance relationship back then, how the hell are we supposed to make it work when he's five hours ahead and a seven-hour flight away? My job at Thrive may not be my forever job, but I just got promoted, and I feel like I'm just now settling in. I'm not ready to give that up.

"You coming?" Parker's voice echoes from the shower.

I try to find my voice, to tell him that I'll be right there, but my throat is dry, and the words catch like sand no matter how hard I try to speak. The uneasiness continues to build up in my chest, and I feel like a weighted barbell is being pressed down on me. I finally found my happiness after years of going through the motions, and now it's all at risk of being taken away from me again.

"Lucky?" I can barely hear the water shut off over the whooshing in my ears. I close my eyes, doing everything in my power to soothe myself. The rational part of me understands this is an overreaction. Yet, I can't stop the anxiety from clawing at my thoughts, threatening to pull me under.

I drop the phone where I found it right before I feel the bed beside me shift. Out of my peripheral, I see Parker sitting on the bed next to me in nothing but a towel. Water droplets stream down his skin, and in any other instance, I would have licked them up, distracting us from the point of the shower in the first place.

"Hey, what's going on?" He tries to place his hand on my lap, but I immediately shoot out of bed, dashing over to the door.

I have to get out of here before the anxiety attack has me in its chokehold.

"I just remembered Amelia needs me tonight. She's got a lot going on, and I told her I would be home early." My breathing is labored, and I can only hope he doesn't notice.

He cocks an eyebrow, clearly not believing a word I say, but he doesn't argue with me.

"Are you okay?" He walks up to me and attempts to pull me

into his arms, but I place a hand on his chest to create a barrier before I can break down in front of him.

I need a moment to process this. Alone.

I wear my best fake smile. "Yeah, I just don't want to disappoint her."

He nods, unsure of what to say yet unwilling to fight me on it. "Okay, are we still on for The Met tomorrow?" I've dreamed of going on a museum date since moving to the city, and the reminder of it makes my heart crack in half.

"I'll call you." I kiss his cheek and hurry to the door, giving him no time to process what I'm saying. As soon as I'm out of the apartment and back outside, I lean up against his building, closing my eyes and planting a hand on my chest. I mentally scan each part of my body, starting with my toes to the top of my head. Once I feel the panic subside, I determine it's safe to start the trek home.

As I walk, the warmth of early summer seeps into my bones, helping to further calm my mind a bit. I don't blame him for not telling me. I've been so hot and cold with him all winter and spring, and it's not like we were dating. I just can't see why he'd want to get into a relationship, knowing there's a high possibility of him moving–especially because he knew how guarded I was.

I can't ask him to stay. We may have a history, but *this* version of us is too new. Far too new to be asking for something that big already. But I'm not sure long distance is something I can go through again. Yes, I am older. I can handle my emotions–though that is questionable right now–better than I could back then. But I just want to be able to enjoy having him in my life again–fully, nothing in our way.

With each step, the heaviness lifts, so I opt to walk instead of taking the subway. As the anxiety lessens, it's replaced with dread. I'm going to have so much explaining to do.

37

DYLAN

When I get home, Amelia is curled up on the couch with a chunky blanket and a sleeve of Oreos, watching the latest trashy reality TV show. Despite feeling heavy-hearted over my behavior and the idea of Parker leaving as we're just getting started, the sight brings a hiccupped laugh out of me.

She perks up when she sees me, turning the TV down. "Hi, Dee. How was your date night?" She sneaks a look at the clock on the wall. That's right, we're mature adults with wall clocks. It has nothing to do with the fact that it looks cute and matches the decor. "You're home early."

I kick my shoes off, drop my purse onto the kitchen counter, and slump on the couch next to her, grabbing an Oreo–or two–in the process. I sigh and run a hand through my hair.

"I fucked up."

She turns her body toward me, crossing her legs and setting the cookies in between us for easier access. God bless her for knowing anything sugary can get me through the trenches. "Fucked up, how?"

"Mia, the night was perfect. He cooked us this beautiful dinner–steak, potatoes, asparagus, a nice bottle of wine. He planned the whole thing to tell me that Evelyn is a New York Times Best Seller. It was so romantic."

Her bottom lip juts out in a pout. "That sounds amazing. So how did you fuck up..." She trails off, confounded.

"I got to tell him the news of the promotion, and he was so damn proud of me. We had some of the best sex we've ever had, and then, as we were getting ready to shower, I picked up his phone by accident."

Her back goes stiff, and her eyes narrow down into slits. The look is so deadly it gives me the heebie-jeebies. "If that fucker is already cheating, I swear I will take a baseball bat to everything he loves. I'll make him regret the day he was born."

I can't avoid the small smile that grows on my face. She's so protective, and it's a reminder of how lucky I am to have her in my life. It's reassuring knowing that even if my world goes up in flames, I'll always have her in my corner. If I go down, she'll be right there with me.

"It's nothing like that."

"Thank God. I'd prefer not to have the cops called on me." She pats my hand. "Just remember that it is on the table should you ever need it, though." She throws me a wink, and I chuckle, shaking my head.

When the laughter dies down, I continue, "I saw an email, Mia. It was from a publisher in London. I couldn't see the full thing, but it mentioned wanting to talk over a job offer they previously discussed. I couldn't even bring it up with Parker like a normal person. I started to have another episode, so I shut down and ran." My eyes tingle with tears, and I push them back, having had enough for one day.

"Oh, babe." She scoots closer to me on the couch and envelops me in a tight hug. I cling to her and let out a shaky breath. "I think that email would've freaked anyone out in a new relationship. Why do you think it made you so anxious?"

"I was immediately brought back to college. We were two very different people back then, but the distance ruined us. I've had to protect my heart every day since he walked away from me last time. I don't want to go through that again."

She brushes my tangled hair down, gently twirling the ends around her finger. I feel her chest vibrate with a small hum as she processes everything. "I love you, Dyl. And I don't blame you for wanting to protect yourself. But that's no way to live. You can't constantly walk around afraid that Parker is going to break your heart. I bet if you asked him about the email, he'd have a very reasonable answer."

I pull away from her grasp and lean against the back of the couch, throwing my arms over my face in shame. "I know. I didn't mean to." My voice cracks, and I feel so small. She pulls my hands away, placing them between us and giving them a light squeeze. Her face transforms into a gentle, reassuring smile.

"I know you didn't. No one faults you for your actions. Trusting someone with something as valuable as your heart is one of the scariest things we can do in our lifetime. It's easy to put your guard up at the first sight of danger. But if we all did that, we'd live in a sad, loveless world. And that's not a world I want to live in if you ask me."

A vision of my life without Parker flashes in my mind. A montage of the past five years plays, and I force myself to swallow the despair that rises in my throat. I have learned so many lessons in that time.

I took myself on solo dates and lived alone to learn how to appreciate my own company. I moved across the country and taught myself that I could do hard things. I watched all of my friends slowly move on with their lives, leaving me alone, and it taught me the most important lesson of all–to be happy in life, I have to be happy with myself.

These lessons are invaluable, and I'm so grateful I was forced to go through them because I wouldn't be who I am today without them.

But when I think about what my future looks like, Parker is by my side. When I'm going through anything that makes me doubt my strength, I want him there to help pick me up. When I have moments where I momentarily lose faith in myself, I want him there by my side to tell me just how much he believes in me. I want him there through it all–even if it means that I get that support from over three thousand miles away. I'd rather have some of him than none of him.

"That isn't a world I want to live in either. I hope he's not mad at me. I did a pretty poor job of rushing out of there." I blow out a sigh, my cheeks ballooning up as I release the hot air and tension that's been building inside of me.

"I'm sure he's more confused than anything, but he'll be understanding. When are you supposed to see him next?"

"Tomorrow. We're supposed to have a date at The Met."

Amelia slams a hand against her chest dramatically, shaking her head. "You two are so damn cute. I need my own Parker."

It's my turn to give her an encouraging squeeze. "He's coming, don't you worry."

She disregards the thought with a flip of her hand. She presses on, "I think you should text him right now and tell him that you're still on for the date. And be honest with him. Tell him you saw the email and panicked. I think he'll be understanding, and you guys can talk about what the future holds for you together."

"You're right." I shift closer to her and rest my head on her shoulder. "Thank you. I don't know what I would've done without you."

"You would've been fine. But I understand sometimes you just need to talk things out even though you know deep down what you need to do."

"Forever grateful shitty social media brought me you," I gush.

"Me too. Thank God you weren't some creep. This conversation would be going very differently," she cracks.

With one last laugh, I grab one more Oreo, give her a hug, and stand. I grab my purse off the kitchen counter and dig around for my phone, which I snatched in a hurry on my way out of Parker's apartment. Turns out I had left my phone in there the entire time. One look tells me that I have two missed texts and a missed call from Parker.

"I'm going to get some sleep. Goodnight Mia. I love you!" I exclaim.

"I love you too, Dee." Amelia turns the TV back up, and our apartment fills with the sound of housewives screaming at one another about god knows what.

When I stride into my room, I throw my purse on a chair beside my bed and plant myself on the edge of my mattress. I reread the texts from Parker, remorse rising in the back of my throat like bile.

> Parker: You seemed upset when you left. I hope everything is alright. Please text me when you get home so I know you made it safely.
>
> Parker: I love you, Lucky

I send him a text back, letting him know that I'm home, safe, and happy. I also let him know that we're still on for tomorrow before changing into a pair of silky pajamas and getting ready for bed. With an absurd amount of skincare products on and my teeth brushed, I climb into my bed, allowing myself to immediately be swallowed by the warmth of my comforter.

I grab my newest romance novel off of my nightstand and read about the love everyone fantasizes about–which I'm now confident I have–until my eyes grow heavy.

38

PARKER

I'm waiting on the steps of The Met, my stomach in knots. I don't know what happened yesterday, but Dylan nearly left skid marks on my floor on her way out. Despite it being almost seven, the sun is still high in the sky, the days growing longer with the summer months approaching.

I do my best to take in the sight of the tall buildings dyed gold, but all I can think about is what could've upset Dylan yesterday. Her texts before bed were normal, but I can't shake the niggling feeling that she was just saying that to get me off her back.

I scan my surroundings, my eyes stopping as soon as they land on the breathtaking brunette approaching me. She's wearing a long white skirt that hits just above her ankles and a black short-sleeved sweater top. Her caramel hair is pulled up into a loose bun at the top of her head with loose tendrils framing her face, and she's wearing that red lipstick that makes my knees go weak.

Every time I see her, it feels like the wind is knocked out of my lungs. My face breaks out in a grin that I wouldn't be able to hide, no matter how hard I tried. Dylan matches it with her own, and the happiness on her face makes my pulse accelerate. We're about to look at some of the world's most beautiful artwork, but I already know that her smile will be my favorite piece of art I see tonight.

"Hi," I whisper into her ear as I pick her up in my arms. Her arms tighten around my neck, and my god, I could stay like this forever. I place her back down on her feet, but her arms don't loosen around me.

"Hi you," she mumbles shyly.

"You look beautiful."

"You don't look half bad yourself."

I roll my eyes but chuckle. "Should we head inside?" I grab her hand and turn toward the museum, but I feel her hesitation. When I look back at her, she's rooted in the spot I placed her, with a look of distress on her face. I try not to jump to conclusions.

Maybe she wants to talk about what happened yesterday. I didn't bother mentioning it once while we were texting today. I knew she'd come to me when she felt ready.

"Do you mind if we sit and talk out here first? There's something I need to get off my chest."

Well, *shit*. That's not the direction I thought it was headed. I nod, feeling like I'm on a roller coaster that won't stop climbing.

My mind snags on the fact that she said she wanted to talk out here first, which means she's not about to break up with me, right? If so, there would be no after–that would make for one fucking awkward date. "Of course." I do my best to play it cool as I sit down on one of the many steps that lead up to the entrance of the museum.

"I feel like Blair Waldorf." She scans her surroundings, clearly delaying whatever she wants to tell me. I don't dignify the procrastination with a response. I'm not in the state to joke around right now, even if I wanted to.

She blows out a breath of understanding, catching onto my

lack of desire to put this conversation off any longer than we have to.

"I saw an email on your phone last night. I went to check the time and see if I had any messages, and I accidentally picked yours up. Before I could put it back, I saw a notification on your home screen. I wasn't trying to snoop. It just kind of happened..." When she's done speaking, her voice is lost to the air, so quiet her words nearly vanish.

My eyebrows stitch together in confusion. I mentally go through my inbox, trying to remember what I could've received that would've upset her, but I come up short.

"I'm not sure I'm following."

"The email was from Thames & Type. It mentioned something about discussing a job offer. I don't know much about the publishing world, but I do know that they're one of the biggest publishers in London."

Fuck. No wonder she ran out of there.

I pinch the bridge of my nose and exhale sharply. I never meant for her to see that, let alone have to sulk with the idea that now that we've finally gotten back together, it's going to be ripped apart by distance for the second time in our lives.

I grab her hand in mine, trying to comfort her in any way I can.

"Shortly after I moved to New York, they approached me about working for them. At the time, I had expressed interest, but I told them I wanted to settle into the city first. I had just made the move across the country. The last thing I wanted to do was move across the world two months later. It was too much to process. And Blake put his neck on the line to get me the job at Blue Bird in the first place. I couldn't accept it and run right after. But I didn't want to turn them down because it's a great offer."

I let my thumb drift across her hand in soothing circles as she tenses. She looks deep in thought, and I fight the urge to smooth out the wrinkle in between her brows that she gets when she's concentrating.

"I couldn't live with myself if I asked you to stay for us." Her eyes meet mine, and the internal battle she's facing reads on her face. She's trying to be strong, but I can tell how much this hurts her.

"Lucky, I'm not taking it. And before you overthink it, it's not because you're asking me to do anything. It's a decision I made on my own–before I asked you to be my girlfriend." A frown tugs at her lips as she chews the inside of her cheek, but before she can argue with me, I power on.

"As soon as I saw you on that flight, I knew I had to give this a fighting chance. I had no idea whether or not we'd end up where we are today. Hell, I had no idea if you'd even entertain the idea. All I knew was that I was going to try. Even if it meant this ended with us being friends. That was a risk I was willing to take. I don't care about the job. I care about you. You've always been my priority, even though I did a terrible job showing you that in the past."

"You didn't do a terrible job." She comes to my defense, interrupting my train of thought. A small rumble of laughter rolls through my chest.

"I did. It's something I've lived with every day since we broke up, but now that I have a second chance, I'm not going to fuck it up again. I don't care about that job. I have everything I want here in this city. I have you. I'm making this decision for me. For us. And I'm sorry that I didn't tell you earlier. I've just been so wrapped up in Evelyn's project and spending as much time with you as possible. It didn't even cross my mind."

"I'm the one who should be sorry. I invaded your privacy and ran off without giving you a chance to explain. Can you ever forgive me?"

I tuck a loose curl behind her ear and place a gentle kiss on her forehead. She leans into my touch, and we sit in silence for a few blissful minutes. When I pull away, I cup her cheek and softly brush her skin.

"There's no reason to forgive you, Lucky. You did nothing wrong. Please forgive me."

She shakes her head adamantly. "You have nothing to be sorry about either. But before all of this is over, I have to ask, are you sure that this is the decision you want to make? Your happiness is most important to me. Distance was hard for us in college, but we're not those same naive kids anymore. We can handle it. I don't mind racking up airline points and gallivanting around Europe with you. I just don't want you to have any regrets."

"The only thing I regret in my life is letting you walk away the first time. I regret not fighting harder to keep you in my life. I regret hurting you. And all I can do now is tell you I'm not letting you go."

As I speak, I see the dark storm clouds that hung over her dissipate. She sits taller, and her eyes become misty, and it's a picture I want to save for the rest of my life. The woman I love in tears on the steps of one of the most famous museums in the world, willing to sacrifice everything to give us a chance.

She presses her forehead to mine, our noses touching. "I love you so much. You're stuck with me now. I hope you know what you've gotten yourself into."

I lower my lips to hers, kissing her softly. "I wouldn't have it any other way," I mumble against her mouth. And just like that, I'm kissing her teeth as she breaks out into a grin so blinding I all but have to shield my eyes.

As much as it pains me, I pull away from her and stand up, wiping my pants off in the process. I reach out to her with a hand, and she immediately grabs it.

"Shall we go see some art?"

She hoists herself up and wraps her arms around my waist. When I look down into her eyes, they're shimmering like a night sky full of stars. They're a galaxy of their own, and they pull me into their orbit.

"There's nothing I'd love more."

We walk toward the entrance, holding onto one another tightly, and I sigh in contentment. I found luck in the city and I couldn't be any happier.

39

DYLAN

The echoes of the museum visitors' footsteps fade as everyone trickles out for the day. Parker and I have spent the last hour and a half walking around the exhibits, laughing, admiring art, and, most importantly, relishing in each other's company.

He handled my overreaction about the email with much more grace than I deserved. If I had just communicated with him, we could've enjoyed our evening together from the jump. But I didn't, and now I know where he stands.

I knew he was serious about us and this relationship, but hearing he's here to stay makes me feel like I can take on anything the world throws at me.

I feel like I've been gliding around the museum, my steps barely grazing the ground. The idea that I get to love this person who felt like mine from the very beginning is something I'm not sure I'll ever be able to accept fully. I've read countless romance novels, but our love story is turning out to be my favorite.

The sculptures are painted in a soft glow from the overhead lights, and Parker and I are the only two left in this wing of the museum. I look down at my watch. It's five minutes until closing, and I'm not ready for this night to end.

I absently trace the railing as I study the statue before me. I'm enamored by the way the marble looks like real flesh, with curtains of fabric draping the body. How something so strong and solid can look so soft and delicate is beyond me.

"You've always loved art." Parker's voice pulls me away from the model. "If it were up to you, you'd spend an entire day here."

I turn around to see Parker sitting on a bench, admiring me as if I were an exhibit, and a spark of excitement dances in my belly. I return my eyes to the art in front of me. "This place is magical at night."

His footsteps grow nearer as he walks over to me, wrapping his arms around my waist. He rests his head on my shoulder, and his words tickle my ear, sending a shiver down my spine. "It is. Especially tonight." His voice is full of warmth, and it pulls a grin from me effortlessly.

I turn to face him, lifting my chin to meet his eye. "You always were a romantic, weren't you?" I scrunch my nose.

"Only with you." His hand begins to trail up my back under my sweater, and the chills come back in droves. I bite my tongue to stop myself from letting out a soft groan at the touch. It's so gentle and innocent, yet my mind runs like the speed of lightning, thinking of his hands skimming down the rest of my body.

I sigh and rest my head on his chest, listening to the steady sound of his heartbeat. It's quick, like mine, and I shut my eyes, losing myself to the rhythm.

"At the risk of sounding like a walking Hallmark card, I can't believe we're here. I can't believe the past few months," I murmur.

"Me neither. But you *are* my lucky charm, so it only makes

sense. With you around, I'll always be the luckiest man in the world."

"Okay, you've got me beat for the Hallmark commentary," I snort.

He barks out a husky laugh, and I look up at him, my heart dangerously close to bursting. This night has been everything I could have dreamed of and more. I stand up on my toes and kiss him gently. The kiss is soft and slow and full of everything I've imagined telling him over the past few years. All of the missed moments, regrets, and longing are replaced with this moment, here and now.

When we finally break apart, we keep our foreheads pressed together.

"This time," I whisper, my voice full of certainty, "we won't lose each other."

He nods, keeping our bodies touching. "This time, we'll make our own luck."

Parker pulls away from me and holds his hand out. My attention shifts to his hand, then back to his face, an unspoken question hanging between us.

"Dance with me."

I giggle and take his hand with no intention of dancing. "There's no music, though. Besides, the museum is officially closed. We should get going before they kick us out."

"Then let's make it quick."

With a swift motion, he pulls me back, and I melt against his chest. We begin swaying to the sound of silence. The only thing we can hear is the quiet sound of our shoes tapping against the floor. In that moment, I know that this is going to be a core memory that I'm never going to forget.

I lose myself in him, cherishing the feeling of our bodies together in a way that's arguably more intimate than if we were in bed together. I'm not sure how long we dance, but the moment is ruined when the sound of a stranger's heavy footsteps grows closer down the hallway.

"Alright, Lucky. I need you to work your charm." Parker pulls away from me and grabs my hand, a playful hint of mischief twinkling in his eye.

"What do you mean?" My eyes widen, and this only makes the grin that he's wearing bigger.

"Run."

Before I can argue, we're running through The Met, hands interlocked, escaping the security guard gaining on us. And at that moment, in a fit of laughter, I know that Parker is my good luck charm, too. And with him by my side, everything is going to be okay.

FOUR MONTHS LATER

"Are you ready?" I call out to Parker from his living room. He appears from his bedroom, clad in a black suit and tie, and I swear it makes me lightheaded. Parker is always good-looking, but seeing him dressed to the nines, walking in my direction, makes my world tilt on its axis.

"Since when do you get ready faster than me?" He frowns.

I fix a few of his rogue curls that are sticking straight up from our late afternoon rendezvous. He grins sheepishly, running another hand through his hair, messing it up further. I roll my eyes, which he responds to with a peck on my cheek.

"It's a skill I've honed over the years. Maybe I can teach you a thing or two," I reply boastfully.

"Oh, I like it when you play teacher. Are you going to tell me I'm a good boy?" He wraps his arms around my waist and buries his face into the crook of my neck, letting out a guttural groan that echos against my skin.

With a giggle, I shove him off of me. "Watch yourself. We're already running late." I glance down at my phone. We've got fifteen minutes until we're supposed to meet with Scarlett and

Blake at Le Bernardin for a celebratory dinner and we haven't left yet.

Three months ago, Blake opened his own publishing agency and convinced Parker to be his partner. We spent many nights making pros and cons lists, and, at the end of the day, we both decided that the risk was worth taking.

After Evelyn, Parker became one of the most sought-after editors at Blue Bird, and thanks to his success, he was fortunate enough to gather a long list of clients before he parted ways. Between Parker and Blake, investors were eager to get a piece of the pie–thus, Beaumont Literary Group was born.

I've never seen Parker happier than I have these past few months. I'd be foolish to assume that our relationship was a key player in that. He wakes up every morning excited to go to work, and when he comes home, all he can talk about is the day that he had. Seeing him beaming with pride only reaffirms that we needed to go our separate ways to become the best versions of ourselves. Now, things couldn't get better–we're moving in together later this month, we're both thriving at work, and we spend our free time exploring the city that we now call home.

With Scarlett as my boss, Katherine has backed off immensely. So much so that I rarely interact with her, which makes my time at Thrive far more enjoyable. I'm regularly given accounts to run, and Scarlett gives me the creative freedom I need to be good at my job, which has already resulted in a few more big wins. It's night and day compared to how it started all those months ago, and I'm so grateful that I waited it out.

"Fine, but I want you to boss me around when we get home." Parker places a rough kiss on my collarbone and drags me out the door with minutes to spare.

✹ ✹ ✹ ✹ ✹

"God, this is delicious," I mewl as I take another bite of the Peruvian dark chocolate tart that Parker and I are splitting. I'm entirely too full from the caviar and salmon I ate, but the dessert is too delicious to pass up. Scarlett eats a spoonful of the banana toffee pudding she and Blake are sharing and moans, wordlessly sharing the same sentiment.

When Blake's brows raise at the almost sexual noise that comes out of Scarlett's mouth, I let out a stifled giggle that I have to hide behind my napkin. We've all split a couple of bottles of champagne, and the bubbles have *definitely* gone to my head. Scarlett's eyes meet mine in question before flicking over to Blake's.

"Save those noises for later," Blake responds to her gaze smugly.

"In your dreams," Scarlett snorts, the usual disgust in her voice missing, thanks to the alcohol. As the night stretched on, the two unconsciously inched closer to one another, like a compass drawn to true north. Their chairs are now inches away from one another, and Blake's arm is wrapped around the back of her chair, a motion that seems as innate as blinking.

"How did you know I dream about that?" Though it's meant as a joke, the way Blake's voice fluctuates makes it clear there's some truth behind the question. If Scarlett notices it, she doesn't let on. She continues to dive into the dessert until the plate is spotless. I do the same, unprepared to go down the rabbit hole that is the sexual tension between Scarlett and Blake at this very moment.

Once Parker and I made things official, he came clean about "Operation-Get-Dylan-Back." Including Scarlett being in on it with Blake. If I weren't so happy with how things turned out, I'd have had some strong words for her. But it'd explain why she was always hiding her phone from me.

She has yet to tell me what that was all about, but I'm choosing to give her the benefit of the doubt. I know she's private about her love life, and she'll tell me whenever she's ready. I also know she doesn't have a malicious bone in her body, so she's doing whatever she thinks is best for others–even if I disagree.

After the bill comes and is paid, we linger around the table, not quite ready to part ways. We've spent the past two hours talking about our favorite memories these past couple of months and dreaming of what the future holds for the four of us. This group, along with Amelia and Evelyn, have become my home away from home, and I'm not sure my experience here in the city would've been the same without them–even Blake.

As much as I hate to admit it, he's grown on me, especially now that Parker and I are together, and I no longer have to worry about him openly undressing me with his eyes. However, I'm wary of rooting for him and Scarlett. She deserves the world, and I can't imagine he'll ever be the man to give that to her.

"Want to keep this party going? Bar Cima's not too far from here, and I could use another drink," Blake questions.

"Ooh, I love Bar Cima! The views are to die for. I'm in." Scarlett perks up in her chair, leaning into Blake's hand, which begins rubbing her exposed skin as if it were a reflex. The movement mirrors the night we got martinis so perfectly that a rush of deja vu washes over me.

Parker must notice, too, because he mimics the motion, which sends shivers down my spine. A glance over my shoulder shows me he's staring at me intently with widened eyes. Telepathically, we agree that we will *absolutely* be debriefing about this once we're home.

"As much as I'd love to, I'm exhausted and have some unfinished business I need to attend to." With that, Parker nips at my earlobe, which makes me squirm in my seat. "You two go. We'll tag along next time," Parker lies, and confusion about why he's letting the two be alone together courses through me.

"You two better make that some of the best sex you've ever had if you're going to ditch us for it," Blake goads. "I'll see you in the office Monday?" He stands and buttons his jacket back up before extending a hand to Scarlett to help her out of her chair. She happily takes it and places the dainty chain of her clutch on her shoulder.

"Of course. See you there, partner." Parker winks.

"It was great seeing you as always, Dylan." Blake tucks his chin and then places a hand on Scarlett's lower back to lead her out of the restaurant. I don't miss the way she's nervously fidgeting with her purse as she leaves with him, and it makes my stomach churn.

"Oh god, what did you just do? You trust him with her?" I press, slapping him gently across the arm.

"He's harmless. Besides, you and I both know that Scarlett would never give him the time of day. She'd chew his head off before ever considering sleeping with him."

As much as I want to believe that, a knot in my gut tells me otherwise. I may have just allowed Scarlett to wade into treacherous waters unattended. Before I can run to stop her from grabbing drinks with Blake, Parker pulls me into his arms, and nibbles at my neck again, leaving me completely at his disposal and utterly distracted.

After a few seconds, when I get my bearings together, I momentarily push out of his arms and text Scarlett a reminder that she can text or call me if she needs me. It's better than leaving her to navigate this alone. I just hope that it's enough.

And with that, Parker and I catch a cab, laughing and ready to get home to tear one another's clothes off.

ACKNOWLEDGMENTS

Where do I even begin? Like many other authors out there, this has been a dream of mine since I was a little girl. I would write countless short stories, daydreaming about seeing my name on the cover of books. Even in my early 20s, it felt like a feat that was impossible. And yet, today, that dream is a reality.

First and foremost, I want to thank my lovely friends Mia, Monica, Denise, Kenzi, Caroline, and Lexie. If it weren't you guys, I'm not sure I would've had the confidence to put this out in the world. From reading every draft created to answering every burning question I had, you've accepted it all with wide open arms. I thank the universe for bringing me you every single day. The same goes to my family, who didn't bat an eye when I said I was going to do the damn thing. I've got the greatest support system a girl could ask for.

Of course, I need to mention BookTok, a community that changed my life for the better. It's because of you that I chose to self-publish my work. A group of what could be considered virtually strangers instilled more faith in myself more than I could've ever imagined, and I'm forever grateful that I joined the silly little app over a year ago.

Lastly, to my best friend and the love of my life, Brandon. When I told you that I wanted to write a book, you never laughed. You never doubted my ability to do it. You cheered me on with zero hesitation–even if it meant I was sitting with headphones on full blast, tuning you out for hours at a time. In moments of joy, fear, stress, frustration, you've been there by my side. You're my very own good luck charm, and I know with you, I can do anything. I love you.

If you're still reading this, thank you for taking a chance on me. Although I am an author, words will never be enough to express my gratitude.

Printed in Dunstable, United Kingdom